THRESHOLD

Also by Jordan L. Hawk

THRESHOLD

(Whyborne & Griffin No. 2)

JORDAN L. HAWK

CHAPTER 1

Trapped. A miserable prisoner, I shifted farther into the corner, hoping not to be spotted. When would I escape? My eyes darted in the direction of the clock, but its workings were surely broken, for it seemed the minute hand had barely lurched forward.

I was doomed.

"Honestly, Whyborne, do stop fidgeting," snapped Christine, fanning herself briskly.

Christine—or, more formally, Dr. Putnam, my friend and colleague at the Nathaniel R. Ladysmith Museum—looked even more annoyed with the world than usual. Neither of us cared much for society, yet our employment required us to attend far too many donor galas and exhibit unveilings. At least she could escape to Egypt for months at a time, during excavation season. As a comparative philologist, my work generally came to me, rather than the other way around.

Tonight marked the grand opening of the newly completed Isley Wing, which would hold a number of large exhibits. Christine's fantastic discovery of the tomb of Pharaoh Nephren-ka would find its home among them, once the mummy and his assorted belongings returned from their world tour. Half of Widdershins society had turned out to stuff themselves with finger sandwiches and cakes, drink champagne, and preen in front of newspaper reporters for tomorrow's society column.

Some of my colleagues enjoyed the opportunity to rub shoulders with the wealthy elite of the city. Having spent my childhood and youth among them, I only wished to get as far away as possible.

"I beg your pardon, Christine," I said automatically. "Perhaps no one will notice if we slip away early?"

"Impossible, I fear." She fanned herself even faster. "It's the one drawback of making a great discovery—one's absence tends to be noticed."

I repressed a sigh. I could hardly fault Christine for her success. I did rather wish she would fan a bit in my direction, though.

An unseasonable heat had settled over the city a day or two before. Not a breath of air stirred within the museum, and the gaslights only added to the misery. As a result, even though we sat in a corner as far from the rest of the festivities as we could manage, sweat had soaked the underclothes beneath my tuxedo.

"Besides," Christine went on, "why are you in such a rush to get away? Isn't Griffin out of town on some case?"

"He was to return on the seven o'clock train," I said, looking to the clock again. Had the minute hand advanced at all? It was after eight; he would have returned to our little house by now. Petted Saul, our marmalade cat. Thrown open the windows against the unseasonable heat. Perhaps stripped off his clothing to expose skin glistening with a thin layer of sweat...

Oh dear lord, I needed to think about something else, quickly. Griffin had been absent for three weeks, and I anticipated his return rather keenly.

"Come along, Whyborne," Christine said, rising to her feet. "I can't possibly endure this heat without a cold drink to brace me."

"You dig in Egypt!" I exclaimed, gripping my chair with either hand, as if I could anchor myself to it. "How can you complain of this?"

"Because it is dry there, and I wear sensible clothing allowing for some ventilation." She snapped her fan closed decisively. "Normally, I prefer whiskey, but at least the champagne is on ice."

She'd only badger me until I surrendered, so I gave up and followed her. We braved the crowd, making our way to the table that held the sweating silver champagne buckets. I tried not to make eye contact with anyone. The waiter poured us each a glass; clutching the flute, I turned to slink back to the periphery.

"May I have your attention!" boomed Mr. Mathison, the museum president.

Biting back a resigned sigh, I stopped in my tracks and turned along with the rest of the crowd. Mathison, the museum director Dr. Hart, and Mr. Isley all stood at the entrance to the new wing. Above their heads hung an enormous banner, Isley's name in letters five feet tall, celebrating the opening. A thick, blue ribbon blocked the entrance to the wing, awaiting the ceremonial cutting.

But first, there would be speeches. I schooled my face into a polite mask and wondered how much longer I'd be forced to endure this, while Griffin waited at home. God, I'd missed him. Until last December, I'd resigned myself to a life of solitude, and believed any passion I harbored for other men to be safely under control. He'd shown me how wrong I'd been—and shown me a great many other things, to our mutual satisfaction.

If I could not be home, I wished he could have been here. He'd posed as

Christine's escort once before, and it would not have caused comment. The sight of him in his formal wear, his overlong hair neatly combed, the cut of his coat showing off his trim waist...

I shifted uncomfortably. Perhaps it was just as well he hadn't been able to make an appearance.

Dear heavens, how much longer could Mr. Mathison drone on?

Christine's fan blurred with speed, as did those of most of the ladies. "Blast it," she muttered to me. "It would at least be tolerable if there was but a stir of wind."

Wind.

Perhaps there was a way I might at least ease the atmosphere of the hall, and banish the collected fumes of the gaslights and the stench of sweat and cigars. Not to mention distract myself from thoughts of everything I wanted to do to Griffin as soon as I got home.

The case which had brought him into my life had brought other things as well. One had been a horrible realization my father, brother, and godfather were all involved in an evil cult, which would have destroyed the world without our intervention. Another had come in the form of the *Liber Arcanorum,* a medieval book of spells, which, to my utter shock, actually worked.

Many of them were horrific, dark things I would never attempt. But some were harmless, or relatively so. A means of setting flame to anything combustible had even saved our lives last winter.

Still, Griffin was uneasy with my experiments with the *Arcanorum's* spells. But he had been gone, and I hadn't really *done* anything—well, except for the one thing, but that had merely been testing the parameters of the fire spell. I needed something to distract me at night, when I lay in my lonely bed. It was only natural I'd taken the opportunity to study some of the other spells, one of which, very innocently, summoned wind.

Surely even Griffin couldn't object to that.

I would just raise a small breeze, to blow through the windows and provide some relief. Just a flutter.

The spell required a sigil to be drawn. Without pen and ink, the best I could do was discreetly trace it on my palm with a finger. Probably it wouldn't even work.

I traced the sigil and murmured the words under my breath. Nothing. As I expected.

Still, I might as well try it again.

Was that a slight breath of coolness against the back of my neck?

Encouraged, I whispered the words and traced the sigil again.

For a moment, nothing happened. Then, with a roar as if the ocean itself had risen against Widdershins, a gale tore through the windows and flooded into the hall.

Hats went flying, half the gas lamps blew out instantly, and two paintings crashed to the floor. Women and men alike screamed, grabbing at fans and skirts and remaining hats as they pelted for shelter. The table with the silver buckets fell over, scattering ice everywhere and sending the fleeing revelers skidding across the floor.

I stood frozen to the spot. As I watched, affixed with horror, the huge banner tore lose from its mooring and ponderously, dramatically fell directly onto Mr. Mathison, Dr. Hart, and Mr. Isley, bearing them to the ground and destroying what last shreds of dignity the event maintained.

Three hours later, I finally reached our gate.

I thought of it as our gate, anyway, even though as far as the world was concerned, I merely rented a room from my good friend, Mr. Griffin Flaherty. The house sat well back from the street, offering privacy to Griffin's clients, and to us as well.

Glad beyond words to be home at last, I hurried down the walk and let myself in. The sight of Griffin's hat and coat hanging in the front hallway made my heart perform a little dance in my chest. "Griffin?" I called, locking the door behind me.

No answer. Perhaps he'd gone to bed, wearied from his journey? It would be a blasted disappointment if he had, although I had no one other than myself to blame for the late hour of my return.

The museum's president, director, and benefactor had to be rescued from beneath the weighty, enveloping folds of the gigantic banner. Gaslights had to be either shut off or relit, to keep gas from flooding the room. Hats were collected, the knocked-over tables righted, and the paintings removed to back rooms to keep them safe from further damage. None of which was strictly my job, except I'd been the one to cause the mess, which made the entire ruined evening my responsibility.

"At least we didn't have to listen to the rest of Mathison's speech," Christine had said, clapping me on the arm, when I confessed to her what I'd done.

Hoping Griffin might have waited up, as anxious to see me as I was him, I peered into the parlor, which served as his office in which he entertained clients. All lay silent and dark, as did the kitchen, so I headed up the stairs to the second floor.

No fire burned in the hearth, of course, but the lamp was on, as if someone had recently quit the room. The only occupant at the moment, however, was Saul, who lay curled in my chair with his fluffy tail tucked over his nose.

I frowned and stepped further into the room. Where on earth was the man? "Griffin?"

Someone grabbed me from behind.

I let out a startled yelp and instinctively threw my weight against the strong arm wrapped around my waist. If I could just break free—

I became aware of Griffin's laughter in my ear. "Very funny," I muttered. "You've given me heart palpitations."

"Forgive me, my dear," Griffin said, although he didn't sound at all sorry. His hold loosened enough for me to turn to face him.

Most would consider his height average—in other words, several inches shorter than me, although broader through the shoulder. Chestnut curls fell across his forehead, unfashionably long, at least among the drawing rooms of the east. He might not have looked out of place around a cowboy's campfire, though. A light dusting of freckles highlighted his cheekbones, and his eyes were green as the leaves budding outside, shot through with threads of blue and rust.

The surge of joy at seeing him again shocked me with its strength. "I was beginning to think the damned museum meant to keep you until dawn," he said, even as he drew my head down for a kiss.

"There was an incident—"

His mouth closed against mine: hungry and urgent. His tongue swirled over my lips, and I parted them eagerly, letting him taste me. I pulled him tight, reveling in the feel of having him in my arms again. My skin ached for his touch, and my member hardened, pressing against the swell of his erection through the cloth of our trousers.

The kiss ended, although we kept our arms about one another. "Poor dear," he said. "I hesitate to ask."

"It can wait," I said breathlessly. "Your room?"

"My thought exactly."

I gladly let him draw me into the room, where he immediately began to divest me of my sweat-damp clothing. I did the same for him, thrilling with each inch of bare skin I uncovered.

Unlike my gawky body, his was a marvel, from the perfect ripple of muscle along his shoulders, to the temptation of his flat, small nipples, to the thickness of his member. I loved even the ugly scar on his right thigh, for no reason other than it was part of him.

He kissed me again, nibbling on my earlobe, before trailing his lips across the line of my jaw, onto my throat. When he shoved aside my drawers and grasped my length, I groaned and pulled him tighter, relearning the shape of his muscles with my hands. God, he felt good. His familiar scent, of sandalwood and musk, filled my nostrils. I ran my tongue over his collarbone, tasting the salt of his skin.

Then the last bit of clothing fell to the floor, and we tumbled into the bed. I reached for his member, the silky hood sliding beneath my palm as I gathered the thick pearl of liquid from the slit. "Shall I taste you?"

"Please," he groaned. "I've been dreaming of having your mouth on my cock again."

I made a small, involuntary sound in the back of my throat. Unlike me, Griffin had never shown any inhibition when it came to bed-talk, and his words fired my blood. He laid back, head propped against the pillows, allowing him to watch. I slid my hand down his organ, peeling back the hood, before bending my head to wrap my lips around him.

I'd spent my life alone, denying even my dreams of other men, until Griffin shattered all of my barriers. How had I come to crave this so quickly? His salty-bitter flavor, the weight and thickness of his cock in my mouth, the way he gasped when I rolled his balls in my free hand: I wanted it all, needed it all.

His hips twitched up, fingers digging into the bedclothes. I glanced up at him; his green eyes shone bright and hot with lust. "We should make love in front of a mirror some time," he said. "So you can see how irresistible you look like this."

Was he joking? Just the thought of seeing my lanky, imperfect body against his made me faintly queasy. I closed my eyes and concentrated on his cock with renewed fervor, taking him all the way in, until my nose pressed against the curls at his base and my throat worked around him.

"Enough," he panted. "It feels too good, and I want to see your face when you come."

He rolled me onto my back and positioned himself above me, pressing our lengths against each other. Seeing what he was about, I loosely wrapped my hand around us both. He began to thrust against me, and I moaned at the heat and friction, the feel of him, stiff with desire. I'd never understand what a handsome man of the world such as him saw in me, but the fact I could make him feel such passion unleashed my own.

"Ival," he whispered the pet name, even as he looked down at me with an expression combining need and tenderness in equal measure. "Missed you so much, my dear love."

I clung to his shoulder with my free hand, arching against him, striving to add to the heat building between us. I spoke thirteen languages, and yet all my words deserted me in these moments. I groaned his name, white heat building in my sack, cresting and cresting, before unfurling in streams of spend across my stomach.

"Yes," he growled, thrusting against my sensitized length once, twice, before joining me in release.

Our ragged breathing evened out gradually. With a soft chuckle, Griffin rolled to one side and propped himself up on an elbow. "Welcome home, indeed," he said with a grin.

CHAPTER 2

I slept more soundly than I had in weeks, waking only the next morning, when the bed shifted under Griffin as he rose. Opening my eyes, I saw him at the washbasin, preparing his morning shave. He hadn't yet dressed, treating me to a view I had sorely missed in his absence. My member roused eagerly, and I rolled onto my side so as not to make too much of a spectacle beneath the covers.

"I missed you," I admitted.

He glanced over his shoulder, shaving cream still covering half his face. "And I missed you terribly, my dear. At least we live in modern times, when we can communicate easily via post. If I'd not been able to write to you and receive your letters, I would have quit the accursed job halfway through."

"Was it very difficult?"

"Not in its particulars. A simple case of theft, as you know. The most difficult part was tracking down the fellow and waiting until he grew bold enough to sell something unique to his former employer. I never minded stalking criminals while in Chicago or out west, working for the Pinkertons. It was part of the game. But knowing you awaited my return, I discovered a new streak of impatience."

My cheeks heated, and I ducked my head, hoping he didn't notice. "I never thought sleeping alone would be difficult."

"I'm glad to hear you've grown accustomed to my presence," he said, as he dried his face. "Shall I make breakfast?"

Our pantry was rather bare, entirely due to my neglect. In his absence, I'd survived on canned beans and bread, with an occasional meal at the lunch counter. "Er, there might be…flour…in one of the cabinets. And milk, if it's been delivered."

He laughed and shook his head. "Pancakes it is. Shall I add your tuxedo to the laundry?"

"Please." He gathered our discarded clothing and left, whistling cheerfully.

I washed quickly then borrowed one of his dressing gowns to cross the hall to my room. A cleaning woman came once a week to tidy up, and we sent our clothing and linens out to be laundered. For appearances' sake, we maintained two bedrooms, his belongings in one and mine in another. In the normal course of things, we slept one night in my bed, and the next in his, ensuring both would be equally rumpled and used by the end of the week. With his absence, I'd been forced to confine myself to my room. In very short order, I'd come to hate the tan wallpaper, not for any fault of its own, but because it reminded me of his absence.

The *Arcanorum* still lay out on the nightstand. I opened the drawer and tucked the book inside, leaving the area bare except for a small paper card Griffin had unexpectedly presented to me on Valentine's Day.

The card was...well, hideous, to be honest, featuring a wretchedly ugly Cupid in a swan-shaped boat. "To My Valentine" was emblazoned beneath the boat, while Cupid appeared to be writing a less-than-inspired poem ending with the words "be mine." Griffin had not signed it, of course, or even addressed it to me.

I loved it.

Dressed in a fresh suit, I hurried downstairs to the kitchen. Griffin stood in front of the stove, a pan in one hand and cooking oil in the other, regarding the wall with surprise.

Oh dear. I'd forgotten about the rather large scorch mark blackening the plaster.

"Whyborne," he said, in a deceptively calm voice, "did you leave the gas on too long before lighting the stove?"

I winced. "Er, no."

"I see." He put the pan on the stove. "Would you care to tell me what did happen?"

I felt rather like an errant schoolboy caught out by a disapproving headmaster, a sensation I did not care for in the least. "Well, I...that is, while you were gone, I, er...experimented."

"Experimented."

"With the spell. The one for fire."

Griffin turned to me, exasperation clearly written across his face. "I thought we agreed you wouldn't use that damnable book without discussing it first."

"You're being quite unfair," I objected. "The spell saved our lives, more than once. Besides, it's only a novice's magic. It's not as if I'm raising the dead, or creating monsters, or calling lightning down from the sky. Although, the last one might be useful..." I trailed off at his expression.

"So you waited until I left town, knowing full well I'd disapprove otherwise, and did what? Tried to set the house on fire?"

"Of course not." I tugged absently at my shirt cuffs, even though they were already perfectly straight. "I simply ran a few tests. I wanted to find out what effects distance might have, and if I could alter the size of the flame produced."

"I take it the answer was yes," Griffin said dryly.

"Forgive me—I'll have the plaster patched soon, I promise."

Griffin put aside the makings of our breakfast and crossed the room to me. Gripping my shoulders with his hands, he looked earnestly up into my eyes. "I don't give a fig for the plaster. I understand you can't help but be curious. Your inquisitive mind is part of what attracted me to you in the first place. But I worry about you."

His words warmed me. "I appreciate your concern. But truly, I'm careful. Er, mostly."

A wry grin slipped across his features. "Well, at least you didn't burn down the house, or set yourself on fire. Just let me supervise the next time."

"Of course." I hesitated, but could hardly put it off any longer. "By the way, the newspaper might contain mention of a 'freak wind' at the museum last night."

"A what? Whyborne…"

"Oh, did I hear the postman?" I blurted, before hastily escaping to the porch.

There was indeed post in the box. I sorted through it as I carried it back to the kitchen. "I've a letter from Dr. Maidstone, one of my old philology professors at Miskatonic. I wonder how he's getting on? Flyer for a new department store…a new issue of the sensationalist trash you subscribe to—"

Griffin rolled his eyes. "Not every work of literature has to be a classic to last the ages. I enjoy reading adventure stories."

"Hmph. Oh, and here's another letter—"

I came to an abrupt halt at the sight of the familiar, thick paper of the envelope and the bold, heavy hand which had addressed it. My throat constricted sharply, and bands tightened around my chest, making it even harder to breathe. Why would my father write to me—and why would he send a letter here, instead of to the museum? I felt as if the sanctuary of our home had been suddenly violated.

Then my eyes caught up to my thoughts, and I read the name on the envelope.

No. Oh no. How *dare* he.

"Whyborne? Is everything all right?"

The expression on my face must have been truly alarming, because Griffin immediately set the pan aside and turned off the gas. "What's wrong?"

I thrust the envelope at him with a shaking hand. "A letter from my father. Addressed to you."

Griffin paled sharply, no doubt thinking the same thing as I. That Father knew of our relationship I had little doubt, considering what he'd witnessed last

December. Given I was already the rebellious child, I'd expected him to simply pretend Griffin didn't exist, rather than risk bringing any scandal on our family.

Apparently, I had been wrong. "If he's threatened you, in any way, I will never speak to or see him again," I said. It would be hard on Mother, but I knew she, of all people, would understand. "We'll go to Europe if need be—I don't care."

Griffin took the letter from me, but the color returned to his face. "Let's not buy our tickets until we've read what he has to say."

The red wax seal, stamped with our family crest, shattered under his fingernail. Unfolding the letter, he scanned the single page, his brows drawing into a frown.

"Well?" I asked, when he didn't say anything. "Where do you prefer to go? The Mediterranean is rather nice, I hear."

"It isn't a threat." Still frowning, Griffin held the letter out to me, as if imploring me to make sense of it. "Or an attempt to bribe me away from you."

"Then what?"

"It seems your father wishes to hire me."

Two days later, we stood on the street in front of Whyborne House, staring up at the pretentious family crest emblazoned above the heavy doors. A feeling of dread curled in my belly; I couldn't imagine what Father was about, but past experience suggested it would prove highly unpleasant.

The offer of hire had included an invitation to dinner, which might have been something of a peace offering, or a tacit acknowledgement of Griffin's status in my life. Or it might have been some new attempt on Father's part to manipulate me, which seemed far more likely.

The butler, Mr. Fenton, opened the door at our knock, the usual expression of displeasure affixed to his face. The staff lived in fear of him. Actually, I'd been rather afraid of him myself as a child.

His eyes flicked dismissively over Griffin, although my companion appeared quite presentable in his best suit and hat, with a lovely new tie, accentuating the threads of blue in his eyes. No doubt the fact he was in my company damned him enough.

"Master Whyborne," Fenton said. Without any further acknowledgment, he turned and led the way inside. A maid took our hats and coats then melted away, leaving us to follow Fenton.

The house looked exactly as it had since my childhood. Marble floors and dark wood, brooding portraits of past Whybornes glaring their disapproval at me. Fenton led the way to a parlor, which disappointed me; I had hoped for the opportunity to speak with Mother before dinner.

Fenton departed, closing the door behind him. Griffin wandered across the room, taking in everything with those sharp eyes, which missed very little. "This is where you grew up?" He sounded strange, as if he hadn't quite realized... what? A house could be this cold and uninviting? Or how garish its displays of wealth might be?

"Unfortunately. At least Fenton put us in the parlor for intimate friends, instead of the formal one. Perhaps it's a good sign?"

Griffin's eyes widened slightly. "This is the informal parlor?"

"Well…yes." I looked around, wondering where his sudden distress originated. Mementos of various kinds crowded the parlor, many of them handed down from previous generations. Photographs in gilded frames sat atop the mantel: a family portrait of Guinevere, Stanford, and myself as children; another of our parents dressed in their wedding attire; the mourning photograph of my twin sister, who had died within hours of our birth. Several hideous, but expensive, vases sported fresh flowers, and an ugly clock crusted with emeralds loudly ticked away the seconds. Father's cavalry sword hung in a place of honor on the wall; he'd served with General Grant in the war.

"These are all family heirlooms," I said, nodding vaguely. "The formal parlor is more concerned with business and, well, money."

Griffin looked at a loss to reply. The opening of the door saved him from having to do so. I turned automatically, expecting Fenton or my father, and instead found Mother, dressed for dinner.

"Oh!" I said, and hastened across the room to her. Her skin held the unnatural pallor of long illness, and deep lines of strain bracketed her mouth, but the smile she gave me was bright as the summer sun. It had been years since she'd attended even the lightest of social duties; for the most part she remained confined to her rooms at the top of the house, and I could not imagine what had changed.

"Mother! I hadn't expected—I mean, are you joining us for dinner?"

She laughed and embraced me. I returned the embrace carefully, painfully conscious of how frail she felt in my arms, like a bird, nothing but bones and a little skin.

"Of course I am!" she said, as if she didn't usually find even family meals to be beyond her. "It's good to see you, Percival. Aren't you going to introduce your friend?"

She'd done this for me, hadn't she? Dressed formally, fixed her hair, put on jewelry, and forced her aching, weak body to navigate the long stairs, just to meet Griffin.

The oppressive atmosphere of the house lightened, and my breath came more freely. There might be no love lost between Father and me, but Mother had encouraged my bookish interests. She'd even sold her own jewelry to finance my degree, when Father cut me off from the family funds.

"Of course; forgive my rudeness," I said, leading her across the room to where Griffin waited. "Mother, allow me to present Mr. Griffin Flaherty. Griffin, this is my mother, Mrs. Heliabel Whyborne."

She extended her hand. Griffin took it with an elegant bow. "Mrs. Whyborne, it's my honor. Your son speaks of you with great fondness."

"Please, Mr. Flaherty, I almost feel you are one of the family. Do address me as Heliabel."

Griffin's smile was surprised but genuine. "If you will do me the honor of calling me Griffin."

"Percival's last letter said you were visiting Vermont. I hope you had a pleasant trip?"

I stood back and watched as they conversed. Griffin led her to a seat, and within minutes they chatted like old friends. Of course, I had never spoken to Mother of my romantic feelings toward my own sex, but she knew my mind perhaps better than any other. No doubt she had divined the truth long ago.

A gong rang from deep in the house, and I stiffened. There would be only four of us at the table, but heaven forbid a servant simply come to fetch us. The pleasant aura of the parlor evaporated, and my muscles tensed once again.

Mother rose, and I offered her my arm automatically. There was a decided gleam in her eye as she took it. Leaning close, she murmured, "He's very hand-some."

She'd spoken in Greek, but the tips of my ears grew hot. "Mother!"

She laughed and tightened her grip. Casting a rueful glance over her head at Griffin, I led the way to dinner.

The dining room felt as cold and forbidding as it had ever been. This time, however, I had Griffin here to bolster me, a fact which filled me with pathetic gratitude.

Father joined us within. He and I did not much resemble one another; he was shorter and stockier, with the look of an aged lion who had not yet given up his dominance of the pride. "Percival," he said in a clipped tone, which was as warm a greeting as he was likely to offer me. "Mr. Flaherty."

Even I couldn't read Griffin's expression. Technically, they'd not been formally introduced. Unless being kidnapped by the cult Father had been involved in counted as an introduction.

"Mr. Whyborne," he responded, cool but not openly hostile.

Father's attention skipped past him and fixed on Mother. "Heliabel! What are you doing up and about? You'll overtax yourself."

"I'm quite all right, Niles," she said with a trace of exasperation. "Don't fret."

He looked as if he wished to object further, but felt restrained by the presence of a guest, so instead settled for glowering. We took our places around the table, and I wondered if Griffin found the arrangement as absurd as I. Twenty people could sit comfortably in the ornate chairs, carved from the same black wood as the massive table. Every sound echoed back from the vaulted ceiling. Suits of armor flanked a fireplace large enough to hold an entire tree, as if in hopes of deluding visitors into believing we were descended from European no-bility, instead of rascals who had fled to the colonies to escape the hangman's noose.

The four of us sat at one end of the table, with Father at its head, Mother to his right, and Griffin to his left. I sat next to Mother. Servants hurried to fill our glasses and offer the first course.

Father usually invited any guests to say grace, but apparently he'd decided Griffin wasn't worth a show of false piety. "Percival," he said, dipping his spoon into the soup, "I hope that museum of yours is spending my money wisely."

I pressed my lips together. Having him acknowledge the existence of the museum was progress of a sort. And he had been very generous in his donations over the last few months, perhaps in an attempt to salve any guilt he might feel over nearly destroying the world. "Finance really isn't my department," I said, swirling my spoon around in the bowl without actually bringing it to my lips.

Father let out an annoyed snort, like an old bull. "I don't know why you insist on wasting your life. If you were serious about things, you'd be aiming for the director's chair, or have it already. Or bought the museum presidency. Your problem is you have no ambition."

I stared at my soup, my fingers clenched around my spoon hard enough for the muscles to cramp. Damn him. Bad enough to be mocked every time I sat at this accursed table, but for him to humiliate me in front of Griffin…

"Shouldn't any man be free to do honest work he enjoys?" Griffin asked. Surprised and gratified, I glanced up, but he gazed fixedly at Father.

"I didn't build the biggest railroad in America with such an attitude," Father shot back.

"Griffin, dear," Mother said quickly, "Percival tells me you used to work for the Pinkertons."

Griffin accepted the diversion. "I was stationed in the Chicago office, but I spent some time in the west as well."

"It sounds fascinating. Surely you must have some stories to share."

Griffin launched into a tale about foiling a train robbery, full of outlaws and horseback riding and other extremely manful pursuits. His natural charm came to the surface, and by the time the servants cleared away dessert, even Father looked impressed. As for myself, I could not help but feel a sense of pride in Griffin's accomplishments.

As the last of the dishes vanished, Mother pushed back her chair, and we all hastily rose. "If you gentlemen will excuse me," she said, and I noticed her pallor had grown more marked. Had she touched much of her meal, or had she occupied herself with pushing it about her plate as I had?

Griffin bowed to her. "It was a pleasure to make your acquaintance."

"And yours, dear boy. Please do call again." She touched my arm lightly as she left the room, just a little pressure of fingers through my coat, but I took it as a gesture of approval.

Then she departed in a rustle of silk and lace. The mood in the room dimmed immediately.

"We'll retire to the study and talk business," Father decreed, and left without bothering to see if we followed or not.

Griffin and I exchanged a glance, before falling in behind him. Griffin's hand brushed discreetly against mine; I desperately wished I could take it outright.

We entered the study. My heart began to race, and my stomach cramped around the small amount of food I'd actually consumed. How many times had I stood in this room, in front of the mahogany desk, while Father picked apart my every flaw? I was twelve years old again, or fifteen, or eighteen.

"Cigars?" Father asked.

"Thank you," Griffin said. I demurred; I hated the reek of the awful things.

Once the cigars were lit, Father poured us each a measure of brandy, indicating we should sit in the chairs provided for us. For himself, he settled in his much larger chair on the other side of the desk. "Well, Mr. Flaherty," he said, "I suppose you're wondering what sort of case I have lined up for you."

"Not at all," Griffin replied. "I only wonder why on earth you'd think I would take hire from a man who tried to kill me."

CHAPTER 3

Father's expression was one of such surprise it bordered on comedic. How long had it been since anyone had dared to tell him no?

"If it's money you're after—" he began, a threatening edge to the words.

"No, sir, it is not." Griffin's voice sounded calm, but cold, all pretense of goodwill abandoned. "The Brotherhood, of which you were an active member, unleashed horrors. Many innocent people died thanks to your activities. My partner in Chicago among them."

"I had nothing to do with Chicago," Father objected.

"Perhaps. But you did have me kidnapped, beaten, and imprisoned with the intention of feeding me to some fiend raised from the dead. Yet you expect me to pretend it never happened. Do you believe I have no pride, no spine, or no scruples, to insult me so?"

They stared at one another for a long moment, cigar smoke swirling languidly in the air between them. My heart swelled with pride at Griffin's defiance, even as I held my breath, waiting for Father to break into a rage. Would he threaten Griffin with ruin, financial and social alike? Or did he realize neither I—nor, it seemed, Mother—would stand for it? Or did our desires ever enter into his head at all?

Father ground his teeth, and his nostrils flared. Then, he took a deep breath, his jaw unclenching with apparent difficulty. "I can see how this might be awkward for you, Mr. Flaherty," he grated. "Rest assured I did not bear you any ill will at the time. You were convenient, nothing more. Whatever your motives for accepting my invitation tonight, whether out of curiosity or for Percival's sake, at least hear me out."

Astonishment robbed me of breath. Niles Foster Whyborne, back down from an argument? *Ask* someone of lesser social status to hear him out? Had some doppelgänger sneaked in and replaced my father?

Or had being misled by the Brotherhood shaken him? He claimed not to have known their ritual would have ushered in the destruction of the human race. It certainly didn't excuse his actions, but a miscalculation of such magnitude would surely be enough to give any man pause.

"Very well, sir," Griffin said, rather more graciously than I would have, under the circumstances. "I will hear what you have to say, though I promise nothing more."

Father looked miffed, but refrained from commenting. Instead, he said, "I don't know how closely you follow the doings of business, but it will probably come as no surprise to learn I own large shares in a number of companies whose main concern is coal mining. One of these is Stotz Mining, which has recently opened a mine in Threshold, West Virginia.

"Threshold Mine began to have difficulties almost immediately—strange accidents, sabotaged equipment, and the like. Disappearances of various persons, mostly hunters and drunkards abroad at night. A band of outlaws, the McCoy gang, fled to the area from Kentucky, pursued by law enforcement. The lawmen cornered them in a blind ravine, from which they could not have possibly escaped—and yet, when the posse finally ventured in after them, no trace was found."

Father took a long pull on the cigar then sent the smoke streaming in a noxious cloud in front of his face, before continuing. "Miners are superstitious fools at the best of times. Most of the men came from outside the area—there wasn't much in the way of a local population—but they've latched onto the native legends to explain their bad luck and the disappearances alike. Tales of otherworldly creatures. There is great unrest and talk of general strike if nothing is done."

Griffin snorted. "You must hold a high opinion of my talents if you meant to hire me to prevent a strike. I am but one man."

"Stotz Mining already has a force of Pinkertons on hand to ensure work continues. Your talents lie elsewhere."

"Oh?"

Father's smile held no trace of humor. "Indeed. I wish to hire you to find out if the miners are right."

Silence fell. Griffin's eyes narrowed slightly. "You think there really is something strange occurring in Threshold. Something otherworldly, as you put it."

"The Pinkerton guards would laugh if I ordered them to investigate a legend. But you have seen things they haven't. You know the possibility exists."

"I see." Griffin's mouth thinned to a tight line. "People disappear all the time, especially drunkards prone to going abroad at night. Accidents happen in a dangerous occupation like mining. As for the gang, it's entirely possible, if not probable, some way out of the ravine existed of which the posse knew nothing.

Do you have reason to think there might be something more happening? Some indicator the legends are true?"

Father's expression took on a triumphant edge I did not like. Opening one of the drawers of his desk, he pulled out a flat, black stone roughly the size of a dinner plate, which appeared to have broken off some larger object. A dense tangle of pictographs covered the surface. Intrigued despite myself, I leaned forward, trying to get a better look at them.

"This stone was found in a cave near Threshold," Father said.

My hands ached to touch the artifact, to bring it closer and attempt to decipher the markings. Father watched me intently. Had I given too much away? "Can you read it?" he asked.

"I-I don't know. I'll need to examine it." But would he take any action on my part as surrender to his wishes? "It might be nothing."

"It might," he agreed.

But he didn't sound as if he believed it.

We escaped shortly thereafter, the stone a heavy weight in my hands. Because of the mild weather, we elected to walk home rather than summon a cab. As we strolled beneath the gaslight, Griffin tilted his head back and stared at the stars crowding the sky above.

"Well. Your childhood home," he said. "It was very…impressive."

I snorted indelicately. "Thank you for attempting kindness, but I know it's horrid. A monument to past glories, meant to overawe the visitor and impress the inhabitants with our own importance."

"Perhaps it seems thus to you."

"What it seemed like to me was growing up in a mausoleum. I'd go back to my student apartment at the university before returning to Whyborne House."

"I suppose one's experiences of a place must taint it," Griffin said. "Your mother seems very kind."

"Visiting with her is the only good thing about going home."

"She was quite gracious to me. I suppose she would regard any close friend in the same way?"

It belatedly occurred to me what he really meant to ask. "Oh! Er, no." My cheeks grew hot, and I was glad for the night and the dim gas lamps. "Perhaps if I had brought home a lady with whom I had an understanding."

"She…knows?" He seemed taken aback. As his own parents had reacted more typically when he'd been caught kissing a neighbor's son, it probably seemed very strange to him.

How to explain it? "Mother has been sick since my birth," I said at last. "While everyone else went out to church, or on picnics, or to visit the neighbors, I remained behind to keep her company. Which suited me quite well, to be honest. Confined as she was, her only escape came in the form of books, sent to her by correspondents the world over. She taught me Greek and Latin when I was a small child, so I could read something close to the original myths instead of the bloodless translations considered suitable for this day and age. We dissected philosophy, theology, and poetry. On each birthday, she would give me some new volume on language, or cryptography, or whatever topic to which my fancy had turned."

"My mother always cooked me an apple pie for my birthday," Griffin said with a wry smile.

I laughed at the idea. "Cooking is what the servants are for. I know it must seem impossibly strange to you. To answer your question, though, I'm not entirely certain. Looking back I think she suspected my...nature...early on. And since she merely laughed and patted my head when I built an altar to Pan in the garden as a child, I think we can agree her religious sentiments probably don't include a hell into which one can be easily consigned." I shrugged. "I'm not certain what else to say. She loves me, and she wishes me to be happy. If you are what makes me happy, she will love you as well."

"I see."

I winced. "I don't mean to imply your mother loves you any less, Griffin. I'm sure she and your father were motivated by what they saw as your well-being. If it's any comfort, Father despaired of me long ago; anything I do only serves to confirm his poor opinion. If he says nothing disapproving, it merely indicates he's washed his hands of the whole business in disgust."

We reached our gate. As I was carrying the stone, Griffin opened it for me then latched it behind us. Once inside the house, I put the stone carefully on the kitchen table, before turning to him. "Do you still feel affection for me, given my family?" I asked, taking his hands. "Having my father and brother try to kill you must surely put a damper on things."

The pensive look melted from his face, and he twined his fingers in mine. "I would still care for you, my dear, even if they were the worst wretches on earth."

"Take me to bed and prove it."

His grin grew wicked, and he drew me after him, pausing only long enough to turn out the light.

The next morning, I made my way to the museum, the mysterious black stone secured in a small Gladstone bag. The usual morning bustle of factory workers, clerks, and shop girls crowded the streets. As the weather was dry and still rather warm, I made my way along the sidewalks on foot, rather than paying for the overcrowded omnibus. The air smelled of fish, thanks to the proximity of the docks, the ocean, and the canning factory.

As I approached the museum, the crowds began to thin out. The day ahead, rather than my surroundings, occupied my attention. When a pair of hands reached from an alleyway to grab me, they took me completely by surprise.

Before I could cry out, a second man shoved me from behind. I stumbled on the uneven cobblestones, even as my attackers grabbed my arms and dragged me hurriedly away from the street. My shoes scraped on the cobbles, and I tried to get purchase, but to no avail.

What did they want? Robbery? Murder? "Help!" I shouted. "Police! Hel—"

A meaty fist buried itself in my stomach, cutting off my cry. Pain bloomed in my gut, and my breakfast tried to claw its way back up my throat. I gasped for breath, but my lungs refused to cooperate. My knees hit the old cobbles as my legs gave out, sending a second shock through me.

One of the men tore the Gladstone from my unresisting fingers. Blinking through a haze of pain, I looked up. Both of my attackers appeared young, barely old enough to be called men, and dressed like simple laborers. Their faces seemed oddly expressionless, betraying no fear or anger, as if they engaged in some perfectly ordinary task.

"Is it in there?" one of them asked in a voice as cool and smooth as the surface of a lake in winter.

The other opened the bag and peered inside. "Yes."

He closed the bag and the two men began to walk away. My lungs unfroze, and I lunged after them, grabbing at the jacket of the nearest one. "No! Stop! Police!"

He turned and, without the slightest look of worry or disturbance, struck me on the side of the head.

My ears rang and light sparked across my vision. The wall of one of the adjacent buildings caught me, and I clung to the crumbling brick to keep from falling again. Nausea returned, and this time I gave up the fight and lost my breakfast.

I leaned miserably against the wall, listening to their retreating footsteps. By the time I was able to raise my head without the world spinning, they had disappeared from sight, and I stood alone in the alley.

"Are certain you're quite all right, Dr. Whyborne?" asked Miss Parkhurst, one of the secretaries, whose desk I had passed on the way to my windowless office in the basement. She immediately became alarmed by the bruise forming on the side of my face, and insisted on tending me. "I can summon a doctor."

I pressed the damp compress she had fetched against the bruise, hoping it didn't swell too badly. My stomach ached from the first blow, although, of course, I did not make mention of it to her. "That won't be necessary. Thank you; you've been most kind."

"Shall I send word to the police?"

Father could afford a bribe to get them to investigate, but I had the feeling such an action would be in vain. "No, no. Don't, er, concern yourself. Truly, I'm fine."

Christine appeared in my open doorway, barging in without an invitation. Not to suggest I would have expected her to do otherwise. "What the devil is wrong with you, Whyborne?"

"He was set upon by ruffians!" Miss Parkhurst exclaimed indignantly.

"Really?" Christine asked. "Whatever for?"

I pulled the compress away and gingerly dabbed at the scrape on my chin, where it had met the wall. "A robbery gone awry, I believe," I said, not wishing to speak further in front of anyone else. "Thank you for your assistance, Miss Parkhurst. I assure you, I'm quite all right."

She looked as if she wished to hover. Lacking an excuse, however, she only smiled and wished me a speedy recovery. As soon as she departed, Christine said, "Well, out with it. What aren't you saying?"

How the devil had she known? No matter. "Griffin will be here soon, or should be." I'd sent the first urchin I'd come across with a note, a penny, and the promise of a second coin if he delivered it to our home with all haste. "But I'll catch you up on the situation."

By the time I explained Father's invitation and the origins of the black stone, Griffin arrived. His eyes widened at the sight of my bruised face. "My dear Whyborne, are you quite all right?" he demanded.

"It appears far worse than it is." It must have looked awful, given Griffin and Miss Parkhurst both wished to coddle me over it. "At any rate, we have a much bigger problem than a few bumps and bruises. The black stone has been stolen."

I related the entire incident. "The men, whoever they were, knew exactly what they were looking for," I finished.

Griffin perched on a corner of my rather messy desk, his lips pressed into a grim line. "They must have known your father had it. If they were keeping watch on Whyborne House, they would have seen us leave with it last night."

"And waited to catch me alone?" An alarming thought. Even more alarming to imagine they'd been behind us in the dark somewhere, while we walked home. Had they lurked outside the gate all night, watching? The thought sent a shiver down my back. Thank heavens we scrupulously kept the doors locked and the curtains pulled over the windows.

"No doubt they wished to see if you would carry the stone to the museum with you—not an unwarranted assumption," Griffin agreed.

"And now we'll never know what it said," Christine remarked with a scowl.

"Assuming we might have translated it to begin with," I pointed out. "With such a small fragment, lacking other context, unless the pictographs proved to be closely related to a known language—"

"Yes, yes, I'm quite aware of the difficulties, even if I'm not a philologist like yourself. Do we know the provenance of the artifact? Was it truly old, or simply a hoax? If we could visit the site—"

Griffin cleared his throat to recapture our attention. "I appreciate your enthusiasm," he said. "The one thing this incident has served to prove is someone didn't want the stone to remain in our possession. Whyborne's father might be right. Strange forces may very well be at work in Threshold."

"You mean to take the case?" I asked.

Griffin looked as if he wished to argue, but his shoulders slumped in defeat. "I can't just leave it. The Pinkertons in Threshold won't be prepared to deal with such possibilities, just as Glenn and I weren't prepared when we went into that accursed basement."

"If we could convince them to close the mine—"

"Based on what? A bit of petty theft?"

"Griffin's right," Christine said. "No one is going to shut down a profitable mining operation without an excellent reason. I'm afraid it is up to us to find such a reason, and, perhaps, put a stop to things."

"Us?" Griffin asked, arching his brow.

"Of course," I said briskly. "As much as I hate to give in to Father's request, there is far more at stake than my pride. I will have to ask the director for time off, of course, but I hardly think he can complain, seeing as I've not had so much as a short vacation since joining the staff four years ago."

"And I'm already on sabbatical," Christine put in. "That's what I had come to tell you, Whyborne—the blasted director wants me to concentrate on my manuscript concerning Nephren-ka's tomb."

"Shouldn't you consider remaining here to work on it?" I suggested.

"Don't be absurd. Do you think I'm going to sit here in Widdershins while you go haring off? One or both of you would end up kidnapped, or eaten, or God knows what. Then who would I talk to at those dreadful formal affairs? Far better I come along."

Griffin shook his head, but an involuntary smile creased his lips. "Indeed. How can I argue with such logic? I shall look into the train schedules straight-away."

CHAPTER 4

A week later, the three of us sat in the first-class passenger car of a train winding its way deep into the mountains of West Virginia. We were the car's only occupants, although I'd seen a few men getting on the second-class car when the train stopped in Charleston. I wondered what business took them to Threshold, and was secretly glad we had a section of the train to ourselves.

We left civilization behind hours ago, and now delved deep into the countryside. Mountains shrouded in green rose and fell around us, the mass of trees occasionally giving away to startling expanses of bare rock. The river alongside the track sometimes ran smooth and broad, before suddenly turning wild and white, like a dangerous animal, which might purr or bite without warning.

"I can't believe we actually managed to remove Whyborne from Widdershins for a few days," Christine remarked from her seat across from us, going through the notes of her manuscript.

Griffin cast me a fond smile. "Is this the farthest you've been from home, my dear?"

"I simply don't see the need to go rushing about all over the country. Or the world," I said, folding my arms over my chest.

"Yes, I know." Christine frowned slightly and corrected one of her notations as best she could with the jostling of the train. "It's why we never married."

"What?" Surely I couldn't have heard her aright. "Married?"

"Of course." She didn't bother to look away from her notes. "It must have occurred to you."

"Good gad, of course it didn't! Are you completely mad?"

Christine rolled her eyes and finally looked at me. "Do try to consider this objectively. It would have given us a bit more respectability, at least in some circles, and I shouldn't have to put up with dunderheads constantly asking what my husband thinks of my career. We would be of no trouble to one another at all, I should think, and it isn't as if we would be the first couple to seal their vows with a handshake rather than a kiss."

"I cannot believe this." I turned to Griffin, expecting him to be equally horrified. Instead, he seemed to be attempting to suppress laughter—and doing a rather poor job of it.

"I don't see why not," Christine went on. "But if we wed, you would be expected to accompany me to Egypt, and I can't see you enjoying such a trip. So I decided against it."

"Thank heavens," I muttered. "And thank you for consulting me in all this, by the way. I can't believe you'd actually think I'd agree to some…some sham marriage! It's a sacred vow!"

"Really? I thought you were a materialist?"

I glared at her, although to no effect, as she'd turned back to her notes. "That hardly implies my oath is meaningless. Nor," I added, turning to Griffin, since he at least paid attention to me, "can I believe you aren't upset."

"I am, my dear," he soothed. "It's only I don't find the idea particularly shocking. It's hardly an uncommon arrangement for men like us."

I folded my arms across my chest and slouched in my seat, glaring at them both. "You find the idea of me moving into a separate house and marrying Christine to be amusing, do you?"

"No, I find the idea of you marrying Christine at all amusing."

"You're both horrid," I muttered, fixing my gaze out the window. "I cannot imagine why I put up with either of you."

Fortunately, we didn't have much farther to go. The train plunged into a long tunnel. Beside me, Griffin tensed. I relented and put my hand on his, in an attempt to alleviate his fear of underground places. In the dark, his fingers curled tight around mine. I wished we were alone, so I might speak some comforting words.

The tunnel seemed to go on forever, before ending in a sudden blaze of light. The mountainside tumbled away sharply beneath us as the train roared over a high trestle, spanning a deep gorge. On the other side, we passed through a much shorter tunnel, before descending a gentle grade as the mountains gradually rose around us. By the time the train began to brake, the green peaks loomed to either side like old men, peering down at the tiny creatures which had dared wake them from their sleep. Only a narrow strip of blue sky remained visible; the hours of direct sunlight must be short indeed.

The train came to a stop at a small depot. Christine gathered her notes and tucked them into a valise, and we soon found ourselves on a busy platform. Men sorted crates, boxes, barrels, luggage, and mail sacks into various wagons. One wall held a series of posters, each one with the likeness of a man, all labeled "public enemy," and warning any who saw them to report to the nearest authorities immediately. The infamous McCoy gang, no doubt, who had vanished mysteriously.

A man with the build—and face—of a whippet approached us. He wore a brown suit, which matched his bowler hat, and a drooping mustache, which matched his morose expression. "Dr. Whyborne?" he asked.

Although the case was technically Griffin's, our trip had put me in a rather awkward position. As the Ladysmith's resident philologist, I was a nonentity as far as most of the world was concerned. It was a state of affairs which suited me quite well, but unfortunately was of absolutely no use in this case. As Niles Whyborne's youngest son, however...

"Er, yes," I stammered. Curse it, Griffin was much better at this. Everyone was much better at this.

The man's gaze took in every detail, from my oxfords to my hat, but his expression told me nothing of his inevitable judgment. "I'm Clark Fredericks. Mr. Orme sent me to meet you."

Mr. Orme operated Threshold Mine for Stotz Mining. I automatically touched the letter of introduction in my pocket. "Oh, er, yes." Who was this Fredericks fellow? An overseer of some sort? A manservant? I held out my hand. "I'm pleased to make your acquaintance."

"Right this way, sir," he said, and turned to lead the way out. Feeling like a fool, I let my hand drop back to my side.

A carriage awaited us outside the depot. Without speaking further, Fredericks climbed into the driver's seat and impatiently waited for us to get in. Trying to contain a scowl, I opened the door and waited while Christine ignored Griffin's offer of assistance and climbed inside. As soon as we settled, the carriage lurched into motion, and we crossed into Threshold.

My first impression of the town was of its roads: utterly unpaved, filled with potholes, and a misery to endure inside a conveyance of any sort. Every jolt threatened to shove my spine into my skull, and Christine let out a series of curses, which would have felled a sailor.

Griffin directed his attention out the windows, however, and it seemed a good idea to imitate him, as he had experience in these matters. I strove, therefore, to gain at least an overall impression of the town as we passed through.

Like many other mining towns, the company had built Threshold. One day, there had been wilderness; the next, loggers cleared vast acreage, while builders followed close on their heels, constructing a brand-new town as quickly as possible. Almost as soon as the first homes were finished, the company filled them with workers.

The narrowness and depth of the hollow forced the town into a long line to either side of the creek. Above, the peaks seemed to lean in, but one towered above its fellows. Was this Threshold Mountain, for which the town and the mine had been named?

And what, I wondered, had the mountain been named for? A threshold to where? Or what? As far as I knew, only untamed wilderness lay on the other side of the ridge, just as it had here until recently.

Chickens and small children scattered out of our way as the carriage jolted along the muddy track. We passed the general store, an enormous, three-story affair whose loading doors opened directly onto the railroad tracks. Beyond lay the town proper, which mainly consisted of row upon row of identical houses, all of which appeared to have been built in great haste using the shoddiest materials available. I glimpsed a church, also cheaply constructed, and a huge, one-story building with a sign proclaiming it the "Threshold Community Center."

Over everything hung a pall of smoke and dust, darkening the whitewashed houses, graying the laundry dangling from lines, and seaming the creased faces we passed. Foul smoke, reeking of sulfur, boiled from the beehive-shaped coke ovens. The sides of the gorge blocked the wind, and the smoke was thick as fog in some places. We rattled across a makeshift bridge over the creek, and the fetid stench of sewage rose from waters stained a bright, poisonous orange.

What an awful place. I longed for Widdershins's fishy breeze.

The entrance to the mine itself lay near the lowest point of the hollow. Mules drew carts laden with coal along a set of rails, back and forth from the mine to a tall, wooden building beside the railroad tracks. Enormous piles of debris—refuse from the mine, I assumed—towered nearby. One of them smoldered alarmingly, adding its fumes to the fog belching from the coke ovens.

The carriage finally came to a halt in front of a wooden building not far from the mine entrance. Griffin hopped out, pausing to assist Christine, who glared at him for his trouble.

"Mr. Orme's office is just inside," Fredericks said. "I'll wait and take you to the hotel when your business is done."

Three men loitered about the porch as we approached, all of them in suits and with conspicuous firearms at their sides. "Pinkertons," Griffin murmured. "Here to act as mine guards. I expect Fredericks is one as well."

The guards watched us coolly as we mounted the steps and crossed to the door. I felt glad to enter the building, away from their judging gazes.

The door opened directly onto a large room, occupying the front half of the building. My first glance took in two desks, a number of filing cabinets, and a pot-bellied stove, cold now in the late spring. Surveyor's maps decorated the walls, marking the locations of coal seams.

Three men occupied the office. One sat at a smaller desk, and I assumed him to be the operator's secretary. The cold-eyed man with a receding hairline and small, neat mustache must be Mr. Orme. As for the third, who sat in a chair in the corner, clearly awaiting our arrival…

My heart sped involuntarily—dear lord, he was handsome! Classic features, firm chin, sculpted lips: my throat went dry just looking at him. He wore his golden hair neatly parted in the center, and the small, trim mustache enhanced rather than detracted from his tempting mouth.

Upon seeing us, his blue eyes widened, and all the color drained from his face. "Griffin?" he exclaimed, rising to his feet. "Griffin Flaherty?"

I blinked then glanced at Griffin, who seemed just as shocked as the handsome stranger. "Elliot?"

Elliot crossed the room and clasped Griffin's hand warmly, putting his free hand on Griffin's shoulder in a friendly gesture I immediately resented. "Mr. Whyborne's letter said a private detective would accompany his son, but I had no idea it would be you!" He stood back, as if to take in the sight of Griffin. "You appear to be doing well—very well indeed."

"I-I am." Griffin swallowed visibly; clearly, this chance meeting had shaken him badly. "You're heading the Pinkerton operation here?"

"Yes. The opportunity was too good to pass up." The man looked as if he wished to speak to Griffin further, had politeness not forbade it. "Are you not going to introduce your companions?"

"Yes; of course." Regaining some of his composure, Griffin turned to me. "Dr. Percival Endicott Whyborne, permit me to introduce to you Mr. Elliot Manning, lately of the Chicago office. Mr. Manning, Dr. Whyborne."

We shook hands; I hoped my palm wasn't too sweaty. "A pleasure," he said, looking me straight in the eye.

He was even more beautiful close at hand. I looked away hastily; the tips of my ears burned. "Yes. Er, I mean, I'm glad to meet you."

Introductions proceeded; as I had guessed, the man behind the large desk was Mr. Orme. He called for his secretary to fetch more chairs from one of the back rooms. Once we were seated, he turned to Christine.

"Forgive me…Dr. Putnam, was it?" he asked. "We are rather rough here in Threshold, and I fear you may find us unprepared to entertain a lady."

"Quite all right," she said, and offered nothing further.

Although I appreciated her stance, I also knew Orme had every right to wonder what her place in the visit might be. "Dr. Putnam works at the museum with me," I explained.

"Surely you must be the lady archaeologist who uncovered the pharaoh's tomb last year," Manning said with open admiration.

Christine seemed surprised he recognized her name, although, of course, it had been in all the papers. "Quite so. Although I prefer to simply be known as an archaeologist, if you please."

"Oh!" the secretary—he hadn't been introduced—blurted out. "I read about that! How astonishing!"

"Yes." Orme's speech had a curious, controlled quality to it. He seemed a man who held back everything of himself, and did his utmost merely to observe those around him rather than participate in life.

Did I come across in the same manner?

"As for why we've come," Griffin said, accepting an offer of coffee from the secretary, "I assume Mr. Whyborne's letter explained his concerns?"

Orme transferred his reptile-cool gaze from Christine to Griffin. "Yes. As did Mr. Stotz's. However, I assure you, there is no cause for concern. As the operator, my duty is to keep this mine running, a task I intend to fulfill. Mr. Manning and his detectives have the workers in hand. They chase away anyone who even looks sympathetic to unions, before they can get any farther than the depot."

"And what about the stone which was found?" I asked.

"Some Indian trinket," Orme replied. "Such things are common enough. Nothing to get worked up about."

I knew better, but doubted I could convince him. "And what of the, er, strange happenings?"

Elliot Manning shook his head, a wry smile on his lips. "Miners are a superstitious lot," he said. "You'd be appalled if you knew all their little rituals to ensure good luck, or ward off injury and the like. They're convinced any rockfall or accident must be caused by ghosts, or spirits, or some other rubbish. If a lad disappears, he must have been snatched by devils, instead of gone to look for a better life away from the mine. A dog growls, there must be bogies in the woods. A band of outlaws escape the sheriff's half-trained men, they must have been dragged beneath the earth by monsters. It's all nonsense."

"I see." Clearly, neither man was inclined to treat the matter with any seriousness. "Still, as my father wished me to make an investigation, we will remain to enjoy your town for a few days."

"Of course," Orme said, although he didn't look happy about it. Perhaps he simply didn't care for the oversight. "I'll have Fredericks take you to your hotel."

Clearly, we had been dismissed. Manning walked us back onto the porch. "Even though you're on a wasted trip, it's good to see you again," he told Griffin, extending his hand.

Griffin stared at the neatly manicured hand for a moment then shook it. "And you," he said.

"Dr. Putnam. Dr. Whyborne. It was a pleasure." Manning gave us a little bow. "I hope we'll have the chance to get better acquainted before you leave."

I retreated into the carriage after Griffin and Christine. As we pulled away, I looked back. Manning stood in the road, watching us depart with a troubled expression on his face.

CHAPTER 5

The porter shut the door as he left, and I sank down into the single chair of my hotel room. The place seemed decent enough; the clerk who'd greeted us had immediately summoned the hotelkeeper himself, Mr. Brumfield. He assured me I would find my stay satisfactory, even if his little hotel wasn't up to the sort of accommodations to which I was accustomed. I couldn't bring myself to tell him I'd never stayed in a hotel of any sort before, let alone one of the grand resorts he no doubt imagined.

The little room was quite spare, with only a bed, chair, wardrobe, and washstand. Brumfield had given me a corner room on the fourth floor, assuring me this would allow me to have two windows instead of only one, and thus be able to take full advantage of the breeze if the night proved warm. It also meant only a single wall adjoined another room.

As if summoned by my thoughts, there came a sharp knock on the connecting door. As soon as I slid back the bolt, it swung open. Griffin, now sans coat and tie, stepped through to take me in his arms.

"I've been wanting to do this all afternoon," he murmured against my lips. His hands strayed, one shaping my back, the other sliding between us.

"There's no time," I whispered, unsure how thick the walls might be. "Not if we're to wash up and dress for dinner. Mr. Brumfield said it is served promptly at seven-thirty."

Griffin abandoned his attentions and stared off to one side, frowning slightly. "I wonder why Orme didn't extend a dinner invitation to you. Since your father owns an interest in the company which employs him, courting your favor would seem to be in his best interest."

"Do you think he might know more about the situation than he let on?"

"He's hiding something," Griffin said with certainty. "What, I don't know. It could be as innocent as removing a bit more than his share of the profits before he sends them on to the company."

I doubted Father would consider such an activity "innocent." Deserving of a hanging, perhaps. But I hadn't come here to worry about such things, and frankly, given Father's dubious actions with the Brotherhood, I hardly thought him in the position to judge anyone. "Would your...friend...Mr. Manning know?" I asked reluctantly.

"I don't know if I would call us friends. Not any more."

"You had a falling out of some sort?" I hoped the question sounded casual. I had never enquired into Griffin's past lovers, save for one occasion, but I cringed at the thought of being compared with the Adonis-like detective.

Griffin let go of me and stepped away, putting some space between us. "Not exactly. I met Elliot soon after I arrived in Chicago. I owe him a great deal."

"I see. And were you two...?" Please let him say no.

"Yes."

Drat. I sank down onto the edge of the bed and tried to keep my face composed. I couldn't possibly measure up to the handsome Manning. Having the opportunity now to compare us side by side, so to speak, Griffin would surely come to his senses. "Oh," I said miserably. A thought occurred to me, which would certainly explain the odd tension between the two men. "I suppose he knew about your, er, confinement?"

Griffin sat on the bed beside me. His career with the Pinkertons had ended in horror and death, compounded with the further agony of being confined to a madhouse, thanks to the unbelievable nature of his tale.

He hadn't been mad, of course. The monsters were real, even if most people didn't know it.

"Everyone knew," Griffin replied. His fingers twined with mine. "And no doubt he's told Orme by now. If Orme thinks me a lunatic and you a gullible dupe, we will need very strong proof, indeed, to convince them something is amiss here. No doubt either Elliot or Orme, or both of them, will try to warn you off me."

"I will have words for them if they do," I vowed.

"No." His grip tightened, and he finally looked me directly in the eye. "That may not be the wisest course. If they seem likely to open up to you, do not hesitate to express your shock, and to thank them effusively for the warning."

"But it seems faithless, to pretend I think you a madman."

A smile bloomed on his lips, dismissing the shadows from his eyes. "I know, my dear. Don't concern yourself. As long as you don't actually change your opinion of me, I shan't worry."

"I love you, Griffin."

"I love you, Ival." He kissed me, and his hands went to the buttons on my trousers, and I decided the world would not end if we were a little late for dinner.

After dinner, Christine retired to one of the private parlors with the stated intent of "getting some work done on the blasted manuscript." After bidding her goodnight, Griffin turned to me with a twinkle in his eye.

"Would you care to accompany me to the hotel bar?"

"Why on earth would I do such a thing?" I asked. Truthfully, I'd only been in such an establishment once before, with disastrous results.

"Because Orme isn't going to give us any useful information—at least, not willingly—and I'm not certain Elliot will go against his employer without compelling reason. Our only remaining avenue is to talk to the locals. As we came in, I noticed an outside entrance to the bar, which means it probably serves as the saloon for the whole town, not just hotel guests. This could be our best chance to find out what—if anything—is amiss in Threshold."

"I see. Will I, er, have to speak to anyone?" I disliked chatting with strangers, one of the reasons I avoided restaurants, saloons, and clubs. "Or play cards?"

Griffin chuckled. "Actually, I forbid you to play cards. We want these men well-disposed to us, not ready to dispense a beating because you've taken their day's wages. Let me do the talking—I have some experience at this."

"Then why must I come at all?" I sounded churlish even to myself.

"Besides giving me the pleasure of your company, not to mention whatever insights you might have?" he asked.

Like an idiot, I blushed—but I also knew a thing or two about how his mind worked by now, at least enough to be certain he had an ulterior motive. "Yes, besides those."

"The unions haven't yet made inroads in the West Virginia coalfields, but not for lack of effort. If Orme has responded to the workers' fears with as much derision as he showed when speaking to us, the situation between miners and management could be very tense indeed. Their instinct will be to distrust us. If they see you're sincere, they'll be more inclined to cooperate with our investigation."

"So I will have to speak with them."

"And drink some. Just look earnest and nod your head."

I sighed, but this was why we'd come in the first place. And even if it hadn't been, Griffin had a way of getting me to agree to whatever scheme he had in mind. I'd like to think it was purely a matter of sympathy between us, but in truth it probably had more to do with his devilish grin and flashing eyes. "Oh, very well."

"I knew you'd see it my way."

The hotel bar was located to one side of the lobby, well away from the private sitting rooms. A haze of smoke greeted us as we stepped inside, and I managed not to wrinkle my nose at the numerous spittoons, not wishing to give what Griffin would consider the wrong impression to the men within.

A few customers looked to be clerks or businessmen, but I had no doubt the majority worked the mine in one capacity or another. Although most of them had made an effort to clean up, I noticed coal dust ground beneath their nails and in the seams of their faces. Their clothing was of a rougher quality, often patched and mended, showing stains at cuff or collar. In the summer heat, many of them had casually stripped off their suit coats and sat about in vests and shirtsleeves. I did my best not to look shocked, but this was a public place.

I wouldn't think of doing such a thing even at home, of course, although Griffin had no such inhibitions.

The clientele wasn't strictly male, although going by the manner of dress of the few women present, they were there in a professional capacity. I removed my hat automatically when one passed by, and received a look of surprise for the simple courtesy.

Our entry garnered the attention of others besides the prostitute. Conversation near us died down, and I felt hostile eyes fix on me. I hunched my shoulders automatically, trying to make myself shorter and more inconspicuous, although it worked no better than it ever had. Why did I have to be tall?

Seeming at ease, Griffin led the way across the room to an empty table in a corner. "Have a seat, Whyborne. I'll be right back with some whiskey." Removing his coat, he hung it neatly over the back of his chair, before making his way to the bar. I tried very hard not to watch his trim form.

I sat very still, feeling like a hunted thing, painfully conscious of other eyes on me. When someone slid into the chair beside me, I started rather badly, but it proved only to be the woman I'd taken my hat off to earlier.

"I ain't seen you around these parts before," she said, leaning over to display her plentiful charms. "My name's Lucy."

Where the devil had Griffin gone? I cast about for rescue, found none forthcoming, and fell back on manners. "A pleasure to meet you, Miss, er, Lucy." What on earth should I say? "P-Permit me to introduce myself. I'm Dr. Percival Endicott Whyborne."

Her eyes widened. "Really? They was saying you're the railroad tycoon's son, but I didn't believe it. Ain't you just a huckleberry above a persimmon! Nothing like the men around here."

She kept leaning farther and farther forward, and I became concerned her bodice wasn't up to the task of containing her bounty. I kept my eyes fixed firmly on her face and silently prayed the dressmaker had known her art. "Yes! Well, that's, er, very kind of you, m-miss."

Her smile turned sultry. "What's a girl got to do to get a drink in this place?"

Oh lord. "Nothing," I said firmly. "Truly." But hadn't Griffin counted a prostitute among his best resources at one time? "However, if you wish to keep me company, of course I will provide refreshment. As a gentleman."

She cocked her head at me curiously. "Huh. Got you a girl back home?"

"My family has certain expectations of me." I spoke only the truth—father expected me to fail spectacularly at whatever I turned my hand to—but I saw no need to elaborate.

"Well, if you're buying, I ain't saying no. Ain't saying no if you change your mind later, either," she added with a grin which revealed several missing teeth. Had she lost them through dental malady, or had one of her "clients" knocked them out? "Stay right here."

Somehow, she managed to get to the bar and back with a pair of whiskeys before Griffin returned. Now truly annoyed, I glanced around and found him deep in conversation with none other than Elliot Manning.

Curse it! I needed to extricate myself from this woman.

"Bartender put them on your bill," Lucy said, slipping back into the chair beside me. "Now, sweetie, what do you want to talk about?"

No, I had to do this. Griffin had entrusted me with it. No doubt seeing Manning again was painful for him, and he wouldn't thank me for interrupting. At least, I hoped such was the case. I knew I ought to be ashamed of the impulse, although I couldn't quite manage it.

"Well," I said, "I suppose about why I've come here."

"Ooh, some big business deal? Bet you have those all the time. You ever been to New York?"

"Er, no. To all the above." I took a bracing sip of my whiskey, and found it not half as foul as I'd expected. Perhaps the barkeep had given me what passed for quality in Threshold. No doubt I would be charged an extravagant amount for it, but Griffin was billing Father for our expenses, and this would simply have to be one of them.

"In truth," I said, "my father sent me here because he's concerned about these rumors of strange happenings in Threshold."

She drew back, wariness blooming in her dark eyes.

"I know Mr. Orme doesn't believe," I went on hurriedly. "But I don't agree with him. Did you see the black stone they uncovered nearby?"

She nodded reluctantly. "Yes. Gave me the crawlies, it did."

"Me as well," I admitted. "Unfortunately, someone stole the stone before we could examine it, so I don't know anything for certain. However, I am, shall we say, open to possibilities others may not be. My partner, Mr. Flaherty, and I tried to discuss the situation with Mr. Orme and Mr. Manning earlier, to no avail. Do you know anything, Miss…?"

She looked at me for a long moment. "My last name is Mercer."

"Miss Mercer."

Her whiskey disappeared in a single gulp. "Most men don't give a damn what my first name is, let alone my last, or whether I'm a miss or not."

I flushed. "Oh! Forgive me for my assumption, Mrs. Mercer."

"Nothing to forgive." She turned and signaled one of the other women. "Hey! Dolly! Come here!"

The miners Dolly had been speaking with didn't look very happy at her abrupt departure. Griffin was probably cursing my name, but he really should have known better than to leave me to my own devices.

"Hello, handsome," Dolly said as she sashayed over. She was as blonde and as fair as Lucy—Mrs. Mercer—was dusky.

"Don't bother," Mrs. Mercer said to her friend. Colleague? "Dr. Whyborne here is trying to get to the bottom of what's going on in Threshold. Serious-like."

"Miss…?" I said helplessly, confronted by another set of breasts at my table.

"Dyhart," Mrs. Mercer said. Dolly looked surprised, but I nodded cordially.

"Miss Dyhart. If you and Mrs. Mercer would be so kind, I could truly use whatever assistance you can give in this matter."

"Well, bugger me blind," Miss Dyhart said. Thank heavens I had been hardened by Christine's frequent exclamations, although at least she kept most of hers in Arabic. "This is going to call for more whiskey."

CHAPTER 6

"Anne just up and disappeared the morning of her wedding," whispered Miss Hatford in a low voice. *"They* said she was just a drunken whore who couldn't be trusted. Bastards."

Somehow, I had ended up the lone male at the table, surrounded by three women of very questionable reputation. A great deal of whiskey had been consumed in the meantime, and I wondered what Father would think if he knew how his money was being spent.

Actually, never mind. If he knew I'd spent the night surrounded by female prostitutes, he'd probably consider it a sign of improvement.

"It's true, Dr. Whyborne," Miss Dyhart added earnestly, as if she feared I'd never believe her. "She loved Thomas. He was willing to overlook her past, give her a home. A real family. She didn't talk about nothing else for weeks before the wedding. She wouldn't have just left."

"How would she get out of town?" Mrs. Mercer asked archly. "Ain't like trains leave Threshold in the middle of the night like they do the big cities. And you ain't going to tell me she just walked off over the mountain, without any of her belongings."

"She went out at night?" I asked, trying to sort through the women's story. "The night before her wedding?"

"She weren't married yet, was she?" Mrs. Mercer demanded fiercely.

Dear God, I'd be lucky if I survived this interview. "I didn't mean it as a criticism," I said, holding up my hands to ward her off. "I only intend to enquire as to the circumstances of her disappearance. Not, er, pass judgment on those circumstances."

They all relaxed, and I let out a glad breath. "That's right," Miss Dyhart said.

"Forgive me, I hate to suggest it, but is it possible she came to harm at the hands of the man she went to meet?" I asked. "Threshold is no Whitechapel, but…"

"Well, ain't you sweet!" exclaimed Miss Hatford.

How could pointing out their profession carried with it the danger of death and dismemberment possibly be "sweet?" But they all leveled fond looks at me, so I refrained from asking. Griffin would be proud.

Griffin sat in one corner, still speaking quietly with Manning. Damn the man, had he entirely abandoned our purpose here?

"Maybe," Miss Hatford said. "But she ain't the only one to disappear."

Miss Dyhart nodded. "The Kincaid brothers didn't just run off. They worked the mine, all three of them, and spent Sunday hunting to get a bit of meat on their mama's table. Their daddy is sick with miner's lung, and he can't work most of the time. They depend on those boys. Worm—sorry, that's what we call Mr. Orme—says they figured they could try their luck somewhere else, away from the mine. But they wouldn't have just left."

"And they would've taken the train," Mrs. Mercer added, to a general round of nodding.

"But there's more." Miss Dyhart leaned in and lowered her voice conspiratorially. "You got to promise me, Mr. Whyborne, you won't tell nobody I said this."

"He's a doctor!" Mrs. Mercer hissed, poking her in the ribs.

"You are?" asked Miss Hatford, reaching for the hem of her skirt, as if she meant to lift it up. "I got this rash—"

"No! I-I'm not that sort of doctor."

"Anyway," Miss Dyhart said impatiently, "you got to promise."

"Of course. On my honor as a gentleman."

The ladies exchanged glances, before nodding to each other in apparent agreement. "Guess honor means something, coming from you," Mrs. Mercer said.

Miss Dyhart's voice grew low and hushed, and all three women leaned in, their eyes gleaming intently in the gaslight. "The men are plum scared," she said. "They'd deny it to their dying days, and give me a good smack across the mouth for saying it, but they're terrified of the mine. Jim Banks swore he heard a voice from somewhere behind him, when he knew for sure he was the last man out of the room at the end of the shift. Others have heard knocking and raps, coming from nowhere they could figure. The whole mine is haunted."

Mrs. Mercer shook her head. "That ain't what Rider said."

"Who?" Was any of this useful or even true? Or just the usual wild tales of tommyknockers and ghosts?

"Rider Hicks." Mrs. Mercer said. "Half-breed Injun who worked the coke ovens. 'Bout went crazy when they brought the black stone back to town. Tried to warn folks, until Worm ordered the Pinkertons to arrest him. The he ran for the hills. Ain't been seen since."

Of course he hadn't. Why should anything be easy? "What did he say?"

"Started screaming about winged devils and yayhos and I don't even know what all. Said they had to take the stone back where they found it, close the mine, and leave Threshold Mountain well enough alone."

"Yayhos," muttered Miss Dyhart with a shiver. "You think they're behind folks disappearing, Dr. Whyborne?"

"Forgive me, but I don't know what a yayho is."

"They're…well, I don't rightly know. I grew up outside of Elkins, and my granddaddy used to say don't go into the hollows, 'cause the yayhos live there. A little girl got swooped up just a few years ago by some flying thing—it was in the local paper and everything. Figure it must've been a yayho."

If only I knew a bit more about regional folklore. "I see. Thank you. Was the stone found in the mine?"

"Oh, no, it weren't." They exchanged looks, apparently surprised I didn't know this detail. "There was a cave, you see," Mrs. Mercer went on. "At the head of the hollow, right below the highest peak of Threshold Mountain. I guess they thought there might be a coal seam there, or maybe part of the same one, I don't rightly know. A bunch of company men went up there. They found the stone in the cave, and one of the boys who'd gone with them ran it back down, thinking it might be worth something. Mr. Stotz, he's interested in antiquities and such, so they sent it along to him. I guess he gave it to your daddy."

Was Stotz in the Brotherhood as well, or did he have less sinister interests? Not that it mattered, in this case. I hoped. "I see. Do you know who else was in the party? I'd like to speak to as many of them as possible."

There came an odd moment of silence. "They was killed, Dr. Whyborne," Miss Hatford said in a soft, frightened voice. "The cave fell in right after. Folks say it happened 'cause they disturbed the funny rock."

"Oh," I said.

"That ain't true," Mrs. Mercer said, but there was a grim note in her voice. "There was one survivor. Came stumbling into town days after, when we'd all given him up for dead."

I leaned forward involuntarily. "Who?"

"The Pinkerton boss. Elliot Manning."

It seemed the ladies had reached the end of their knowledge and speculation, both. "We'd best be back to work, before the boys get too rowdy," Mrs. Mercer said. She finished her whiskey in a single swallow and stood up.

I hastily rose as well. "Well, er, thank you, ladies. You've been most helpful."

"Thank you for the drinks, Dr. Whyborne. I figure you're something special. I sure hope the girl you got back home appreciates you."

She sauntered off, along with Miss Hatford. Miss Dyhart hesitated—then abruptly leaned over and kissed my cheek, before hurrying off.

"I can't leave you alone for ten minutes," Griffin said at my elbow.

I jumped, as if he'd caught me doing something unsavory. "I could have used your assistance!" I snapped, keeping my voice low.

"I think you were getting along quite well without me. Really, I must acknowledge your prowess. I turn my back for a few seconds, only to discover you entertaining every whore in Threshold at once."

My face felt hot enough to fry an egg. "I'd thank you not to refer to them in such a vulgar manner. They were quite kind to me, after all. Unlike some persons whom I shan't name."

"Forgive me," he said, without looking even slightly penitent. "Shall we depart?"

"Finished reminiscing with Mr. Manning, are you?"

A shadow went over his face, and I wished I hadn't been quite so blunt. "For now. Let's speak further in private."

We left the bar and went up to our rooms. As there was no one else in the hall, I deemed it safe to enter through Griffin's door. "Don't be put out with me," he said, shutting and locking the door behind us. "When I saw you had engaged a…companion…I assumed you would get whatever information you might out of her. It made more sense to divide our efforts."

"How do you know I was gathering information?" I asked recklessly. "Perhaps I was setting up a-a commercial transaction. Perhaps they are all three to come to my room later."

Griffin burst out laughing, curse him. "Because, my dear, in all the months I have known you, I have never seen your eyes stray even once in the direction of a woman."

"Or, I hope, a man."

"You're subtle about it, but I've learned the signs." He slipped his arms about my waist. "Come now. Don't be cross with me. You know I only mean to tease."

I sighed. Griffin did not play fair at all, gazing up at me through thick lashes, the tip of his tongue just visible against the plump swell of his lower lip. "I just wish you wouldn't change your plans without informing me," I said in defeat.

His hand stole up my back, beneath my coat. "A detective learns to be flexible," he murmured, pressing closer. "Are you…flexible?"

Parts of me grew anything but. "I don't even know what you mean. Besides, I thought you intended to tell me if Manning had anything of interest to say?"

"And I shall. Later. After I've gotten you out of these clothes." He caught my tie in one hand and used it to haul me down for a kiss.

"My room," I mumbled against his lips. "It has no adjoining wall save this one." In other words, it was far less likely someone would hear us.

"An excellent suggestion."

I caught his hand and drew him after me, through the connecting door and into my room. Griffin shut it behind us, perhaps to further muffle sound, before all but tackling me, his hands busy at the buttons of my vest, then my shirt.

I loved his passion. I didn't entirely understand why he directed it toward me, especially having been with someone like Elliot Manning...

Who had been the only survivor of the group which had found the stone. I must remember to mention it to him. Which meant we would have to talk to handsome Elliot yet again, reminding Griffin of past times both terrible and good.

What had they spoken about earlier? And was Griffin comparing us even now?

How could I possibly compete? I'd never even kissed anyone prior to Griffin, whereas Elliot struck me as a man of the world. Not to mention how blasted handsome he was, in direct opposition to my scrawny, gawky self.

Griffin pulled back slightly and cocked his head. "Is everything all right?"

"Fine," I lied.

"Are you certain?" His hand brushed my flagging erection. "It's been a long and tiring day—if you wish merely to sleep, I understand."

Wonderful. This would surely make a fantastic showing. Elliot was probably some sort of sexual athlete. "It's fine," I lied again, even as my skin heated with shame. "Come—lie on top of me."

As I leaned back on the bed, however, something crinkled beneath my elbow. Startled, I sat back up, my skull nearly colliding with Griffin's nose.

A folded piece of paper, which had certainly not been there when I'd left for dinner, lay atop the bedclothes.

I picked it up and opened it. The script inside was written in an almost childish hand, as if the writer hadn't been afforded much in the way of an education.

"Not everyone is who they seem to be.
Don't trust any as have been to the woods.
Signed,
A Friend"

"Whyborne?" asked Griffin worriedly.

I passed the note to him in silence. He read it, the line between his brows growing deeper. When he looked up, all passion had been replaced by grim intent.

"Perhaps you should tell me what you learned," he said. "And we shall ask ourselves who has access to your room."

I told him all I had heard, from the tales of yayhos, to the Indian who had seemed to know something about the black stone, to the fact only Elliot had returned alive from the cave where it was found. He paced the room as I spoke, brow furrowed in thought. I donned my nightshirt and sat on the bed, watching him.

When I finished, his expression eased into a smile. "Well done, my dear. We'll make a detective of you yet."

My cheeks heated at his praise. "It was nothing."

"Nonsense." He came to the bed and pressed a kiss to my forehead. "At least we have some avenues of investigation now."

"I'm glad to have been of assistance, then. So are you, er, coming to bed?"

Griffin shook his head. "Whoever gained access to your room must be hotel staff. Or one of the Pinkertons, I suppose, trained in lock picking. It isn't likely they'll come back in the middle of the night, but we should be cautious."

"Oh." I watched in disappointment as he took my chair and carefully wedged it beneath the door knob. I understood his reasoning, but it didn't lessen my desire for his company.

He paused long enough to kiss me again. "Sleep well, my dear," he said.

"And you," I answered, but he had already shut the connecting door between us.

Despite Griffin's wish, I slept poorly that night.

At some point before dawn, I half-woke—or dreamed I did—to the sound of voices coming through the window I had neglected to close. One of them spoke in normal human tones, but the reply came in a hateful buzzing voice which filled me with an inarticulate dread.

I finally awoke alone to a damp room and a headache. Only one night in this dreadful town, and already I wished to flee back to Widdershins.

I rapped on the connecting door before dressing. When I received no answer, I made my way down to breakfast alone.

Long tables filled the hotel dining room. Last night they had been crowded, with locals as well as guests partaking in the meal, but this morning they were sparsely occupied. Christine and Griffin sat at the far end of a table, well away from anyone else, engaged in deep conversation. They looked up at my approach.

"I was just telling Christine about your admirers," Griffin said.

"Yes," Christine said, vigorously cutting into a slice of calf's liver. "Amazing how women react when you treat them as human beings, isn't it?"

"You're being quite unfair," Griffin objected as I seated myself beside him.

A waiter hurried over with a menu card. I selected coffee, eggs, and oatmeal.

"Perhaps," Christine allowed. "But you would not be above flirting if you thought it the easiest path to your goal."

"Did you tell her about the note?" I asked.

Griffin chewed thoughtfully on a bite of toast. "'Don't trust any as have been to the woods.'"

"It would have been nice if they could have left us a straightforward warning," I complained, sipping the coffee the waiter poured for me.

"No doubt it seemed quite straightforward to them," Griffin replied. "A local, or anyone who has been here any time at all, might know exactly what it means."

The eggs were rubbery, and I shoved them away with a grimace. "What is our plan?"

Griffin tapped his knife absently against the edge of his plate, usually a sign of deep contemplation. "I think we should go into town and ask around. Perhaps talk to the relatives of the missing men." He took a deep breath, which he let out with a sigh. "At some point, we should speak with Elliot as well, although it might be best to give him today to…consider things."

"You don't sound very pleased," Christine said, eyeing Griffin closely.

"Let us say our friendship suffered a strain when I left the Pinkertons," he replied evasively.

"Hmm." She transferred her sharp gaze to me. I busied myself with the oatmeal, which was much better than the eggs. "Do you mean to take him into your confidence?"

"No," Griffin said. "Not yet, anyway. For one thing, he is in the employ of Mr. Orme, who doesn't seem at all keen on our investigation. If we find any proof he might accept, however, I would like to recruit his aid."

"Whyborne, please stop attacking the oatmeal," Christine said crossly. "You're making a terrible mess."

"Oh!" My cheeks grew hot, and I quickly wiped at the splattered oatmeal with my napkin. Both of my companions regarded me with alarmed curiosity. "So, er, you wish to go into town?"

"I think I will remain here and work on my manuscript," Christine decided. "Going about talking to the locals sounds dreadfully boring. But if you find you need anyone shot, send word and I'll come at once."

CHAPTER 7

Once we'd finished with breakfast, Griffin and I descended into Threshold proper.

My impression of the town on foot was similar to the one I'd formed in the carriage. The hollow was nothing more than a narrow slot between peaks, whose tree-shrouded hillsides blocked both the early and late light, allowing full sunlight only when the sun stood at its highest point in the sky. Threshold Mountain loomed over all, like a giant disdainful of the tiny creatures seeking to pierce its skin and steal its riches.

The heights blocked the prevailing west-east breezes, leaving the air stagnant and still. Mosquitoes hummed above pools of water in the unpaved streets, and sweat prickled my neck beneath my collar. I longed for a bit of shade, but the lack of trees anywhere within the town made it a forlorn hope.

As we penetrated farther into Threshold, we passed the general store, the church, and a medical clinic. Beyond lay a few other shops, then the main part of the town, where the miners lived. The houses were packed together by necessity, given the narrowness of the valley, each one identical to all the rest. A few residents had made an effort; one house had a fresh coat of yellow paint, while another sported window boxes filled with sickly flowers. Several had attempted vegetable gardens, none of which seemed to be prospering any more than the flowers, as if something about the land or the water carried within it a blight. Given the creek was little more than an open sewer, with the added foulness of effluvia from the mine, I could well believe it.

The thick air reeked of fetid water and burning coal. As before, the coke ovens sent out a vast sheet of mephitic smoke which diluted the sunlight from burnished gold to watery gray. A fine layer of ash and coal dust coated everything, including the wash hung out to dry between houses. A few very young children played in the streets, along with an assortment of chickens, ducks, and geese. We passed a handful of scrawny hogs digging through the trash, watching us with small, unfriendly eyes.

Griffin's first case in Widdershins had taken us to the docks, and there I'd seen a certain amount of squalor. But the sheer wretchedness of the flimsy houses and filthy children, of the smoke and nasty creek, was beyond everything I'd ever imagined.

"What a horrid place," I said, aghast. "How do people stand to live here?"

Griffin's mouth twitched. "Because this is where the work is. Coal mining doesn't pay much, but for a man with no other skills, looking to feed his family, it's better than nothing."

"I suppose, but surely the houses could be improved, or the streets paved."

"All of which would cost the company money." Griffin gave me a half-smile, but his eyes were sad. "I almost envy your shock."

"You don't find it so?"

"I've been in slums far worse. At least here it's only one family to a house, not five."

"Oh." I felt like a fool. I'd grown up in the desiccated splendor of Whyborne House, but in my student days, I'd lived in a small room in a boarding house, on a diet consisting largely of beans and bread. I'd thought myself practically a martyr at the time. But my clothes had been clean, and I'd spent my days studying with some of the foremost scholars in America.

In truth, there had never been any real danger of falling too far. Mother might have had to pay for my education by selling her own jewelry, but if I'd ever found myself in dire need, I had only to humble myself by showing back up at the door to Whyborne House and apologizing to Father. It might have meant a certain death of the soul, but at least I wouldn't have starved.

We walked farther into the settlement. No men besides ourselves seemed to be about; no doubt they worked in the mine, for the most part, or fed the coke ovens, or ran the machine shops. Domestic chores occupied the women: sweeping the coal dust from their stoops, hanging out the wash, working the small gardens, or carrying pails of water.

Our first destination was the home of Rider Hicks, the runaway Indian. Griffin had asked a few casual questions of one of the hotel porters, and discovered Mrs. Hicks remained behind in Threshold.

Griffin led the way to the line of houses nearest to the coke ovens. These, I could not help but notice, were exclusively the domain of immigrants and blacks—and presumably Indians, as Rider Hicks had lived here. The ash from the ovens laid a greasy film over every surface, and formed a scum on the pools of standing water.

I spotted Mr. Fredericks and two other Pinkerton guards standing in front of a house. The house itself was the neatest I'd yet seen in the ramshackle town, cheerfully painted and surrounded by patches of flowers, which had managed to bloom where others had only withered.

The presence of the Pinkertons couldn't be a good sign. Griffin and I exchanged a look and picked up our pace.

"You've got fifteen minutes," Fredericks said as we came up. "So shut your damn mouth and get to it."

The object of his ire was a young black woman, whose dress and headscarf were worn from many washings, but patched with careful stitches and spotlessly clean even amidst these surroundings. Her eyes went wide as if with fear, and she clutched an infant to her breast, as though seeking to protect it from Fredericks.

I disliked the smug expression on Fredericks's face. His companion held a shotgun loosely in one hand, which made me no happier.

"What's going on here?" I asked, more sharply than I'd intended.

Fredericks tipped his hat at me. "Just taking care of some company business, Dr. Whyborne."

"Business?" Griffin asked. I could feel the coiled tension in him when he stopped shoulder-to-shoulder with me.

"These houses are for miners or those who tend the coke ovens," Fredericks said, scowling at having to explain himself. "Bertie's man done run off, which means she's got no right to stay here."

"You chased him away!" she broke in. "Please, sir, I don't have anywhere else to go! I have work—"

"This town already has plenty of whores," Fredericks said.

My belly tightened, not just at the insult, but the dismissive way he said it. Certainly, as Mrs. Mercer had said, this was a man who didn't care anything for the familiarity of her first name, let alone whatever identity she wished to claim. "Surely you can spare her a few days in which to find somewhere else to go."

For the first time, he turned his full attention on me. "This ain't a charity, Dr. Whyborne. This is a company town, and she ain't working for the company. If Rider comes back, well, she can keep the house. Seems fair, don't it?"

This was Rider Hicks's wife. Was there more to this than the fact of his absence? Did someone hope he would return if his family was at risk?

"As I understand it, Mr. Hicks left town after being threatened with jail," I said. Acid roiled in my belly. Thank goodness I hadn't eaten the overdone eggs. "Unless you have workers waiting on housing, what harm will come from letting her stay another few days?"

Fredericks eyed us uneasily, perhaps remembering my parentage. At first, I thought he wouldn't listen. Then he gave a single, sharp nod. "Fine. But unless Hicks is back and at work in a few days, she leaves."

"As you say," I agreed, knowing I was lucky to have gotten even this much.

"Come on," Fredericks said to his men.

Once they left, I shook my head and turned back to the woman on the porch. She'd transferred her wary gaze from the Pinkertons to us, but dropped it quickly when she saw me looking. "Thank you, sir," she said, giving as deep a curtsey as she could manage with a sleeping baby in her arms. Her voice trembled, though, and I wondered if she expected us to demand some vile repayment.

I removed my hat and stepped just close enough to have a civil conversation. "Mrs. Hicks?" I asked.

"Yes," she said warily.

"Please, allow me to introduce myself. I am Dr. Percival Endicott Whyborne, and this is my associate, Mr. Griffin Flaherty. We've come to Threshold to investigate…well, any strange goings-on."

"Your husband seemed to recognize the black stone found in the cave on Threshold Mountain," Griffin added.

"I don't know nothing about it," she replied quickly.

Was she telling the truth? Considering her husband had been threatened with jail for spreading stories, I wouldn't blame her for lying. "Mrs. Hicks, I assure you, we take this matter very seriously indeed. If you know anything at all, it would be a great help if you would tell us."

After a long moment, she slowly shook her head. "I don't know much, sir. Rider worried about moving here. He said the Shawnee didn't much come into this area except for hunting, because something lived in the hills which didn't take kindly to people. But we needed the money, and we came anyway. He didn't say nothing more about it. Guess he didn't want to scare me."

My shoulders slumped. Another dead end.

Griffin glanced around carefully. He spoke in a lowered voice, as if he wished to make certain no one overheard him. "We must speak with your husband. Do you have any idea where he might be hiding?"

Mrs. Hicks's eyes widened, and she glanced around quickly. "N-no."

She was lying; even I could tell. "Please," I said. "We don't wish him any harm. I'm not allied with the Pinkertons, and you have my word neither of us will tell them or Mr. Orme. We came here to help, if we can, not make things worse by jailing the only man who might be able to tell us what's happening."

Her arms tightened around her baby, as if wishing to protect it from the consequences of her choice, whatever they might be. "I'm sorry, sir. I just don't know. Now please, I got to get to work."

Then she was gone, the door slamming shut between us.

Our next destination was the home of the parents of the missing brothers. Unlike Mrs. Hicks, who had clearly been terrified of us, Mrs. Kincaid gladly invited us inside her house.

"It does my heart good to know somebody besides us is worried about my boys," she said, ushering us inside. "Now that an important man like yourself is involved, surely something will turn up, and I'll have them home soon."

The weight of her faith bowed my shoulders. She thought me far more than I was, far more than I wished to be. Certainly far more than I *could* be.

"We'll do our best, ma'am," Griffin said, when I failed to reply.

"Er, yes," I agreed. "If it's within our power."

The house was of simple design, with a single, large, front room and two smaller rooms in the back, one of which appeared to be a kitchen. The front room had clearly been used as a bedroom for the three brothers, given the heaps of bedclothes and general untidiness. Mrs. Kincaid hurriedly cleared off two chairs for us. "Can I offer you gentlemen tea? Coffee?"

"Coffee would be lovely," Griffin said, giving her a dazzling smile. She blushed and smiled, taking a decade off her weary face.

A deep, wracking cough came from the back bedroom. "My husband," she called from the kitchen. "He's got the miner's lung. Lots of days he can't work anymore. That's why I know the boys didn't just run off like those Pinkertons say. They wouldn't just leave us, knowing their daddy can't work half the time."

"Did the Pinkerton guards say why they concluded your sons ran away instead of met with foul play?" I asked. "With outlaws and other, more natural, hazards in these woods, I would have thought they would attempt a more thorough investigation."

"Not what they're being paid for, is it?"

"She's right," Griffin said with a glance at me. "They're being paid to keep the peace in Threshold and to keep the unions out. Not investigate random disappearances."

"But if they're to act as the law here, surely they should do so in truth," I objected.

Now they both looked at me pityingly. Apparently, I once again demonstrated I had no idea how the world actually worked.

Within a few minutes, Mrs. Kincaid brought our coffee. It was too sweet and full of grounds, but I choked it down with a smile.

"Do you know where your sons went to hunt?" Griffin asked. "Threshold Mountain itself, or one of the lower peaks, or…?"

She shook her head sadly. "No. I'm afraid I don't. It couldn't have been too far, though, because they meant to be home for dinner."

Griffin nodded, as if she had been in any way useful. "I see. Is there anything you can tell us? Were your sons worried about something, or had they noticed anything odd? Anything which seems relevant might help."

Mrs. Kincaid frowned, rocking back and forth on her chair, while her husband coughed and choked in the back room. "I can't rightly think of anything. They worried about their daddy, of course, but otherwise you wouldn't have thought they'd had a care in the world. Always laughing and playing jokes." A fond smile creased her lips. "Everyone loved them. Oh, but would you like to see a photo? We had one made when we first got here, along with some of the other families. For the company records, they said, but we could buy a print if we wanted."

"Please."

She carefully took a photo in a paper frame from a drawer and brought it to us. "Here. Those are my boys: Thomas, Ben, and Lucas on the right there."

I took the photo from her. It showed the family, standing in what was doubtless their Sunday best in front of the house. Mrs. Kincaid and her husband posed in the center, surrounded by the three boys. The one on the right, Lucas, was unfamiliar to me.

The other two, however, I knew all too well. They were the thieves who had attacked me in Widdershins and stolen the black stone.

CHAPTER 8

"What the devil can it mean?" Christine wondered, scowling out over the veranda toward Threshold, as if the town itself might give her an answer.

We had excused ourselves from the Kincaid home shortly after viewing the photograph, Griffin noticing my sudden anxiety. I'd had no wish to accuse Mrs. Kincaid's sons in front of her. Or two of them, anyway; what had become of the third and youngest?

"I don't know," Griffin said. He leaned against the railing, peering out at the road. "But I've sent word to Elliot to meet us here."

I started. "You did?"

"These circumstances are ordinary enough. Odd, but without requiring him to believe anything particularly strange is going on."

It made sense, I supposed. Having the aid of the head of the Pinkerton division would be an asset. I should welcome his presence.

Perhaps if I kept repeating it to myself, I might even begin to believe it.

We didn't have to wait long for his arrival. He strolled up in a cream-colored summer weight suit, with striped trousers and a colorful blue vest.

I glanced down at my attire, which consisted of differing shades of brown, and found I'd managed to splash mud all over my shoes.

Elliot greeted us cordially, but with clear puzzlement. The four of us settled on the veranda, sipping glasses of lemonade while Griffin explained the situation to Mr. Manning.

The detective frowned, turning his piercing gaze on me. "You're certain of your identification?"

I stiffened at the implication. "Of course. I hardly think I would forget the faces of the men who assaulted and robbed me in an alleyway.”

“I mean no disrespect, Dr. Whyborne,” he said, holding up one hand.

“Whyborne isn’t given to fancies,” Christine said, coming to my defense. “The question you should be asking is why on earth would two young miners suddenly decide to follow the mysterious stone all the way to Massachusetts, without telling anyone and with no apparent motive?”

“Indeed.” He frowned in thought and sipped his lemonade. “Did you ask Mrs. Kincaid?”

Griffin shook his head. “I doubt she would have volunteered to show Whyborne the photograph if she knew anything. Nor did she strike me as a woman playing a game with us, but rather a mother genuinely worried for her sons.”

“I see.” Manning leaned back and clasped his hands over his stomach. “Dr. Whyborne, would you say the stone might have been valuable?”

“I can’t say for certain. I didn’t have the opportunity to examine it,” I replied slowly. What was he getting at?

“But it might be the sort of thing a collector would buy?”

“Possibly.”

“I think I begin to see what happened.” He nodded slowly to himself. “The Kincaid boys saw the artifact when it was brought back into town, just as everyone else did. When they heard it had been sent to Mr. Stotz, they hatched a plan to steal it. Perhaps they assumed it must be valuable, or all artifacts are, after the recent newspaper stories about Dr. Putnam’s discoveries. At any rate, it must have seemed more glamorous and profitable than mining. They took on the mantle of thieves, sneaking away without anyone’s notice, and followed the trail of the stone until they had the chance to seize it. No doubt they’ve either sold it or are trying to sell it as we speak.”

“Perhaps,” Christine said dubiously. “It seems like a great deal of persistence and trouble to go to, for three young men who’d never done such a thing before.”

“All outlaws must get their start somewhere,” Manning said with an easy smile. “And if you doubt the persistence of the criminal mind, ask Griffin about the Dixon robbery sometime.”

Griffin laughed. “I had entirely forgotten that case!”

“How could you? Don’t you recall we—”

“What about the other strange goings-on?” I broke in. “The sounds in the mine, for instance?”

Manning’s smile faded. “They have a natural explanation, just as the disappearances did. If you wish to investigate further, perhaps you should ask Mr. Orme for permission to tour the mine.”

“I think I shall,” I replied recklessly. I noticed Griffin’s face pale and immediately regretted my words.

Manning rose to his feet. “I must get back to my office in the Pinkerton barracks,” he said. “A pleasure to see you again, Dr. Putnam, Dr. Whyborne. And Griffin…thank you. You’ve only been in town for a day, and already you've solved an incident which has vexed me for weeks."

Griffin returned his smile, more warmly than I liked. "I would say I learned from the best, but, in truth, happenstance led to the solution, not any investigative ability on my part."

I waited until Manning was safely gone, before blurting out, "Surely you don't believe his ridiculous explanation!"

Griffin gave me a startled look. "You are entirely set against it?"

"Yes." I folded my arms over my chest and glowered at him. "Don't you agree, Christine?"

"Hmm." The traitor actually seemed to be considering the possibility Manning was right. "It would explain the facts, you must admit."

"I don't have to admit any such thing. What of the sons simply leaving their parents in the lurch? There's a fact Manning's theory fails to cover."

"If they believed they could get good money for the stone, their intention may have been to give a portion of it to their mother," Griffin speculated. He sank into a chair and leaned forward, his elbows on his knees and his fingers steepled thoughtfully. "Or the family bond was not as tight as their mother believes. She would hardly be the first parent to delude herself in such a way."

"And there is a market for artifacts, obtained legitimately or not," Christine added.

"You're both accepting this far too easily," I pointed out—quite reasonably, I thought.

Griffin and Christine exchanged a glance. "Will you share your theory with us?" Griffin asked.

"Well…" Blast the man. "I haven't had time to come up with one yet."

"Perhaps your visit to the mine will clarify things," Christine suggested.

Griffin blanched slightly and glanced aside. "I'll speak to Orme tomorrow," I said. "There's no need for all of us to go."

"I'm certainly not," Christine said. "A tomb is one thing, but I've no intention of crawling about in a coal mine."

"I should accompany you," Griffin said reluctantly.

"There's no need. Your time would be better spent talking to people." Inspiration struck. "Perhaps you can find out what others thought of the Kincaid brothers. If it seems likely they would turn to robbery."

He clearly didn't like the prospect, but finally nodded. "Very well, my dear. We'll do as you say."

That night, a muffled cry awoke me.

I rolled over, and almost fell out of the dratted bed. Alone, as Griffin slipped back to his own room after we'd made love.

Griffin. Had the cry belonged to him?

I extricated myself from the twisted bed sheets. My nightshirt stuck unpleasantly to my sweaty skin as I crossed the room to the connecting door and knocked on it. "Griffin?"

There came no reply. I strained my ears, trying to catch any sound from within, or from the hall outside. Was he having one of his fits? Had anyone else heard him call out? Did I have to worry about someone knocking on his door and discovering me within, or would the fact of our connecting door be enough to avert suspicion?

I hated I even had to consider such things. Devil take it, here I was dithering while my lover needed me.

I opened the connecting door and stuck my head inside his room. "Griffin?"

In the darkness, I could just make out his form, sitting upright in the bed. As he seemed in no position to complain about my use of magic, I lit his night candle with a word, even as I hastened to his side.

All of his muscles were locked, his eyes wide and staring into a horror I, mercifully, couldn't see. His breathing came short and shallow, and his skin felt icy cold when I touched him.

"No," he whispered. "Please don't. Please. I'll be good. I won't—I won't—I won't—"

"Shh." God, I hated these fits. I hated the men who hadn't believed his tales of monsters beneath a basement in Chicago, and I hated the doctors at the insane asylum who had done this to him even more. "It's all right, darling. You're safe. I'm here." Had the knowledge I'd be going into the mine tomorrow brought on the fit, or was it the strain of seeing Elliot again? Or some other reason altogether?

He began to shiver uncontrollably, despite the hot, stuffy air. I lay down on the narrow bed. He resisted at first when I tried to pull him down, then gave in and let me wrap my arms and legs about him.

We lay together for a long time, until sweat had completely drenched my nightshirt. Eventually, however, he stirred in my arms. "Whyborne?" he whispered.

"Of course."

A shudder went through him, and he gripped me tightly. "I thought I was back in the madhouse." My heart broke to hear the fear in his voice. "Where are we? The bed—"

Waking in a strange place surely had done him no good. Not for the first time, I wished us back in our little house in Widdershins. "We're in your room, in the Brumfield House hotel in Threshold."

"Oh. Yes. Of course." He sounded stronger now. "You shouldn't be here."

"No one else heard you cry out," I reassured him. "Or if they did, they didn't come to investigate."

His emerald eyes looked almost black in the dim light. "Still, we shouldn't risk it. I'm better now."

I disliked the idea of leaving him. Usually when he had his fits, he'd lay shivering in my arms for hours after. "No one is going to come around in the middle of the night."

"And if we oversleep, and a maid lets herself in?" He stroked my face gently. "I'm much better. Go back to your own bed."

"Are you certain?"

He nodded. I kissed him, then reluctantly slid out of bed and padded back to my own room. As I turned to shut the connecting door behind me, though, I saw him curl up with his back to me, knees drawn up to his chest, hugging himself like a child afraid of the dark.

The next morning, I went to the mine office alone. The Pinkerton guards watched my approach, but their expressions betrayed no curiosity or surprise. One tipped his hat to me as I passed by, but thankfully they didn't question my business.

The clatter of typewriter keys filled the air inside, courtesy of Orme's secretary, whose name I still didn't know. Their cadence slowed as I passed by, and I guessed he hoped to eavesdrop on my conversation with his employer. Orme sat behind his desk once again, and I noticed he seemed almost preternaturally still, only his head and eyes moving to track my progress across the room.

"Dr. Whyborne," he said in his emotionless voice, "how may I be of assistance?"

"Er, well, I wished to speak further about my investigations," I tried not to fidget; his stillness made me hyperaware of every movement. "I'm told there have been strange sounds heard in the mine. Knocking and the like."

"All mines have their sounds," Orme replied coolly. "The earth is not still. It shifts and groans, like a sleeper in its bed, but we only hear it when we burrow beneath its hide."

"Yes, but, that is, surely some of the men here have worked other mines. They would be used to such sounds. You aren't at all concerned this is something different?"

"No."

Curse the man, he wasn't going to give me any opening at all, was he? "I'd like to see the mine for myself, if I might," I said.

Orme turned his beady gaze onto his secretary. "Fetch Mr. Manning."

The secretary hurried from the room, leaving us alone. Orme returned his gaze to me and simply stared, without speaking. It was like being gazed at by a Gila monster, or some other species of cold-blooded thing. Fortunately, I didn't have to endure it for very long. The secretary returned within a few minutes, Elliot Manning behind him.

Manning crossed the room to me, his hand extended. "Dr. Whyborne, good to see you again."

He sounded as if he genuinely meant it. His physical beauty struck me afresh; he could have made a fortune on the stage. And this man had once been Griffin's lover?

If I'd known this was whom I was no doubt being compared to, I would have insisted on making love only in the dark. Or never worked up the courage to take off my clothes in the first place.

"Mr. Manning," Orme said, "please escort Dr. Whyborne to the mine. Have one of the miners who reported the noises show him the face where he heard it. I believe Mr. Johnson will do."

"Johnson?" Manning asked, and I couldn't interpret the look he gave Orme.

Orme did not return it. "You heard me."

"Yes, sir." Manning's smile flared back to its full brilliance as he turned to me. "Come with me, Dr. Whyborne. I hope you have another suit; if not, perhaps you should consider a change of clothing before going into the mine."

"Oh. Er, no. I mean, yes, I have another."

"Good. Shall we be on our way?"

"Of course." I forced myself to look back at Orme. Why the man repelled me, I couldn't say, other than something about his mannerisms struck me as unnatural. "Thank you, Mr. Orme, and good day."

"Goodbye, Dr. Whyborne," he said, and I felt his gaze on me, like a chunk of ice pressed against the back of my neck, until the door shut safely behind us.

Manning led the way from the office, toward the mine itself. The entrance lay not at the very bottom of the hollow, but close to it. "I thought it would be higher up on the hill," I said, gesturing vaguely.

Manning shook his head. "This is a slope mine—it means a tunnel slopes down into the coal seam, rather than boring straight into a hillside, or descending as a straight shaft. Mules haul the mine carts up to the coal tipple." He pointed to a large, multi-story building which extended over the railroad tracks. "It's sorted there, by grade and size, then lifted up to bins for storage until it's time to load the train cars. You can see the sheave house at the very top, where the pulleys are."

I wondered where the coke ovens came in. Most likely the entire process was far more complicated than I realized. "I see. Thank you."

"I take it Mr. Flaherty didn't choose to accompany you?" Manning asked. The question sounded casual, but the look in his eyes was sharp.

An unexpected surge of anger boiled through my chest. This man had stood by while Griffin went to the madhouse and done nothing to save him. How dare Manning ask after him now!

Unless…unless Manning realized his mistake in treating Griffin badly.

Did he want Griffin back?

"Dr. Whyborne? Are you quite all right?"

I forced a smile onto my face. "Forgive me. I was woolgathering. Griffin had other business." Let Manning wonder what it might be.

"I see." Manning's look turned pensive. "Is he…forgive me, but am I mistaken in saying you're good friends?"

What did he mean? Was he asking if we were lovers?

"We live under the same roof," I replied. In other words, yes, and he might as well give up now if he had any thought of rekindling his relationship with Griffin.

Manning didn't look terribly surprised, and I wondered if Griffin had mentioned it to him, the night they'd spoken in the bar. Or if he'd even wired a contact with Widdershins to inquire about us. Either way, he only nodded and asked, "Is Griffin happy?"

I hadn't expected such a question and, for a moment, didn't know how to answer. Was he? I thought him content with our life in Widdershins, in our little house with our cat, solving whatever cases came his way. But what if he missed his old life in Chicago? His work with the Pinkertons had surely been far more exciting than whatever Widdershins had to offer a private detective.

Certainly the men were better looking, if one could judge by Manning.

"He seems to be," I said finally. "He has his own agency." It wasn't much of an answer, but I honestly didn't know what else to say.

"I'm grateful." A cloud passed over Manning's handsome face. "I'm happy to see he's doing well. After the Pinkertons fired him, I worried about him a great deal."

I stopped in my tracks, blinking. "Fired?" For some reason, I'd assumed Griffin had voluntarily quit, after the betrayal of their disbelief. But of course a detective agency wouldn't keep a madman on its roster.

Manning winced. "I'm sorry—I thought you knew. Griffin was fired after having some…mental distress…about a case."

"He seems quite sane to me," I replied stiffly.

"Indeed he does," Elliot agreed. "No doubt the doctors affected a cure, something for which I'm profoundly grateful. When last I saw him…a policeman found him crawling through a slum, a wound on his leg, screaming and raving about monsters. I rushed straight to the hospital when I heard. It was not a pretty sight. He was convinced unholy creatures lived beneath the streets of Chicago, and one of them had *eaten* his partner. Nothing could persuade him otherwise. He finally had to be restrained to keep from injuring himself or anyone else."

My tongue felt thick in my mouth. I wanted to shout at Manning, tell him Griffin wasn't insane, and the monsters were real. But if I did, would he think me a madman as well? I didn't care, but if Griffin believed his assistance would be valuable, I shouldn't drive him away. Griffin had even warned me of this, and yet I did not know what to say.

"I know comes as a shock," Elliot said, misinterpreting my silence. "As I said, he seems to have been wholly cured. I would think on it no more, were I you."

"I won't."

I couldn't tell whether he believed me. "I'm glad to hear it." He met my gaze squarely. "I hope you'll accept my assistance in your investigation. The safety of the mine is my job, and if there is something more to this, I wish to know of it."

He seemed sincere, at least. "Thank you, Mr. Manning."

"Please, call me Elliot."

"I don't go by my first name." Why on earth was I almost apologizing to the man? "But, er, Whyborne will do." Inspiration struck. "If you wish to offer your assistance, perhaps you would be kind enough to show me where the expedition found the black stone?"

His features shifted briefly into an expressionless mask. Mrs. Mercer had said only he returned from the expedition. Surely the deaths of those other men must haunt him. I was a wretch to have asked so bluntly.

At last he nodded. "Of course. Will tomorrow suffice?"

"Yes. Thank you. I know what I've asked is not easy for you." Now I was apologizing again.

"Quite all right," he said, more graciously than I might have in his position. "Shall we continue on to the mine for now?"

CHAPTER 9

The mine entrance lay deep in the shadow cast by the mountain above. The creek ran nearby, its waters less tainted than further downstream. Not a breath of wind reached down from the heights to stir the close air, and mosquitoes hummed in my ears and raised welts on my wrists, around my cuffs. I slapped at them irritably.

As we approached the entrance, Elliot bid me wait, then went to speak with some men working nearby. I assumed one of them must be a foreman of some sort, but, in truth, I had only the vaguest idea what sort of hierarchy might exist within the daily operations of the mine itself. As I waited, mules pulling carts full of coal emerged one by one from the darkness. The handlers walking them out glanced at me curiously. Their faces and hands were black with coal dust. Most of them went without coats, their shirts and trousers dark gray with filth. The poor mules were equally covered in dust, and their raspy breathing reminded me of Mr. Kincaid, coughing himself to death in the back room of his home.

"Here," Elliot said, approaching me with a cloth cap and a carbide lantern in his hands. He already wore another set himself. "You might wish to leave your coat outside."

"I-it wouldn't be proper," I objected, although, as I'd already noted, many of the men who worked the mine had dispensed with such formality.

"We'll hope it can be cleaned successfully, then," he said with a wry smile. "If you're ready, we can ride inside one of the coal carts."

I didn't feel at all ready, in fact, but my only other choice was to back down from my insistence on seeing the mine and return to the hotel. I followed him to one of the returning carts, which had paused to wait for us. He leapt in easily, then helped me half-climb, half-tumble in after him.

Coal dust covered the interior, of course, and a few pebble-sized bits still rattled about on the floor. Despite the rails, the ride was hardly a smooth one, and I clutched the sides of the cart in an attempt to remain upright.

"I suggest you duck often," Elliot said, as we passed through the entrance.

Thank heavens I'd successfully talked Griffin out of coming with me. Darkness enclosed the cart as the earth swallowed us. The tunnel leading down to the coal seam had been cut with just enough clearance to allow the mules and laden carts to pass, and no more. The only light came from the carbide lanterns on our caps. To our left, other carts made their way up the other set of tracks, and their handlers exchanged insults and curses with the man leading our mule. A few of them glanced curiously at me, but those whose eyes found Elliot usually fell silent and passed by with hostile glares. Apparently, the Pinkerton boss was not loved by the miners.

The cart slowed as the slope leveled out. "Here we are," Elliot said to me. "Within the coal seam itself."

The air of the mine felt much cooler than outside, but far fouler, heavy and damp, thick with fine particles of coal dust stirred up by the work of the miners. The stink of burned powder blended with the scent of the raw coal itself, combining with the gases put off by the carbide lamps. The rattle of carts mingled with the sounds of picks and shovels, and the voices of the miners, to create a surprising din.

I climbed out of the cart behind Elliot. The ceiling forced men of average height to stoop, let alone someone as tall as I. Within minutes, my back began to ache.

Elliot spoke to some other men. I looked about, taking in the rough-cut timbers holding up the ceiling, the narrow-gauge tracks for the coal carts, and the obscene words or pictures scrawled on walls or timbers by the miners. Graffiti, barring the language it was written in, had changed little in the last four thousand years. Whether Egyptian, Roman, or modern American, it mainly consisted of names, boasts of sexual prowess, and crude depictions of penises. I could only imagine what Christine would have to say on the matter.

"Whyborne?" Elliot said at my elbow. I jumped guiltily, nearly ramming my head into the ceiling. "Johnson is working a face not too far from here."

"Oh. Lead the way," I said.

A boy of no more than fifteen did the honors, escorting us deeper into the darkness. I all but felt the weight of the mountain pressing down on us, and I wondered how the men endured it. Did they simply grow accustomed, or did they feel it anew every morning when they began another long shift?

As we walked, Elliot pointed out features of the mine. According to him, the pattern of digging was known as room-and-pillar, in which square "rooms" were dug out of the seam, with pillars of coal left in place at each corner to support the roof. Areas of active mining were known as "faces." A team of three men worked the face of each room, undercutting it, setting charges to break up the coal, then shoveling it into carts.

Still, none of it really meant anything to me, until the boy led us into the room worked by Johnson and the other two men on his team. Ahead of us, I saw a ragged wall of coal. Augurs waited, propped against the wall, until it the time came to drill a hole for the blasting charge. Two men sat on wooden planks, eating out of their lunch pails, while a third lay on his side at the bottom of the face.

It took me a moment to understand just what he was doing. A pile of broken-up coal lay to one side, removed from the base of the coal seam. The man on his side dug farther in, swinging his pick as best he could to deepen the cut. The planks of wood jammed into the cut were presumably meant to keep the coal above from falling in on its own and crushing his arm.

"Johnson, you got visitors!" the boy said. Then he went back the way he'd come, no doubt considering his duty done in delivering us. Hopefully, we'd be able to find our way back through the maze of pillars without him. At least we had only to follow the tracks to reach the surface eventually.

The two men stood up, and the third extricated himself from under the cut. One of the first two nodded warily at us. "I'm Johnson. What can I do for you, Mr. Manning?"

Although the words were polite, their tone held mixed fear and hostility. Had there been some strife between the Pinkertons and the miners, or was it natural wariness?

"This is Dr. Whyborne," Elliot said. "He wants to ask you about the noises you heard."

"I'm here to investigate any, er, strange occurrences," I said, since Elliot didn't seem inclined to offer any further explanation. "Mr. Orme said you reported sounds not normal to the mine?"

"Told you not to say anything," one of the other men muttered.

Johnson cast him a look of defiance. "We all did," he said. "You hear lots of things down here: creaks, groans, and tapping."

"Tommyknockers," said one of his companions with a shiver.

"Yeah, well, this weren't no tommyknockers. It was a sort of humming sound, coming from the other side of the rock. Never heard nothing like it. And there was a buzzing, too. Later on the same day, after we'd got the cart loaded, just as we left for the end of the shift."

"Buzzing?" I asked.

"Yeah. Like some kind of bee. Only it sounded almost like…like words." Johnson swallowed heavily, and his expression reminded me of a child whispering of monsters in the dark. "Like something talked to us. Something not human."

A shiver trailed up my spine. "What did it say?"

"It said it'd show us a good place to open up a new face, if we'd just come with it." He shuddered.

One of the other men shook his head. "I think you were hearing things. If it did say something, it weren't clear enough to make out."

A shiver crawled up my spine, and the lights seemed to dim, the dark bulk of the mountain pressing down. "And it occurred in this, er, room?"

Johnson nodded. "Yes, sir."

I moved closer to the raw face, my carbide lamp throwing a dim cone of illumination over it. The rough coal glittered in the light, revealing nothing beyond the marks left behind by the work of the miners.

What had I expected to see? Pictographs? A crack leading to some hidden space, filled with yayhos? The very notion was absurd. The miners and Elliot must think me a fool.

I drew back. "Yes. Well. Thank you for, er, speaking with me."

"Yes, sir." Johnson glanced at his companions. "If it's all right with you, we ought to get back to work."

"Of course."

Johnson took up the pick and laid down on the mine floor, extending his arm and upper torso beneath the overhanging cut. What awful, awful work. I couldn't imagine spending ten hours a day, six days a week, in this claustrophobic place, unable to stand up straight and with the weight of the mountain bearing down on me. Let alone the actual strain of the labor involved.

Elliot led the way from the room. We had gone no farther than the first line of pillars, however, when there came a loud groan, almost as if the mountain itself were in pain. There followed a series of sharp cracks, shouts of alarm, a crash—and screams.

Elliot and I ran back the way we had come. The rock face behind us had transformed into a pile of rubble, a set of legs and the arm of another man protruding from beneath what must have been tons of coal. The hand convulsed, fingernails scratching across the mine floor, before falling still.

I froze, my heart pounding madly in my chest, bile rising in my throat. All around me, the mine came alive, men rushing from nearby rooms, crying out to one another. The only survivor of the three men we had spoken to screamed the names of Johnson and their other companion, clawing at the pile of rock.

Elliot seized my arm. All the color had vanished from his face, other than the thin layer of coal dust adhering to it. "I need to get you out of here, in case there's another rockfall," he said, tugging me after him.

"But…" I wanted to render assistance, and yet what could I do? A dozen trained men were already on the spot, with more hurrying to the site every moment. I would only get in their way. "Yes. All right."

We were forced to walk all the way out of the mine. Word of the rockfall had spread, and Elliot answered the questions shouted to him as we passed other workers. One of the boys, on hearing two men had been killed, sped out of the mine ahead of us to spread the word.

By the time we emerged, a crowd had already begun to gather. It consisted mainly of women, panic and fear in their eyes as they wondered if their brothers or fathers or husbands would emerge alive. Even Orme had left his office and stood near the mine entrance, although his impassive face showed no emotion of any kind.

"Are you all right, Dr. Whyborne?" he asked.

"Er, yes."

"Johnson and one of the other men were killed," Elliot told him grimly. "But the rockfall seems to have been localized. They were undercutting, and must not have braced up the face correctly."

Orme nodded. "I see. Have your men watch this crowd, just in case their mood turns. As for you, Dr. Whyborne, I suggest you retire to your hotel. You must have had quite a shock."

Uncertain what else to do, I turned my steps toward the hotel. People called out to me for news as they hurried toward the mine, and I answered with what little I knew: two had died, but there didn't seem to be fear of a larger disaster.

Griffin and Christine found me before I'd crossed half the town, both of them panting and out of breath, having apparently run from the hotel. When he saw the coal dust on me, Griffin's eyes widened. "Oh God! Are you all right?"

"Of course he is," Christine snapped, as Griffin seized me by both arms. "He wouldn't be strolling about town if he was horribly injured, would he?"

"I'm quite all right," I assured Griffin. "There was an accident, though. A rockfall crushed two men near me."

I shuddered at the memory. Griffin's hands tightened on my shoulders, and I knew he would have embraced me, had we been alone. "Tell us," he said.

When I finished, Christine's eyes narrowed in thought. "You talk to a miner about strange happenings, and the room he worked in collapses only moments later. Coincidence?"

"I don't see what else it could be," I said uneasily. "Surely Elliot is right, and they simply didn't use enough bracing. Or they missed some flaw in the rock."

"Says the man who can light fires by speaking a few words," Griffin replied, finally letting go of my arms. "What if we're right and there are unseen forces at work here in Threshold?"

"Then why kill poor Johnson, not to mention the other fellow? And why not kill all three?"

"Because one had to live to spread the warning." Griffin turned his gaze up to Threshold Mountain, his mouth set in a grim line. "Anyone who gives away the mountain's secrets will die."

CHAPTER 10

As the day waned, a line of thunderheads built over the peaks to the east, sweeping in to cover the hollow in an early darkness. The humidity intensified, but a breeze sprang up, bringing with it the scent of rain and the distant rumble of thunder.

The weather matched the mood of the town. The remains of the dead men left the mine as they had entered, within one of the mule-drawn carts, while the church bells tolled somberly. I wondered if the next shift would be tasked with shoveling up coal soaked in their blood.

The accident served as a grim reminder of the dangers of the mine, even to those who didn't share our fear something otherworldly had caused the rockfall. Only a handful of locals showed up for dinner at the hotel, although the bar seemed to do an even more rousing business than the night before, as men tried to drink away their fear and grief.

I retired to my room early. Griffin declared his intention to return to the bar, to gather more information, but I heard his door open and close before long. The scrape of a chair announced he had chosen to brace it further against possible entrance. With any luck, the precaution meant he intended to join me in bed.

A moment later, he knocked on the connecting door, and I bid him enter. "Did you learn anything further?"

"No." His face wore a dark scowl. "Nor am I likely to. We aren't the only ones who noticed Johnson and his companion died only moments after talking to you. Half of the miners are convinced there is some awful spirit in the mine, which will destroy anyone who speaks of it aloud. The other half laugh...but don't speak either, because they secretly fear it's true."

"Drat." The curtains over the half-opened windows stirred in the freshening breeze, and thunder growled nearby. I stood up, using the chair to brace my door as well, before unbuttoning my coat. The suit I'd worn earlier in the mine had been taken away for cleaning; I hung my coat up carefully, not wishing it to be creased. "Perhaps we'll find clues at the cave."

"The cave?"

The rockfall had driven it out of my mind. "Yes—forgive me, I quite forgot to tell you. Elliot offered to show us the cave where they found the black stone."

"Elliot, is it?" Griffin asked, an odd note in his voice.

"Well, er, yes." Had I misunderstood his wishes? "I thought you wanted me to recruit him as an ally, if possible."

"Elliot's a good detective. He taught me almost everything I know," Griffin admitted. "I was only surprised to hear you speak of him familiarly."

"I'm sorry."

"You have no reason to apologize. But let's not speak of Elliot. Not when we could be doing far more pleasant things."

Hooking his fingers around my suspenders, he yanked me to him. His lips sealed over mine with almost bruising force, muffling my startled squeak. His tongue invaded my mouth boldly, and my thoughts began to unravel.

Thunder crashed, nearer now, and the curtains whipped into the room. The wind smelled raw and clean, of wet earth and green sap. It felt cool on my heated skin as Griffin loosened the buttons of my shirt, pressing a kiss against each inch of bare flesh thus revealed. My cock swelled against my trousers, aching for his touch. I grabbed his hair with one hand, dragging his head back up for another kiss. His lips tasted faintly of whiskey from the bar.

The wind blew out the night candle, leaving behind only the flashes of lightning to reveal tantalizing glimpses of Griffin's naked skin, as he removed his clothing. I scrambled into the bed, and a moment later he crawled in on top of me. I reached to hold him, but he caught each of my wrists in one of his hands, pinning me to the bed. He kissed me again, with the same urgent heat, then worked his way down my throat, where he bit and sucked the flesh, hard enough to bruise.

God! I bucked against him, savoring the feel of his bare skin on mine, his length hot and hard as an iron bar against my belly. I tugged against his hold, not because I truly wished to be freed, but because being held down by him fired my blood. I wanted to be his; I wanted him to forget about Elliot and everyone else he'd ever been with.

Griffin fastened his teeth around one of my nipples, the sensation riding the fine edge between pleasure and pain, eradicating my ability to think. I swallowed back a cry and struggled to rub against him, as he switched his attention to the other side of my chest.

He released my wrists in order to work his way lower, biting lightly at my stomach. He licked the crease at the top of my leg, before nuzzling my thigh, nudging my knees further apart. His hair felt like silk against the underside of my sack as he licked and kissed each thigh.

"Wider," he murmured hoarsely against my skin.

Lightning flashed just outside, making me jump—then jump again as his tongue touched my fundament. I closed my eyes and clutched at the sheets as he traced the puckered flesh. It felt incredible: warm and wet, and shockingly intimate, especially when he stabbed at the hole with the tip of his tongue. I bit my lip hard to keep from crying out.

He rose up to his knees. I moved to give him more room—and nearly fell off the narrow bed, letting out a startled yelp before Griffin pulled me back.

"Curse this narrow bed," I muttered. "How on earth is one to manage?"

"One can manage fine. Two is the difficulty." Griffin turned sideways to lean his back against the wall. "Here. Straddle my lap."

I did so, the position bringing our lengths into contact. He felt exquisitely hard and hot, sensitive flesh pressed to sensitive flesh. This was the best feeling in the world, this undeniable proof he desired me the way I did him.

His hands gripped my buttocks, urging me to move. I wrapped one hand loosely around our cocks, to keep us together.

The lightning strikes came faster now, one after the other. A light sheen of sweat slicked our skins, my thighs rubbing against his as I thrust against him. "Feels wonderful," he whispered in my ear, voice husky with desire. "Don't stop, please."

I kissed him in response. His lips parted wantonly for me, and I slid my tongue into his mouth, then out, and in again, matching the rhythm of my hips. He moaned, sucking frantically on my tongue. His fingers tightened on my buttocks, and his cock twitched against mine. Everything spiraled up and up, until it was too much: musky desire and sweat-slick skin, fingers and mouths, his body arching beneath me even as the storm exploded around us.

I flung my head back and cried out, the sound lost in a titanic crack of lightning. My fingers drove into his shoulder, while hot semen spilled over my other hand, everything reduced to a fiery epicenter of heat and pleasure. I pushed against him again, and again, until my sensitized organ could take it no more, and he groaned and bucked and spent himself beneath me.

I collapsed against him. The air of the room had gone damp and wet, and smelled of rain. Thunder growled again, but more distantly now, the storm moving on. Griffin's hands gently stroked my back, and he made little sounds of contentment in my ear.

We remained thus for a long time, until the rain outside died away. Then Griffin slid out of bed, closed the window, and slipped back through the connecting door, leaving me alone.

We met Elliot immediately after breakfast. The clouds were gone, and the sun struggled to peer over the mountains and through the thick haze of the coke ovens. The rain, which had seemed refreshing last night, now formed stagnant pools already humming with mosquitoes.

For our expedition, Christine had donned her rational dress, and carried her rifle slung on her back. Griffin had his revolver and sword cane. As for myself, I carried the *Arcanorum* in my breast pocket as usual. In addition, we carried rope and lanterns, in case the cave proved accessible to exploration.

Elliot raised a brow at the sight of us. "Expecting trouble?" he asked, with a nod at Christine's rifle.

"Are there not bears in these woods, Mr. Manning?" she returned.

"Yes, although they don't tend to be aggressive, unless their young are threatened." He looked as if he wanted to say something further—perhaps suggest she remain behind if she feared bears—but thought better of it. "Let's go."

He led us along the slope, above Threshold proper, although within the cleared area. Once we were past the town, we descended back into the hollow as the trees closed around us. Here the creek ran clear and cool, and the scent of wet earth and growing things saturated the air. The thick canopy cast us into gloomy shadow and blocked out the wind. Sweat soon pooled in my armpits.

From now on, I would insist Griffin only take cases in New England, if this was what I could expect from other parts of the country.

The rough terrain forced us to pick our way slowly along slopes more suited to a mountain goat. Thickets of laurel and rhododendron choked our path, and rocky outcroppings left us no choice but to make long detours. If only I'd had the foresight to purchase a pair of boots. My oxfords continually slipped on the ancient accumulations of fallen leaves, and the seepage of hidden springs slicked the rocks. Surely, even an experienced woodsman might become disoriented amidst the maze of trees.

Of course, Elliot seemed confident of his direction. He'd come equipped with suitable footwear, as well, curse him.

After we had hiked for what seemed like hours, but in reality was probably less than one, Christine asked, "So, Mr. Manning, you and Griffin knew one another in Chicago?" Annoyingly, she didn't even sound winded, while I panted like a bellows from the unaccustomed exercise.

Elliot's gaze sought out Griffin, while a smile shaped his mouth. "Indeed. We worked at the agency together—well, eventually. We didn't meet there."

Griffin glanced away, a faint flush suffusing his cheeks. Why? "Elliot arranged for me to be hired by the Pinkertons."

"Only because I knew you would be a tremendous asset." Elliot turned his attention to me. "Would you believe it, when I first encountered Griffin, he could barely make it through a sentence without saying 'ain't' or 'shucks' or the like. And his accent!"

"Truly?" I asked. Although I knew Griffin had been brought up on the plains, it had never occurred to me his speech must have once had a rural flavor.

Griffin's mouth thinned with embarrassment. "Elliot, please."

"Come now, Griffin, you should be proud of how quickly you improved, once you set your mind to it. Within a week, I knew he would be natural at undercover work. He's a regular chameleon, but, underneath it all, I daresay the heart of a Kansas farm boy still beats."

I wasn't at all sure Elliot was right. I tried to imagine Griffin doing…well, whatever one did on a farm. Milking cows, or chasing goats, or tossing hay bales about. Weren't square dancing and barn raisings involved as well?

"We didn't come out here to discuss my past," Griffin said. "Do you mind if I ask some questions about the cave-in, while we walk?"

Elliot step hitched slightly. "If you wish."

"The other men on the expedition didn't make it back, correct?"

"Correct." All the earlier cheer had drained out of Elliot. Good. I hadn't liked the overly familiar way he'd smiled at Griffin. The man had no manners whatsoever, if he thought such warm looks to a former lover were appropriate in front of a current one.

"And you were almost lost as well." Griffin's tone softened sympathetically. "It took you several days to find your way back to Threshold, did it not?"

"I was disoriented," Elliot replied tightly. "I exhausted myself trying to dig the others out; by the time I gave it up as hopeless, night had fallen. They'd taken all the lanterns inside with them, leaving me without light. Men get lost in these mountains even on cloudless days."

"Of course." Griffin used his cane to scramble up a steep pile of rock, dirt, and roots, then held his hand out to me. I clasped it and he hauled me up, my shoes slipping the entire time. "Where did you say the black stone was found, exactly?"

"Just inside the mouth of the cave. One of the boys we'd brought grew very excited, and the lead geologist gave him permission to run back to town with it, as long as he returned immediately."

"You had children with you?" I asked. Or panted, more like, from my exertion.

"Yes, a pair of small boys. Normally they sort the coal, but we brought them along in case portions of the cave proved too narrow for an adult to get squeeze through. The other died in the collapse, I'm afraid."

His voice trembled slightly; surely the deaths of the other men and the boy weighed heavily on him. I tried to imagine being in such a wild, lonely place as this, all my comrades suddenly dead, exhausted and with night coming on. "I'm very sorry," I said. "It must be painful for you to return here."

Sadness drew shadows on Elliot's handsome features. "Thank you for the sympathy. It is difficult, but as I said, I wish to aid you in whatever way you deem necessary."

"I'd like to speak with the other boy, the one who took the stone back to town," Griffin said. "Just to be thorough."

Elliot's expression of sadness only grew. "I'm afraid it isn't possible. He was run over by a mine cart and killed."

Christine batted irritably at an insect. "This boy, the geologists, Johnson.

Do this many people normally die in your mine in such a short time?"

"It's dangerous work, Dr. Putnam. Stotz Mining Company has far fewer deaths than other operations, I assure you."

We emerged from the dense tangle of trees into open air. Ahead of us stretched a steep bald of rock, free of everything but moss and the occasional small flower, growing from a crack. The peak of Threshold Mountain loomed overhead, its heights seeming no less mysterious for being nearer at hand. On the other side of the bald, a narrow opening gaped in the face of the mountain. The vegetation around it had been torn away, and piles of rubble lay outside, along with discarded timbers, all, no doubt, from the attempt to rescue the men lost in the collapse.

Griffin came to a halt, staring at the narrow opening. His hands clenched, then relaxed when he seemed to remember himself.

A thought occurred to me, as I observed the detritus of the rescue effort. "Why didn't you go inside with the rest, Elliot?"

"There was no reason for me to accompany them. I'm no geologist or engineer. I remained outside, guarding the mules and horses against bears. As I told Dr. Putnam, black bears will seldom attack a human, but the animals would have made tempting prey."

"Why didn't you ride back to town to fetch help, instead of getting lost and wandering around the countryside?" I asked.

"The mine collapse was very loud. They broke their traces and ran away."

"And none of them made it back to town? I suppose they were all eaten by bears?"

Elliot stiffened. "I don't know what you mean to imply," he said.

"I'm sure Whyborne didn't mean to offend," Griffin said quickly, cutting a sharp look at me.

Actually, I rather did, but I kept my mouth shut.

Whether Elliot believed Griffin or not, he chose to behave as if he did. "Here is the cave. Please be cautious if you choose to go inside, not that there is much to see. As for me, I have other duties to attend to back in town." He tipped his hat to Christine, then glanced at Griffin. "If it's convenient for you, I'll dine with you at the hotel, and share any findings?"

Griffin looked surprised, but quickly covered it. "Of course."

"I look forward to it." He nodded to me and turned his back on us, the trees swallowing up his figure within minutes.

CHAPTER 11

"Honestly, Whyborne, what is the matter with you?" Christine asked, as soon as Elliot had left. "You sounded as if you meant to accuse the poor man of something nefarious. You all but asked him why he didn't have the decency to die along with his companions!"

"I most certainly did not!" I turned to Griffin for support, but he also frowned at me.

"Christine has a point, although I would not have put it quite as strongly," he allowed. "You were a bit rude."

"Well, I'll have the opportunity to apologize over dinner, won't I?" I snapped. "Come, let's have a look at the blasted cave."

Griffin touched my elbow lightly. "Don't be angry with us, my dear. It's just not like you to be so…forthright, shall we say."

"It's not my fault if I'm not as taken with him as the two of you seem to be."

"Oh dear lord," Christine muttered, rolling her eyes. "I beg you, spare us any melodrama, and focus on the task at hand. Now, it's unlikely we'll find anything directly around the cave, or even within, given the extent of the rescue operations. The entire area is disturbed. Unfortunately, it would take a far larger force than ourselves to give the surroundings a proper survey."

"Do what you can, Christine," Griffin said. "I suppose…well, there may be nothing to see inside the cave, but we should at least check."

"I'll go," I offered hastily.

"We'll go together," Griffin said, although he didn't sound at all certain.

"Don't be silly," Christine said. "*If* there are any traces of carvings or what-not, they must be subtle enough to escape the notice of the rescuers earlier. I will accompany Whyborne, while you begin a transect."

I took a lantern from our gear and lit it with a match, while Christine lectured Griffin on how to conduct a proper survey. When done, she rejoined me, and together we ventured into the cave.

My heart picked up its pace as we closed on the black maw of the cave opening. The tumble of stones, cast aside by frantic rescuers, served as a mute reminder of the lives lost at this spot. We entered the cave cautiously, both of us seeming afraid to breathe, lest we bring the roof down on us. The rescuers had shored up the ragged roof with hastily placed timbers, but it was far too easy to imagine them coming down on our heads. At least we could stand upright; my back was still sore from stooping in the mine yesterday.

As Elliot had indicated, the area cleared of rockfall was quite shallow. About twenty feet in, a truly enormous boulder blocked our progress.

"I wonder why the rest of the cave was filled with smaller rocks," I murmured, staring at it in the light of our lantern.

"Perhaps they undertook a blast during the rescue," Christine suggested. "Now do shine the light on the walls, where it might be useful."

I obeyed. There was little hope of finding anything, however; the walls were nothing but ragged rock from the collapse. Even so, Christine scanned the walls closely, pausing to pick up a bit of broken stone every so often. Eventually, she shook her head and stepped back. "Nothing. It was a bit of a stretch to hope for more, I suppose."

We went back outside. The day had grown darker, and thunder rumbled ominously again in the distance. "Blast these storms," Christine muttered, holding her hat in place as she tilted her head back to glare at the sky. I merely blushed and looked away, remembering the night before.

"Well," she went on. "I've set Griffin to walking transects to the north side of the cave. You take the south. I'll walk the quadrant directly in front of the cave, to a depth of one hundred yards to either side."

I made my way up the slope with the intention of keeping my path as straight as possible. The roughness of the terrain and the slickness of my shoes quickly put an end to my plan. I peered at the exposed rock and poked about at the base of the scrubby trees which clung doggedly to the steep slope, but I was no archaeologist. I feared I might be missing obvious signs.

The day grew progressively hotter, and the thunder remained in the distance, passing to the south and eventually dissipating. Some sort of large insect insisted on buzzing around my face and hat; I tried to dash it away, fearing it meant to bite.

This was why I preferred not to leave Widdershins. I was no good in this savage wilderness, full of bugs and caves and trees. I was meant for gambrel-roofed houses, and sidewalks, and omnibuses to take me where I needed to go.

Lost in thought, I scrambled around one of the larger outcroppings. There seemed to be a slight depression beyond, but I paid no mind to it—at least, until the ground gave way beneath me.

I let out a startled cry, scrambling back as the thick matt of leaves and roots gave under my weight. But I wasn't fast enough, and in a rush of crumbling rock, I plunged into darkness.

I twisted as I fell, dirt and rotted leaves raining down with me into the depths below. I struck something hard, slid, then fell again, only to come to a sudden, jarring stop.

For a moment, I lay absolutely still, save for my rapid breathing, my lungs unable to draw in enough air. Darkness surrounded me, the only light streaming down from a fissure above and behind me. An odd reek underlay the scent of damp stone. Although faint, it reminded me of ammonia.

I'd fallen. Into…a cave? Perhaps another part of the same cave? Had the earlier collapse weakened some other portion of a more extensive system? "Hello?" I shouted weakly. "Help?"

"Whyborne!" Griffin's voice was faint but frantic. "Where are you? Is everything all right? Whyborne?"

"Here!" I struggled to my feet, taking stock as I did so. I ached abominably and had lost my hat, but at least my bones seemed intact.

"Whyborne!" Christine added her voice to the shouting.

"I'm here! Please—be careful! The ground isn't stable."

Within moments, Griffin appeared, framed against the sliver of light. "Ival? Are you hurt?"

"No. Well, bruised, but I'm on my feet and everything seems to be in working order."

"I'll fetch the rope," Christine said.

"Bring a lantern as well!" I called after her.

"Why?" Griffin asked suspiciously.

I didn't answer. A few minutes later, Christine reappeared. "Shall I tie the lantern on and lower it down to you?"

"No!" Griffin objected. "Whyborne, you can't mean to wander about down there by yourself."

"I just wish to have a quick look around," I said. "I'll be fine, Griffin."

He didn't reply, his face nothing more than a shadow against the bright sky, but I suspected he was not at all pleased with me. Christine lowered the lantern, which I freed from the rope. I considered fumbling about in the dark for matches, but that seemed ridiculous, so instead I lit the lantern's wick with a few words. Griffin's sigh drifted down from overhead, which I pointedly ignored.

Shadows swung and shifted alarmingly when I lifted the lantern, before settling into recognizable shapes. The passage around me seemed oddly level. I knew little about such formations, of course, but didn't they usually twist and turn, the ceiling growing higher or lower as the stone dictated? This seemed more like the tunnel leading down to the mine in Threshold than any natural formation.

Something on the wall caught my eye. Frowning, I stepped closer. "Christine?" I called.

"Yes?"

"Would it be possible for Griffin to lower you down?"

"Why?"

"Because there are carvings on the walls. Pictographs, similar to those on the stone."

There came the sounds of a brief argument. Predictably, it ended with Griffin lowering Christine down via the rope. "What have you found?" she asked, even before her boots touched the ground.

"Look here."

I held the lantern close to the wall, revealing row upon row of carved pictographs. Christine let out a gasp and leaned in to examine them. "And they're the same as those on the stone?"

"A similar style, at least. Without a direct comparison, I can't say with absolute certainty, but I believe them to be."

"Damn, I wish I'd brought paper and charcoal to make rubbings. Later, perhaps." Her eyes gleamed in the lamplight. "Do the symbols seem at all familiar to you?"

I studied them carefully. Many of the pictographs were highly stylized, and their grouping suggested they might form sentences. "No. That is, they could be, but at first glance they don't seem to be related to any language with which I'm familiar."

"Do you realize what this could mean?" she asked, and her voice trembled with an excitement I'd never seen in her before. "What if we have discovered a heretofore unknown civilization?"

"Of yayhos? Don't start writing a paper just yet."

"Assuming these yayhos even exist," she reminded me. "We haven't met anyone who has claimed to actually see them, and the buzzing voice in the mine could have been produced by some strange trick of acoustics."

We worked our way slowly along the wall, and I began to grow excited myself. The repeating nature of the symbols convinced me this was indeed a system of writing. If only there was some way to know how ancient or recent the carving might be. I longed to have an accurate reproduction in my hands, to compare with other known systems of writing. Were there connections, or did I view the work of wholly alien beings?

What if Elliot had been right and the theft of the stone was nothing more than the work of men who had decided the wrong side of the law offered more opportunity than the mine? What if these carvings represented the work of men? If Christine and I uncovered evidence of a new civilization, to rival those discovered in Mexico and South America…

As we worked our way along the wall, the hieroglyphs—for such they seemed to be—began to be interrupted by scenes meant to depict specific happenings. The first showed some sort of creature, which resembled a winged crustacean, like a prawn, with an oddly pyramidal head.

"A god?" Christine suggested.

"A yayho?"

Her mouth pressed into a line of annoyance. "Before you dragged me into the business last December, it wouldn't have even been an option."

"I didn't drag you into anything," I reminded her.

"Hmph."

The next pictorial display showed the crustacean-thing interacting with a stylized human, dressed in Indian clothing. The human knelt and bowed his head, as if the creature dominated him in some fashion. Was Christine's suggestion correct, and this depicted a god of some kind?

Christine's frown turned uneasy, but she didn't comment. We continued on.

"Odd," she said, after we had gone a bit further.

"The carvings?"

"Well, yes, but the cave itself. I've been in more cracks and crevices than I can count. Any left open to invasion by animals invariably collect some sort of occupants. Snakes, scorpions—"

"Not here, I hope!" I exclaimed with a shudder. Surely this blasted place didn't have scorpions, did it?

"Spiders," she went on, undeterred. "Bats. At the very least, I'd expect to see cobwebs or guano. But there's nothing."

"Which means…?"

"That the area is too regularly disturbed for animals to find it a safe haven."

I didn't like the sound of that.

More scenes appeared amidst the carvings. Crustacean-things, humans, and strange jars seemed the most common depictions. But the humans were frequently…wrong. Their right and left arms depicted on the wrong side of their bodies. Missing limbs. Extra limbs. A body rigidly laid out, while a crustacean-thing cut into its skull with some odd implement.

If these carvings had been made by human hands, they were strange indeed, for they never showed a man in ascendance, only dominated or operated on by the creatures.

Before long, our exploration brought us to the other side of the rockfall. Or, rather, the other side of the enormous boulder we had commented on earlier.

A few smaller rocks had fallen on this side, but the main damage seemed to have occurred at the very front of the cavern, where the unfortunate men and boy had been found. I held the lantern close to the walls and floor. Looking for what, I wasn't entirely sure. The boulder fit almost unnaturally into the tunnel, but just above it, I made out the ceiling of the cave.

Wait a moment. If the boulder had fallen, shouldn't there be an equally large hole in the ceiling above?

"Look at the size, the shape," I murmured to Christine. "It almost looks as if someone put it here to block the entrance."

The line between her brows deepened. "It can't have been. The geologists would surely have sent back for blasting powder, and possibly men to help move the rubble after, when they let the boy run the black stone back to town."

"Unless it was put in place after the collapse," I said uneasily.

"Impossible! If that were indeed the case, the stone would have to have been fit into place from the inside. From deeper within the mountain."

We were silent for a moment, contemplating the possibilities. I didn't care for any of them, and with the hideous carvings added to the mix…

"Perhaps we should return to town, and come back later with more hands," I suggested, my voice just a touch higher than normal.

Christine swallowed visibly. "Yes. Let's."

We hastened back to the ragged hole in the roof of the cave, where Griffin waited. "Are you coming up?" he called down.

"Yes, at least for now," Christine said.

The reek of ammonia had grown stronger in our absence. I found myself glancing worriedly into the deeper part of the cave. More carvings stretched off into the blackness, decorating the wall with even more distorted human figures.

Was that the scrape of something hard, like a claw, against the rock deeper into the cave?

It was probably just a bear. Dear heavens, let it just be a bear.

Christine gripped the rope; she'd tied heavy knots into it before being lowered initially, to give purchase to her feet and hands. At the sound, however, she too turned to the darkness.

"Whyborne?" she asked.

"Go." I backed up toward her, my eyes fixed on the tunnel. "Hurry, damn it!"

"Haul me up!" Christine called, and Griffin must have heard the urgency in her voice. Earth and pebbles tumbled down from above, accompanied by a curse.

There came another scrape, closer, like a crab shell on stone. No, I was only making the comparison thanks to the blasphemous carvings. They'd put the idea in my head.

It was just a bear. Or a mountain lion. Or—

The rope fell back down to me. "Whyborne! Grab hold!"

I dropped the lantern and ran for the rope. Footsteps sounded behind me, and I grabbed the rope with all my strength. "Go! Go!"

They hauled me up immediately. But I was only a short distance off the floor, when a hand wrapped around my ankle.

I let out a cry of alarm and looked down. A young man who seemed vaguely familiar clung to my foot, adding his weight to mine. "Let go!" I cried, but his eyes were flat and black, more like the unmoved gaze of an insect than the desperate stare of anything human.

I tried kicking him in the face with my other foot, but with all my weight on my arms, my strength failed. I fell heavily to the stone floor, sending great spikes of pain into my hip and shoulder. And still he clung to my ankle, trying to draw me back, deeper into the cave.

"Whyborne!" Christine shouted. "Don't move!"

I went limp. An instant later, her rifle spoke, deafeningly loud in the close confines of the cave. My assailant jerked, blood bursting free from his throat. His grip loosened on me, and he collapsed to one side, gurglingly loudly.

The stench of ammonia was overwhelming.

Griffin and Christine both yelled at me to return to the rope. But I had recognized the young man at last, and I staggered toward him, one hand outstretched.

"Your mother—" I started. But there was no flicker of recognition, of warmth.

Then it was too late, his features shifting from impassivity to the slackness of death. The chemical stench receded, and I sucked in great gulps of air, fighting to breathe and calm my racing heart.

"Whyborne!" Griffin shouted. "Hold on—I'm coming down!"

"No." I held up my hand, even though my head spun. "We need to get him out of here. Back to Threshold."

"Why?" Christine asked.

I swallowed against the tightness in my chest. "Going by the photograph we saw, I believe this is Lucas Kincaid."

CHAPTER 12

"It ain't true! He wouldn't have hurt nobody!"

Mrs. Kincaid's voice carried through the front window of the Pinkerton barracks, before dissolving into an inconsolable wail. Elliot had ordered his men to bring the body here, after retrieving it from the hillside where we had left it concealed. The lower level of the building contained an iron-barred cell, which served as the town's jail, Elliot's office, and a large front room. They'd laid out Lucas in this latter area, before sending for his parents and the company doctor.

"Fredericks, please take Mrs. Kincaid home," Elliot said. Apparently, Mr. Kincaid had been too sick to leave his bed. A moment later, the door opened and Fredericks led the sobbing woman across the porch. I was deeply glad she didn't look over to where Griffin, Christine, and I sat amidst the growing darkness. Her cries tore my heart; I couldn't imagine how she must feel. I glanced at Christine, but she had turned her head away.

"He would have killed me," I said quietly.

"I know, Whyborne. Don't be stupid." She rubbed impatiently at her face.

Elliot stepped out onto the porch, his expression grim. "I'm sorry I abandoned you earlier," he said. "If I'd imagined anything like this would happen, I would never have left."

"You had no way of knowing," Griffin said tiredly.

"Why do you think he attacked us?" I asked Elliot.

Elliot shrugged. "At a guess? He and his brothers found the carvings in the cave while out hunting. They remembered the stone sent to Mr. Stotz and decided it might be valuable. The elder two left to find the stone, and Lucas remained behind to guard their find."

I recalled Lucas's impassive expression, far too similar to the look on the faces of his brothers when they'd accosted me. Elliot's explanation was perfectly reasonable, but I didn't believe it. The blank-eyed man in the cave barely even seemed like the same person as the laughing, smiling youth in Mrs. Kincaid's photograph.

From inside, the doctor let out a muffled exclamation. "What the devil?"

Griffin hurried to the door. Elliot swore. "Blast it, Griffin, this is no longer part of your investigation!"

Christine and I followed them inside. The dead man had been laid out on top of a large table, hopefully not one used for dining. A heavy sheet had been placed beneath him to catch any blood. The doctor stood by the body's head, his skin almost matching the corpse's in pallor.

"What is it?" Griffin asked.

"I…I was just doing a quick examination, to fill out the death certificate," the doctor said.

"How much of an examination do you need, man?" Elliot asked indignantly. "I would have thought the gaping hole in his throat would be enough to attest to cause!"

The doctor blinked, but seemed too stunned and confused to properly react to Elliot's ire. "It was, Mr. Manning. But I have an interest in phrenology. I wondered if there had been any obvious signs as to Kincaid's criminal nature, and decided to examine his skull. And I found…this."

He pulled back a section of the dead man's hair, exposing the scalp. "Bring a lamp," Griffin ordered. The doctor's servant fetched one and brought it near enough to see a line of very fine stitches.

"An injury?" I asked, confused.

The doctor said nothing, only continued to pull the hair aside, exposing more sutured skin. The wound—if wound it had been—wrapped in almost a complete circle, all the way around the back of his head. As if someone had tried to scalp him. Or open up his skull.

"Dear God," Christine breathed. "What could it possibly mean?"

A short while later, I sat in one of the private parlors of Brumfield House, along with Christine and Griffin. We had ordered a bottle of brandy, and sat nursing it in silent, horrified contemplation.

"I must say, gentlemen, I don't care for any of this," Christine said at last, breaking our silence.

"Nor do I," Griffin agreed. "Although I can't say what any of it means."

"Someone performed surgery on him," I said, clasping my hands about my knee. "Not the company doctor, clearly."

"I can't imagine there are many practicing surgeons in the wilderness," Christine mused.

"We know there's at least one," Griffin said wryly.

I leaned forward and lowered my voice. "You didn't see the carvings, Griffin. One of them showed a creature cutting into a man's skull. It can't be a coincidence."

Griffin paled. "Why? Did the carvings indicate what it was doing to him?"

"The writing probably did, but I can't read it. But none of the Kincaids acted at all like the men their mother described. Perhaps whatever procedure was performed on Lucas turned him into a slave of the things—the yayhos. Doubtless it was performed on his brothers as well."

The line between Griffin's brows deepened in thought. "Perhaps," he murmured.

"Even if I'm wrong, the rockfall was deliberate," I said. "And now we're attacked by one of the missing men, whose brothers assaulted me in Widdershins? Even if we don't consider the deaths of Johnson and the boy who brought the stone back to town, it all seems very odd."

"Yes." He tilted his head back and frowned. "And Elliot the only survivor."

A chill touched me. "Do you think he's involved?"

Griffin chewed on his lower lip, his eyes staring at something far away as he considered. Finally, he shook his head. "No. I've known Elliot for too long—his shock when he heard Kincaid attacked us was genuine. Elliot has many faults, to be sure, but he joined the Pinkertons because he truly wished to do good, not just cash a paycheck."

A soft knock sounded on the open door. A small man with very large ears stood there, wearing a bowler hat and a suit, which was slightly too big for him, and an enormous camera hanging from a strap around his neck.

"Yes?" Christine asked suspiciously.

He tipped his hat to her, then to us. "Toby Webb, from the *Threshold Times*," he said. "Reporter and photographer. I'd like to interview you about the shootout, and maybe get a few photographs, Mr. Whyborne."

"Dr. Whyborne," I corrected automatically. I disliked his ingratiating smile.

"Of course, of course. Your father is Niles Foster Whyborne, right? The railroad tycoon?"

"And what if he is?" Griffin asked stiffly. Apparently, I wasn't the only one who'd taken an immediate dislike to our guest.

Webb sidled farther into the sitting room and gave us a little bow. "Word is, Mr. Whyborne sent you lot to Threshold to investigate the mysterious happenings here," he said, his voice lowered but no less oily.

"Is this for your newspaper article, Mr. Webb?" Griffin met the reporter's smile with a cool glare.

"Not at all," Webb replied, undeterred. "In fact, it's about what Mr. Orme told us *not* to print."

I straightened. "What?"

"Thought that would get your attention, Mr.—sorry, Dr. Whyborne. Right after the Kincaid boys disappeared, the dogs sent up a ferocious barking on the end of town nearest the mine. One of the Irishmen who works the coke ovens swore some kind of creature was up on his porch, looking inside. I figured he'd been drinking, but I went out the next morning anyway, and there were the damnedest—pardon my language—prints in the mud outside his house. Not like any animal I'd ever seen. Figured maybe it was them yayhos Rider Hicks was on about, before he ran off. I took some photographs to run in the paper—we've got a nice half-tone printer—but Mr. Orme nixed the article. Said he didn't want us stirring up folks."

Was this the clue we'd been looking for? "Can we see the photos?"

Webb's expression grew sly. Curse it—I'd given too much away with my eagerness. "I still have the prints and the negatives," he said. "I'll be glad to share them with you…for a price."

"And what is your price?" Griffin asked, his green eyes narrow.

"Two hundred dollars."

Griffin laughed. "You're having quite a joke at our expense. They're worth fifty at most."

"One-fifty."

"Seventy-five."

Webb glanced at me, then back at Griffin. "Your boss is heir to the biggest railroad in North America." I wondered if I ought to tell him I wasn't likely to inherit as much as a dime. "One-twenty five."

"Seventy-five," Griffin said severely. "Take it, or we go to the editor at the newspaper and demand they be handed over for nothing."

Webb scowled, but nodded. "Done. Meet me here for lunch tomorrow, and I'll bring them with me."

"I don't have seventy-five dollars!" I exclaimed, when the photographer had left.

"No, but your father agreed to pay expenses. He'll pay for this." Griffin glanced down at my muddy oxfords. "And for a proper pair of boots."

The next morning, Griffin and I left Christine and her manuscript ensconced on the hotel veranda, and went out into Threshold. On Griffin's insistence, we visited the general store, which stood along the railroad tracks. A young man busily swept the porch, and a trio of women conversed nearby, while their children toddled around in the road.

The first floor was dedicated to receiving and storage; we took the stairs up to the second, where the store proper was located. The shelves sagged beneath the usual dry goods: bolts of cloth, hardware for home repair, tools, hats, and carpets. I noted a wide selection of canned food, sweets, coffee, and anything else a denizen of the town was likely to need. Including shoes.

Like everyone else in town, the storekeeper knew my identity and mistook me for the favored son. At least it guaranteed us quick service; within minutes, I found myself trying on a series of thick-soled boots. Griffin, in the meantime, drifted away to chat up the shop boy and the female customers.

When we eventually departed, I sported a brand-new pair of boots. The soles were much thicker than my trusty oxfords, and caused me to tower over everyone else even more than usual. I hunched my shoulders and wished I could disappear.

We spent an hour or so sitting on the store's porch afterward, loitering about while Griffin did his best to strike up conversation with the passing locals. Although everyone was civil, it soon became clear no one wanted to talk to us.

No wonder. First Johnson died after conversing with me; next, we shot a young man who must have been well known to everyone in the community. Did they think us dangerous, or simply unlucky?

We returned to the hotel just at noon. Both hotel guests and residents from the town came in for lunch, it seemed, although the latter were mainly those who worked at the general store, the livery stable next door, or the newspaper. Christine awaited us at the end of a long table, and we took our seats with her just as the waiters began laying out our meal of pork chops, potatoes, and carrots.

"No sign yet of Mr. Webb," she reported. "I hope your morning was profitable?"

"Not at all," I replied gloomily. "Besides obtaining these horrible boots, anyway. I hope you had success working on your manuscript?"

Christine launched into a long explanation of funerary jars, frequently interrupted by outbursts against colleagues who disagreed with either her theories or her methods. I listened with half an ear, nodding and murmuring agreement at the appropriate times, but, for the most part, I kept watch for the newspaperman. Where on earth was he? With the promise of seventy-five dollars in exchange for some photographs we'd not even seen, I could scarcely believe he wouldn't bother to even meet us.

He did not, however. Lunch soon ended, and under the cover of scraping chairs, I asked, "What should we do next?"

"Perhaps he was detained at the newspaper," Griffin said. "After all, he could hardly tell his employer he had a meeting to sell the photographs he was ordered to suppress."

"He could have at least sent word, or thought of some other story," I objected, but Griffin had a point. Possibly the man was simply rude. He'd certainly seemed it last night.

Leaving Christine to her work, we returned to the streets of Threshold to visit the newspaper office. It sat beside the train depot, no doubt for ease of access to the telegraph office within. As soon as we stepped inside, I felt the floor vibrating from the printing press in the back room. The smoke from cigarettes and pipes mostly obscured the large front room. A typewriter clattered noisily, almost drowning out an argument between two red-faced men. I assumed the loudest one must be the editor.

The only man not engaged in shouting caught sight of us. "Can I help you?" he called over the din of the press.

"We're looking for Mr. Webb," Griffin said. "Is he here?"

The man shook his head. "No—haven't seen him all day. His desk is there." He stopped typing long enough to wave a hand at a desk directly across from him.

Griffin and I exchanged a glance. "It's very important we speak with him," Griffin said. "Can you tell us where he might be?"

"Home, sleeping off the gin?" The man shrugged. "He's married, so he doesn't stay in the boarding house with the rest of us."

A bit more badgering on Griffin's part elicited the location of Webb's house. Once we were back outside where we could hear ourselves think, I said, "Do you think he's right and Webb stayed home?"

"He seems the type of have celebrated a windfall before actually having it in his pocket," Griffin said. "Let's hope his colleague was correct, and he's merely suffering from a hangover."

Webb's domicile was a small, single-story structure built on the same plan as the worker housing. The location, however, was relatively pleasant. The house stood on the uppermost edge of the cleared area, far enough away from the creek to keep down the stink. There was a bit more space between itself and its neighbors as well, and a small garden occupied the rear of the lot.

The trees loomed close enough to cast shadows over the walls, and I welcomed an escape from the sun. The humidity still made my clothing stick uncomfortably to my skin. Buzzing insects whined in my ears. I hoped Mrs. Webb would offer us a cool drink before our walk back.

I stared to step onto the porch, but Griffin abruptly caught hold of my arm. "Hold up. Something is wrong."

Startled, I examined the structure more closely. Smeared mud tracked across the porch, and the front door hung open, although only by an inch.

Griffin drew his revolver. "Stay behind me," he warned.

The wooden boards of the porch creaked beneath his feet, the sound unnervingly loud. Moving slowly, he pressed his eye to the crack between door and jamb. All his muscles tensed, and he flung the door open, sending it crashing back into the wall.

Only silence greeted us, broken by the soft creak of the door as it started to swing back again.

"Damn it," Griffin said.

We entered the house. A foul odor thickened the air, as if someone had spilled a bottle of ammonia and neglected to clean it up. The single, large room, which took up the front half of the house, was a ruin: drawers pulled free from the desk and papers scattered everywhere.

Two rooms formed the rear of the house: a kitchen and dining room, and a bedroom. The bed had been overturned, the mattress torn and shredded in places. A low, flat trunk lay near the door, its lock bent and broken as if it had been violently ripped open. Whatever had been inside the trunk was gone now.

Of Toby Webb and his wife, there was no sign.

CHAPTER 13

"Griffin," I began, then trailed off. That someone had ransacked the house looking for the photos seemed evident. As for the former occupants...

Griffin's mouth thinned into a taut line, and his gaze took on a steely quality as he surveyed the wreckage. He went to the bed, inspecting the rents in the mattress, before dropping to his knees to peer carefully at the floor.

I watched him work, fascinated. I'd never seen this part of his investigations before. My involvement had inevitably come during the monsters-and-screaming portions, and it was a pleasant change to see his talents at work in this fashion.

Finished with the bedroom, he moved to the largest room, examining the drawers, which had been yanked free from the desk. "Look at these scratches," he said, pointing at the face of one of the drawers. Deep gouges marred the wood to either side of the pull.

"Was it locked, perhaps?" I asked, although the marks seemed in an odd location for someone trying to force the drawer open.

"This type of desk doesn't lock," he replied, putting the drawer aside and examining another, which bore the same sort of scratches.

"Er, should we...summon someone?" I suggested weakly.

"The only law in Threshold is the Pinkertons, and they work for the very company which didn't want the photographs published," Griffin replied. "We will alert Elliot, of course, but not until after we have an opportunity to look around. If you would, please go through the papers and make certain there's nothing of use to us. If anything seems at all relevant, take it now and we'll read through it later."

I went to the scattered papers and picked them up, hoping to find some sort of order. "My dearest pudding pie," I read aloud.

"Yes, my little turnip?"

"Hilarious," I muttered. "If you ever call me anything of the sort again, we shall have words. There is a great deal of correspondence here, but it mainly seems to have been saved from their courtship." I scanned a few paragraphs at random as I sorted through the papers, and the tips of my ears grew hot. "It, er, mostly describes the liberties she hoped to take with his person. Dear lord, the man must have been an acrobat if she hoped to accomplish *that!*"

Griffin cleared his throat. "Please stop reading the licentious affairs of others and return to the matter at hand."

"Oh, er, yes." I blushed again and hurriedly put the letters aside. Unfortunately, the other papers consisted merely of mundane items such as receipts of sale and recipe cards. Nothing connected with our investigation, and no photographs of any kind.

Griffin finished his inspection and beckoned me outside. Dropping to his knees again, he peered at the muddy marks on the porch. "Odd," he murmured.

"What?"

He sat back and point to the prints our boots had left. "Do you see the general roundness of a footprint? There is an oval shape, even when scuffed or smeared. These are more like crescents."

"What does it mean?"

"No idea." He rose to his feet in a single, graceful move. I trailed him off the porch; he inspected the soft ground in front of the house, then moved around to the side. When we came to the area beneath the bedroom window, however, he let out a soft hiss and dropped into a crouch. "Whyborne! See here!"

I hurried to his side and mimicked his posture. In the soft mud beneath the window was pressed a single...well, it wasn't a footprint. Rather, the crescent shape more resembled the claw of some gigantic crustacean.

Griffin and I reported the Webbs' disappearance to Elliot. Clearly disturbed, he promised to investigate, although I doubted he'd uncover anything more than Griffin had already. Not knowing what else to do, we returned to the hotel. While Griffin updated Christine, I went to my room, intending to change back into a comfortable pair of oxfords, as opposed to clunking about the hotel in thick-soled boots.

As I approached my room, one of the hotel maids let herself out, no doubt having just finished her work of straightening up. She shot me a nervous glance as we passed in the hall, but with her uniform of a black dress with white collar and cuffs, and a plain white headscarf, it took me an instant to recognize her.

"Mrs. Hicks!" I exclaimed.

She froze, like a startled deer. "Sir?"

"I had no idea you worked at the hotel." Although there was really no reason I should have; I'd merely assumed she'd referred to her duties as a house-wife when she'd spoken of getting back to work during our previous conversation.

"Yes, sir. Please, I'll be in trouble if I don't get my work done quick enough."

"Oh, er, of course, please forgive me." But as I started to turn away, I realized she didn't carry anything I would expect a maid to need in the course of her normal duties. No feather duster, or dirty linens, or anything of the sort.

She had already started to leave. "Stop!" I called.

I half expected her to flee, but she seemed to realize the futility of it. I disliked the way her shoulders hunched, though, as if she thought the order would be followed with some show of physical violence.

"You left the note in my room," I said, careful to keep my voice down. "And you've just left another, haven't you?"

"Sir, I…"

"Stay here. Please."

I ducked swiftly into my room. As I'd thought, a small, folded note lay atop my pillow. Snatching it up, I went back out, before unfolding it. In the same childish handwriting as before, it said:

> *"Mr. Kenkade weren't himself.*
> *Don't trust those as have gone to the wood.*
> *Signed,*
> *A Friend"*

"My daddy was a house slave," she said unexpectedly. "When he was a little boy, he'd carry the master's son's books to school, then sit in the back and listen. That was how he learned to read and write, even though it weren't legal, and he passed it on to me."

Although her voice was soft and she didn't raise her eyes to my face, her shoulders tilted defiantly, as if she felt she had to explain her literacy but couldn't quite suppress pride in her father.

A sort of horror washed over me, quite unrelated to the case. Books had been my salvation as a child; I could not imagine what might have become of me without them. And although I was perfectly aware many of my own race were unable to read, to have it actually be illegal to even attempt to learn seemed a monstrous injustice.

No doubt Griffin would call me a fool, to think this the worst thing humans had done to one another. And I knew he would be right, yet, somehow, this instance struck home and made things real to me in a way other examples might not.

"I see," I said, because I didn't know what else to say. "Well. I, er, hope you will pass along the skill to your own child." Or would it be allowed to attend the town's school? I didn't know.

She gave me a quizzical look, but some of the fear had eased from her face, at least. "Please, Mrs. Hicks," I said. "I don't understand what 'going to the woods' means. If you can shed any light on what's happening in Threshold, help me."

Her teeth flashed white against her lower lip, worrying it uncertainly. "I don't rightly know the extent of it myself, sir. Just what Rider told me. But you seen for yourself the truth of it. Those Kincaid boys wouldn't have run off and left their mama and daddy in such straits. Certainly not to become robbers and murderers, without any cause at all. They went into the woods, and now they ain't…them anymore. And Mr. Orme is the same."

"What?" My heartbeat quickened. "Mr. Orme?"

Mrs. Hicks nodded. "My cousin is a maid in the operator's household. After all this started, with the black stone and the yayhos and such…Mr. Orme, he changed. Turned cold. Not mean, just…different."

A chill walked up my spine on spider feet. I wondered suddenly if the Webbs would return, the sly photographer replaced by a man with Orme's reptilian gaze. And the Kincaid brothers—hadn't I noticed their icy demeanors?

"That was when Mr. Orme ordered Rider arrested," she went on quietly. "And why Rider ran. Because them as go to the woods and come back different don't mean us any good."

"Mrs. Hicks, please. The only person who seems to know anything about what is happening is your husband. I swear to you, I mean him no harm whatsoever, and will do everything in my power to protect him. If you know where to find him, tell me, I beg you."

She trembled, and, for a moment, I truly did not know whether she would speak or not. "I leave a cache of food and suchlike for him every few days," she said, her voice so soft I had to strain to hear her, even as close as we stood in the hall. "He can't be far from it."

She told me the location of the cache; her directions meant little to me, but I repeated them back dutifully.

When she finished, she took a step away from me. This time, I let her go. "Thank you, Mrs. Hicks."

Her eyes were sad and frightened. "Help Rider, if you can, sir," she said in a small voice. Then she hurried away down the hall, leaving me alone in silence.

Naturally, I rushed back downstairs immediately to inform Griffin and Christine. I repeated the directions to the cache back, before I forgot them entirely. Griffin listened intently.

"Yes," he said. "Give me a half an hour, then meet me at the livery stable."

At least I'd never gotten around to taking off my awful boots.

We did as he asked, taking the opportunity to grab a bite of dinner before leaving the hotel to meet him. The air remained stubbornly humid, even after the setting of the sun. At least there was a breeze now, although it was accompanied once again by the distant grumble of thunder. Apparently, evening thunderstorms were the norm here in the spring, rather than the exception.

I'd hoped I'd mistaken the intent behind Griffin's suggestion we meet outside the livery stable, but as we approached, the light of the lantern he held limned his handsome face in gold—and gleamed in the eyes of the three horses tied up behind him.

I came to a halt, but Christine strode directly up to the beasts. "Oh, excellent. I'd worried you meant to hike about in the dark. Have you selected one for yourself?"

"The black, I think," Griffin said, patting the creature in question.

I took a tentative step closer. "You can't mean for us to...to *ride* about, can you?"

Griffin frowned at me. "Surely you can ride, Whyborne."

"Well...yes. I've ridden before." My childhood friend Leander had loved horses, and insisted I join him on little tours around his estate. Of course, I hadn't been on one of the beasts in a decade, instead riding in cabs, like a civilized person.

"Then mount up!" Christine exclaimed. She swung easily into the saddle, as if she did such things all the time. No doubt she rode horses and wrangled camels as a matter of course in Egypt.

I stared at the remaining creature. I could barely make it out in the dim light, but I thought it was brown in color, with a white blaze on its forehead. What was more obvious was it was very tall and very large.

"Do you need help adjusting the stirrups?" Griffin offered kindly.

"No! Well, yes."

Griffin assisted me up onto the towering monster's back and adjusted the stirrups to fit my long legs, before stepping back with a grin. "Don't fret, my dear—you'll be fine."

I rather doubted it. Griffin swung up onto his mount with the same ease Christine had shown, and I remembered his tales of chasing train robbers and the like across the west. Of course he was an accomplished horseman. No doubt Elliot rode like a cowboy as well.

Griffin's steed responded to a light touch of his knee and headed away from the livery stable at a brisk walk. Mine followed, more or less by default, as I'd done nothing to encourage it I was aware of.

"Buck up, Whyborne!" Christine called from behind me. "They can sense fear, you know!"

Wonderful. I'd be trampled to death by midnight.

Griffin led the way up along the cleared area, avoiding the bulk of the town. I clung grimly to the reins, every step—trot—whatever—of the horse jarring my spine. As we approached the woods, Griffin glanced back and me and winced. "Try to sit more loosely," he advised. "You're bouncing along like a sack of wet laundry. Move *with* the horse."

"Oh, yes, why didn't I think of that?" I muttered under my breath. As for what he even meant to begin with, I hadn't the slightest notion.

Thunder growled over the mountain, louder now, and my horse let out a worried snort. I rather shared the sentiment. The wind picked up, rattling the trees as they closed around us, and bringing with it the scent of rain. The temperature dropped quickly, the oppressive feeling of the air giving way to something wilder.

I looked about worriedly, but the tossing trees already blocked the scattered lights of Threshold. Cloud rack covered the sky from horizon to horizon now, and our lanterns seemed to be the only points of light in all the world.

Griffin slowed his horse and cast about. "Listen," he said.

"I don't hear anything except the wind."

He nodded. "Exactly. The frogs and whippoorwills have fallen silent."

My skin crawled, and the horse seemed to agree, snorting and tossing its head, tugging at the reins in my clenched hands. We surely couldn't have penetrated far into the forest, but in the dark I had no idea which direction would lead us back to Threshold and which deeper into the hollow.

"How much further?" I asked. Surely Mrs. Hicks wouldn't have journeyed too deep into the countryside, given the dangers lurking in the woods.

"Not very—did you hear that?"

The wind howled down off the mountain, and the trees thrashed, branches rubbing together with obscene moans. But underneath it all, nearer at hand, there came the sound of something moving over the forest floor, snapping twigs and crunching leaves.

Christine pulled her rifle from her shoulder. "There's something moving in the woods."

Fear prickled along my arms, and the hair on the back of my neck stood up. Every shift of the trees seemed to herald an attack. Griffin drew his revolver, guiding his nervous horse in a circle with his free hand.

The edge of the lantern light fell across something moving toward us.

My blood froze in my veins at the sight. The shape was poorly lit, but I could just make out its general outline: huge and menacing and utterly inhuman. There were multiple legs, and wings, and what might have been a pyramidal snout in place of a true head. The reek of ammonia gusted over us, strong enough to make me gag. The horses whinnied in terror, their eyes rolling, even as Christine and Griffin both opened fire on the half-glimpsed horror.

Something hard and sharp, like a pincer, grabbed me from behind.

CHAPTER 14

My horse and I both let out shrill cries at the same instant. Then my mount heaved under me; I clasped my legs tightly to its sides as it sprang away from whatever had tried to grab us. The cloth of my suit coat tugged and tore, and the lantern fell from my grip as I clung to the reins with both hands.

A better rider might have controlled the horse, but I could only hang on for dear life. It plunged madly away from the creatures, heedless of where it ran. Branches tore at my face and hands, and I bent low over the horse's neck in an attempt to shield myself.

Thunder roared almost directly overhead, and a deluge opened up. Rain pelted us even through the heavy canopy of trees. The horse's hooves slipped in the layers of wet, rotting leaves, and the world tilted—

I fell, the leather reins whipping through my fingers fast enough to burn. My shoulder hit the ground, and I found myself tumbling down a steep slope. I grabbed wildly for something—anything—to stop my fall, thin branches striking my face, until I fetched up painfully against a tree.

I clung to the solid trunk, gasping for breath, my head spinning as I tried to make sense of my surroundings. I had no idea how far the horse had carried me, or even what had become of the wretched beast. All I saw was utterly black, except for the occasional flashes of lightning. I was alone, and had no idea if Griffin and Christine were all right, or if the things had—

My heart lurched painfully in my chest at the thought. No, please, no, nothing had happened to them. They had surely fought off the creatures and even now searched for me. I couldn't let myself be distracted by fear, not when I was in such a dangerous position myself.

I needed to do something, but what? How could I possibly find my way back to them? And where were the monsters—the yayhos? One could be standing behind me right now.

A hand closed on my elbow.

I spun with a shriek, striking out blindly. They would not take me without a fight, even if a pitiful one.

"Shh!" A hand—a human hand—closed over my mouth, muffling my cry. "Be quiet, you damned fool! They're all around us!"

I froze. A crack of lightning revealed the man standing pressed against me. I received the impression of a hawk nose and dark eyes, high cheekbones and glossy black hair. Surely this must be Rider Hicks.

Seeing I had calmed, Hicks removed his hand, then pulled me down the slope behind him. Another flash of lightning showed me a low stone wall and a wooden door: the remains of a spring house, almost invisible amidst the stones and fallen branches littering the hillside.

He dragged me inside, shutting the door behind us and pressing his ear against it. I followed suit, although I didn't know if I'd be able to hear anything over the pounding of my heart. The wood felt damp and slimy against my ear, and the fetid odor of mildew and wet rock choked my nostrils.

I don't know how long we stood there in the blackness, listening to the rain pound the leaves and the wind whip the trees. It seemed like years, or at least hours, as if dawn should have come and gone a dozen times over.

A branch snapped loudly, as if something had stepped on it.

Probably just the storm. Or even my horse, come to put an end to me with a heart attack, as it had failed to murder me with the fall.

A soft crunching sound, as of feet against the leaves and stones, followed. Not my horse. In truth, it sounded more like a drunken man staggering about than something more sinister. Lightning struck nearby, the flash seeping through the cracks in the crumbling door, and Hicks's eyes went wide in horror. Then we were in darkness again, and I heard him groping about.

"Do you have a weapon?" I whispered.

"My hunting rifle." His voice was barely audible above the falling rain, the scraping steps coming closer and closer. "I'm trying to light a torch—fire is the best defense against the yayhos. They hate the light. But if it isn't one of them…"

I reached out blindly in his direction, and my fingers encountered the rough length of wood, wrapped in cloth stinking of kerosene. "Give it to me, and get your weapon at the ready."

He swore softly, but did so, not having much choice. Together the two of us waited in the dark. Had whatever was out there heard us? Was it standing outside even now?

The door swung inwards. Calling out the name of fire, I thrust the torch in the general direction of the interloper.

The torch exploded in flame, blindingly bright after the darkness. I looked

—and almost vomited on the ground at what was revealed.

Whatever I had glimpsed before—or thought I had glimpsed—this was no monster. No thing of multiple legs and chitinous joints, of wings and reeking flesh. And yet, it was a thousand times more terrible.

In short, it was nothing more than the missing photographer, Toby Webb. But the way he moved turned my stomach, even before I consciously understood why.

Whatever stood before us retained his face and the general outlines of his aspect. He still wore shoes, but the rest of his clothing was gone, revealing lines of delicate sutures across his hips and arms. His legs bent in the wrong direction, as if they'd been removed and put on backwards. And as he reached to grab me with a ghastly, mewling sound, I saw his left and right hands had been swapped.

I froze, unable to move or think. But Hicks had no such difficulties. His rifle spoke, deafening in such close quarters. The shambling thing with Webb's face staggered, then collapsed awkwardly, its joints all askew.

Hicks didn't wait to see if it lived, only grabbed me by the sleeve and pulled me with him. The rain had lessened, and the torch remained lit as we rushed into the open.

I had no idea where we were going, but Hicks did, guiding me with shouts or tugs on my arm. We ran for what seemed forever, until my lungs burned and my side ached. At last, Hicks slowed to a stumbling stop.

"Here," he said, taking the torch from me. I followed him along the fold of hillside, until we came to what at first looked like nothing more than a tumble of rocks and debris. Bending down, he shifted some of them aside, revealing an opening of sorts, into which he promptly vanished. Not wishing to be left outside in the rain with monsters, I got down on my hands and knees and crawled in after him.

From the inside, the pile turned out to be a lean-to of sorts, which took advantage of a natural crack in the rock to form a shallow cave. The torchlight revealed it to be quite dry, and nicely stocked with food and a small stack of books. A heap of blankets in one corner must have been the bed; I simply sat on the bare earth floor, my knees drawn up to my chest, and hoped the seat of my trousers would survive.

Hicks rearranged the debris covering the entrance, then lit a small lantern, before dousing the torch. The light illuminated his face from below, sparking in his dark eyes and making his features seem even harsher.

"Now," he said, "who the hell are you?"

My hands shook, and a thousand questions boiled in my mind. I couldn't stop seeing the horror Toby Webb had become, shambling and flailing. The images Christine and I had examined in the cave took on a new significance, and my stomach turned.

"Wh-what happened? To Mr. Webb?" I asked, dazed.

Hicks glared at me. "Who are you? I saw what you did with the flame!" His hand shifted to rest on his rifle. "Are you some kind of sorcerer?"

"Me? Oh, no! No, I j-just translate old languages. I mean, yes, I know a few little tricks, but nothing more. I'm no sorcerer. Er, my name is Percival Endicott Whyborne."

"You're not in league with the yayhos, else they wouldn't have been chasing you through the woods," Hicks mused, but his eyes remained suspicious. "Did the Pinkertons send you?"

"No. Certainly not. I came here with my friends to investigate the disappearances and other strange goings-on. Thus far, it seems to me you know more about what's happening than anyone." I spread my hands apart helplessly. "So we came to find you."

Hicks studied me in silence, and the tips of my ears grew hot with embarrassment. How must I look, covered in mud and leaves, my hat gone and my hair sticking up in every direction? Surely, he would laugh at the idea of a man such as myself attempting to thwart creatures like the yayhos.

"This is how it was told to me as a boy," he said at last. "The Winged Ones came down from the stars—from the Great Bear, some say. They came for the same reason people do today—to mine something they couldn't get anywhere else."

"Coal?"

He nodded. "No man knows when the Winged Ones first burrowed into the mountains, but my ancestors learned the hard way to steer clear of them. Hunters came here, tracking game. Sometimes they'd hear things, strange buzzing voices offering them gifts in exchange for working for the Winged Ones. Other times, though, the hunters would return home changed. As if they'd become different people altogether."

"Like Mr. Orme."

"Exactly."

"But why? And why do…what they did…to Mr. Webb?"

He shrugged. "They're curious. They want to study us. But they also fear us. Before, they've gone about their business, sending spies into our midst and taking anyone who got too close, but keeping to themselves, for the most part. Now the railroads have come in, with the town and the mining company, and they fear discovery more than ever. They have to know if the army realized they were up here—and I mean knew for sure, with hard enough proof to convince anybody—they'd be wiped out."

"Then we must get proof."

Rider shook his head, black hair gleaming in the lantern light. "Don't you understand? The yayhos aren't going to just wait for the army to show up. They'll do whatever they can to keep the word from getting out in the first place. That's why I've begged Bertie—my wife—to leave Threshold. Before it's too late."

My blood ran cold. "Too late?"

"Before they wipe out the whole damn town." He shivered. "They hate the light, like I said. A few of them will come out when there's only a weak moon, but most stay underground. But the new moon is in three days."

God. We had to do something. "If I talk to Elliot—Mr. Manning—perhaps I can convince him to listen to you. We can take Mr. Webb's body back with us as proof something horrible is going on."

Hicks hesitated, and I glimpsed longing on his face, before he hid it quickly. No doubt he missed his wife and child terribly. "Come back with me," I cajoled. "We can sit down and continue this discussion in more secure surroundings."

To my disappointment, he shook his head slowly. "It isn't safe out here. But Mr. Orme is the yayhos' spy. He'll order the Pinkertons to throw me in jail. I'll be dead by dawn."

I wanted to argue, but in truth I couldn't. "I understand."

"Convince Bertie to get out of Threshold, if you can. She'll say she doesn't want to leave me, but I'd die if anything happened to her."

"I'll do my best."

He reached for the lantern. "Come with me, and I'll get you back on the path to town."

"My friends are still out here." I'd managed to put aside my fear for their safety, but now my heart quickened and my stomach churned.

"We'll never find them in the dark," Hicks replied with a shrug. "Come on."

We left the lean-to, Hicks holding the lantern. The rain had swept away, taking the clouds with it, and leaving behind the thin nail-paring of the waning moon. Even though I knew Hicks was right, I wanted to rush off into the night. Griffin could be anywhere on the mountain, lying injured, cold and wet—

No. As soon as I returned to Threshold, I'd go to Elliot. He'd surely raise a force to men to search. Christine and Griffin would be found, confused but whole—

"Whyborne! Damn you, answer us!"

—or they would find me.

I cupped my hands around my mouth. "Christine! I'm here!"

The lantern light went out. Startled, I turned, but Hicks had vanished.

"Whyborne!" Griffin shouted. His voice sounded rough, as if he'd been yelling my name across half the mountain.

"Here!"

Within a few moments, I caught sight of their lanterns through the trees and hurried to meet them, stumbling over every branch in the accursed forest on the way. Griffin swung down off his horse, set his lantern aside, and ran to meet me.

"I thought they'd carried you off!" he exclaimed, and pulled me to him.

I returned his embrace. He held me tightly, his body trembling. I'd been worried about him and Christine, but it had never occurred to me they might be equally frantic over my fate.

"I'm quite all right," I assured him. He smelled like sandalwood and wet horse, spiced with gunpowder. "The only thing to carry me off was the damnable horse."

Griffin let out a shaky laugh, before letting me go. "Thank God. Christine and I were out of our minds with fear."

"With good reason. I found Rider Hicks. And Mr. Webb."

"Mr. Webb?"

"Yes. I-I'll explain on the way to retrieve his...body."

But by the time we located the old springhouse, no trace remained of the mutilated corpse, save for a few stains of blood.

CHAPTER 15

So," Elliot said slowly, "you're saying you were attacked by the missing Mr. Webb, who had some sort of terrible surgery performed on him for inexplicable reasons, and the entire town is in danger from creatures from outer space."

"Precisely," Christine agreed.

Outside the small building, which served both as Elliot's office and the company jail, the first rays of the rising sun illuminated the western peaks, although the hollow still lay in darkness. A wren began its morning song, just outside the window. Exhausted as I was, I could not help but resent its sprightly cheer.

The night before, we wandered far from our original course. It took several hours to navigate the steep ravines and unforgiving stones of the landscape, especially since we operated with only the light of our two lanterns. For my part, however, the ride back had been more pleasant, if only because the loss of my horse obliged me to sit behind Griffin on his mount. At first I started at every sound, but once the peeping of the frogs and the grating of the crickets had resumed their usual din, I'd relaxed enough to become aware of the firmness of his backside pressed against the front of my trousers.

Feeling me harden against him, he cast a wink back over his shoulder, his impertinent grin enough to make me wish we were alone. As we were not, I kept my hands quite properly to myself, and merely imagined what I might do to him once we returned to the hotel.

Alas, it was not to be. I'd assumed my horse had come to some misfortune during its mad flight, but the demonic beast had instead made straight for its own stall in Threshold. Upon seeing it return alone, the stable owner had grown worried and raised the alarm. A force of searching Pinkertons, with Elliot at their head, met us on the way down the mountain.

Now it was dawn, and sleep the only thing I felt up to doing in bed. With the maids performing their daily chores, Griffin and I couldn't take the risk of even dozing in one another's arms. And of course it had all been for nothing, judging by the open skepticism in Elliot's voice.

Blast it.

In the chair beside mine, Griffin stiffened. "We all saw them, Elliot," he said. "This was no delusion."

Elliot held up his hand placatingly. "Of course. I do not question you saw something."

"But?"

"But I question what you saw." He gave us an apologetic look. "It was dark, on an almost-moonless night, in the middle of a storm. That you were attacked I have no doubt."

"And what do you think attacked us?" I asked, not bothering to conceal my frustration.

"The McCoy gang, most likely."

"Are you seriously suggesting we mistook a group of bandits for winged abominations?" Christine demanded.

Elliot eyed her warily, as if afraid she might reach over the desk and throttle him. "I mean no disrespect, Dr. Putnam. But in the dark, with the wind blowing, a coat or loose poncho could easily be mistaken for wings. A handkerchief tied across most of the face, in combination with a hat, might give the appearance of a monstrous head. Especially if the idea had already been implanted in your minds by the carvings you found."

"And Webb?" I demanded. "Or did he run off and turn criminal as you claim the Kincaids did?"

Elliot's mouth tightened. "I question if it was Mr. Webb in the first place. But even if it was, did he really attack you? Or was he stumbling around in the dark, lost and afraid? As for what happened to him after, of course he ran away once the damn Indian shot him."

"What about the claw prints on their porch and beneath their window?"

"Those marks could have been caused by anything."

"Then why would he have left town, to wander about in the woods?" Griffin countered. "He thought he was going to be paid a handsome sum for the photographs he offered us."

"Unless he didn't really have any photographs. *I* didn't see them, nor did anyone else I've spoken to." Elliot shook his head. "And there is the explanation for your 'claw prints,' Griffin. Mr. Webb promised mysterious photographs, which he attempted to fake himself in the mud beneath the window. At some point he realized they weren't convincing enough, panicked, and fled the town, rather than confront Dr. Whyborne's wrath at his attempted swindle."

I closed my eyes, then forced them open again as weariness descended upon me. "You're determined not to believe us, aren't you? You have an answer for every argument, and nothing will change your mind."

Elliot gave me a sympathetic look. "You must admit, it sounds rather incredible."

I didn't have to admit anything of the sort. Griffin, however, sighed and rubbed at his eyes. "I know it does, Elliot, but at least consider the possibility something strange happened in the woods last night."

"I am. And I agree you were certainly attacked. I'm putting a moratorium on anyone leaving the settlement and going into the woods for any reason. It's simply too dangerous."

The door to the office burst open. My heart leapt into my throat, and I was on my feet almost without realizing it.

"Sir!" One of the other Pinkertons stumbled into the office, cast us an uncertain look, then focused on Elliot. "It's Bill Swiney, sir! He's causing trouble outside the community center—trying to tell the other men not to start their shift!"

"Excuse me," Elliot said. "I must attend to this."

We shuffled out, and he shut the door behind us. As he hurried off with the other Pinkerton, I exchanged a baffled gaze with Christine.

"Who the devil is Bill Swiney?" she asked.

"One of the miners," Griffin murmured, watching Elliot stride away. "Some of the men look to him as a leader. Let's go hear what he has to say, shall we?"

The community center was easily the largest building in Threshold. What it was normally used for, I had no idea. Weddings? Dances? Traveling entertainers?

At any rate, its whitewashed walls made for a commanding backdrop behind the man currently standing on the stairs leading up to its porch. My height allowed me to glimpse him despite the great press of people gathered round, most of them men dressed for a day of work in the mine, their caps perched on their heads and pickaxes in their grimy hands.

"We can't ignore this any more! Stotz Mining knows something is going on here!" he boomed, his beard jutting out angrily in front of him.

"Enough, Bill," Elliot said. He and a small force of Pinkertons closed in from one side, and I noticed most of them carried visible weapons. A murmur swept through the crowd, mixing fear and anger.

"There's no conspiracy," Elliot went on, directing his words at the crowd more than at Swiney. "Just a lot of superstition and wild talk."

"You lie, and there is the proof!" Swiney insisted—and pointed dramatically at me.

I shrank back as a host of unfriendly eyes swung my way. The nearest men shifted away slightly, grumbling as they took in my disheveled appearance. Griffin and Christine both moved closer to me, and I had the sudden, sickening vision of them fighting to defend me against the mob.

"Would Niles Whyborne send his son here, if he didn't know there was something wrong in Threshold?" Swiney went on. "People are disappearing and dying, but *he's* here to help cover it up!"

"Johnson died right after talking to him!" another of the miners shouted.

"Enough!" roared Elliot. One of his men fired a gun into the air, and the attention of the crowd instantly swung away from me. "You're a drunken fool, Bill Swiney, as is anyone who listens to you. If I hear another word out of your mouth against Dr. Whyborne, I'll take it as a threat, and toss you into jail to rot. As for the rest of you, get to work, before you're late. The company owns your houses, and I *will* evict anyone who isn't in the mine or at his station in half an hour. Have I made myself clear?"

Unsurprisingly, the men didn't like it. A grumble ran through them, and for a moment I thought violence would erupt. Then a few men deserted the edges of the crowd, headed in the direction of the mine. Within a minute, the mob dissolved into a collection of muttering individuals.

Swiney's eyes narrowed as he focused on Elliot. "This isn't over, Pinkerton. Our blood has been spilled. Only fair if we get some payback."

"I'm not your enemy," Elliot replied coldly. "Nor is Dr. Whyborne. Go to the damned mine, or pack your things. I don't care which. Just do it now."

They glared at each other for a long moment. Swiney looked away first and very deliberately spat on the ground, before striding off in the direction of the mine.

Elliot watched him go. "I want a man on him at all times," he said, and one of the Pinkerton guards immediately left the group to follow Swiney.

It seemed the excitement had ended for the moment. We started in the direction of the hotel. As we walked, Christine said, "What now?"

"We need proof," Griffin said. "Something more damning than a line of sutures on a scalp, something Elliot can hold in his hands and believe. And if Rider Hicks was correct, and the yayhos mean to attack the night of the new moon, we need it soon."

"Orme," I blurted. "Mrs. Hicks said he'd changed. Perhaps we could find something in his office, or in his house?" What I had no idea, but surely it was worth a try.

"His office would be simpler to gain entry to at night, but I doubt he would leave anything too suspicious there. His house, however…but how to get inside?"

Christine snapped her fingers. "I've an idea. Give me a few hours."

What her idea was, she didn't say. We returned to the hotel, and I went straight to my room and collapsed into bed.

When I awoke several hours later, much refreshed, I dressed and made my way downstairs, where I found Christine sitting on the veranda, sipping lemonade. "There you are," she said. "Is Griffin still asleep?"

"I imagine so. I didn't knock on his door, not wishing to wake him."

A porter came out onto the veranda, and we fell silent. "A letter for you, ma'am," he said, passing an envelope to Christine.

"Ah, excellent!" Christine exclaimed. "Tip the man, won't you, Whyborne?"

I fumbled in my pockets while Christine opened the letter. Once the man left with his earnings, she said, "Perfect. While you napped, I took the opportunity to send a letter to Mrs. Orme, expressing my delight in the town and hinting I hoped for permission to call."

"Brilliant!" Could gaining admittance to the house truly be this simple? "Did she grant it?"

"Even better—she has invited you and me to dinner." With a smile of satisfaction, she folded up the letter and tucked it away. "Go see your best suit is brushed and ready, and I shall pen our reply. Tonight we dine at the operator's house."

Mrs. Orme sent the carriage around for us, letting Christine and I ride to the operator's house in some comfort. We had dressed carefully, and Griffin even assisted with oiling my hair, so it didn't stand up quite as badly as usual.

The house sat high on one of the slopes, overlooking the town and upwind from the coke ovens. Three stories tall, it bore graceful porches and ornate trim in the Queen Anne style, painted in cheerful colors. I couldn't help but compare it to the cheaply built miners' shacks in the town below, with their grimly utilitarian design. Or, when the maid let us inside, the opulent interior with the sparsely furnished houses of the Kincaids and the Webbs.

No sooner had the maid taken our coats and hats, than a matron who must have been Mrs. Orme appeared, followed by two younger women.

"I'm very glad you wrote, Dr. Putnam," she said to Christine. Although her dress was neat and hair perfect, I noticed lines of strain around her eyes and mouth. "I'd heard of your fiancé's arrival, of course, but I had no idea there was a woman in the party."

"Er, no!" I exclaimed. "That is, Dr. Putnam and I are colleagues. Not...not anything else."

"Really?" Mrs. Orme said, her smile taking on a predatory edge. "Please, let me introduce my daughters, Philomena and Amelia."

Christine used her skirts to cover the delivery of a swift kick to my ankle.

"Excuse my husband's absence," Mrs. Orme went on. A high, nervous note came into her voice, although her smile remained fixed. "I sent word to him we were to have guests, but—"

"I'm here, wife."

The cold voice sent a shiver through my blood. The two girls shrank behind their mother slightly, and Mrs. Orme straightened, as if through some protective instinct. "Y-Yes, husband. I was just greeting our guests."

His reptile eyes slid over us, and I knew he was not pleased. How would he communicate his displeasure to his wife later, after we left?

"I believe dinner is ready," Mrs. Orme said. "If you'll come this way."

In short order, I found myself seated at the dinner table, with Philomena on one side and Amelia on the other. "So, Dr. Whyborne," said Amelia, as the servants laid out our meal, "have you saved many lives?"

Heat suffused my cheeks. "I, er, no. I'm not a medical doctor."

"Dr. Whyborne studies languages," Mrs. Orme said.

"Really?" Philomena leaned in from the other side. I tucked my elbows as close as possible to my ribs to avoid touching her. "Oh, do say something in a different tongue!"

I cast about for something—anything—to save me. Christine rolled her eyes, which was not at all helpful. Desperate, I blurted out the first thing which came to mind.

"How romantic!" Amelia gushed. Considering I had just called her grandfather a donkey in Hindi, I merely nodded like an idiot and hoped no one asked for a translation.

Mrs. Orme inadvertently saved me by turning her attention to Christine. "I am in awe of your accomplishments, Dr. Putnam! How brave you must have been to go on such an expedition as the one which uncovered the tomb of the pharaoh!"

"I did not 'go on' the expedition," Christine said briskly, sawing on the mutton in front of her. "I led it."

Mrs. Orme looked taken aback for a moment, before hurriedly smoothing her expression. "I see. But surely, having had such success, you must hope to secure a husband and achieve the very height of womanly ambition?"

Christine snorted. "Are you daft? Why on earth would I want to do that?"

I risked casting a glance at the ladies seated next to me. Both of them stared at Christine, a mix of curiosity and horror on their faces. As for Mr. Orme, he showed no expression whatsoever, as if he didn't realize there was anything odd about the conversation.

Was Christine not even bothering to mince her words in hopes of exposing him somehow? Or...

Her foot connected rather sharply with my shin beneath the table. Startled, I jumped.

"Oh! Are you well, Dr. Whyborne?" Mrs. Orme asked, transferring her attention to me.

"I, er..." Christine gave me a pointed look I was at a loss to interpret. "I..."

"Has your illness from earlier returned?" she asked, practically glaring now.

"Oh! I mean, yes."

One of the servants materialized at my side. "This way, sir."

My face burning, I followed him out of the dining room, silently cursing Christine. The house was opulent enough to have indoor plumbing, and the servant left me at the water closet on the second floor.

I went inside and waited for his steps to disappear. Once certain he had left, I slipped silently out and leaned back against the door. Clearly, Christine meant me to search the house while she distracted its occupants. Now, if only I knew what to look for.

I started down the hall as stealthily as I could. The board beneath my foot immediately let out a loud creak.

Damn it. I was no good at this. If only Mrs. Orme had the decency to invite Griffin along as well.

Several doors lined the second-floor hall. I opened the first, and discovered a bedroom which no doubt belonged to the lady of the house. I shut the door hastily.

The next bedroom I glanced into seemed meant for the daughters. Two doors remained: one would surely belong to Orme's bedroom, but I was less certain of the other. I opened the first I came to, and found myself confronted by a masculine study, complete with books, a worn leather chair, and a desk. Might I find something here?

I moved across the floor as quietly as I could. Perhaps there was some odd correspondence, or a diary. Because clearly Orme would commit whatever villainy he was involved in to paper, where I could find it, yes?

If only Griffin were here.

I couldn't linger. If I was away from the table much longer, a servant would surely be sent to see if I needed the doctor. And when they realized the water closet was now empty, they would come looking for me.

Almost ready to declare defeat, I swept my gaze one last time over the study. There, on the desk: a daybook.

I hastened across the room and cautiously turned back the cover. Orme's name was written inside. The book seemed filled with quick accounts and one or two sentence summaries of the day.

I flipped through until I came to the latest entries. There were no more daily summaries, only notes about the household accounts…and in a different hand.

Was someone else writing them? Or had Orme's handwriting undergone a mysterious transformation?

A creak just outside the door. The house settling, or…?

I stuffed the book into my coat hastily, turning to face the doorway. An instant later, Orme's silhouette appeared.

"Dr. Whyborne?" he said, watching me with those cool eyes.

"I-I'm sorry," I babbled. "I got lost on the way back from the water closet."

The lie was absurd—this wasn't Whyborne House or Somerby Estate, with their labyrinths of hallways and rooms. But I couldn't think of anything else to say.

We stared at one another for a long moment: him utterly emotionless, me shaking in my shoes. Then he stepped back and gestured toward the hall.

"This way," he said.

I slipped out past him and headed down the stairs. And the whole time, I felt his eyes boring into my back, and knew I had just made a dangerous enemy.

CHAPTER 16

Christine and I returned to the hotel only an hour later.

I must have been pale when we returned to the table, because no one questioned my indisposition when I weakly declined to linger after dinner. The girls seemed disappointed, and Mrs. Orme…grim.

How much did Philomena and Amelia know or guess? That Mrs. Orme wished to protect them I gathered, but surely she couldn't have hidden her husband's strange alteration from them. Did they believe him to be under some sort of strain, or did they watch him in uncomprehending fear?

As the carriage bore us away, I felt as if I abandoned them to some terrible fate.

I told Christine of my findings, whispering them into her ear as we bumped along, for fear the driver might report back. When I finished, she shook her head.

"What the devil is going on here, Whyborne?" she asked. "I thought perhaps Mr. Orme had been mesmerized, or had some sort of brain surgery performed, but it wouldn't account for his change in handwriting."

"No. It wouldn't." I shivered. "I don't know what's happening."

We rode the rest of the way back in silence. As we had returned far earlier than expected, I went first to the public areas of the hotel, expecting to find Griffin on the veranda, or in the bar, having had a more pleasant dinner here than Christine and I had been subjected to.

I didn't find him in any of those places. Had he retired to his room already? Surely not; the evening was breathlessly hot, and there couldn't be much air to be had, with only a single window. Unless he wasn't feeling well, of course.

Concerned, I climbed the stairs to our floor, sweating profusely by the time

I reached the top. I left the landing, turned the corner into our hall...and stopped as Griffin's door swung open.

Elliot stepped out. His hat was in his hand, his hair tousled, his cheeks flushed...from the heat? Or something else?

Griffin's voice drifted from inside the room, "...nothing like what I have with Whyborne."

Nothing like what he had with me? What wasn't? Who wasn't?

But the answer to my question stood right in front of me, did he not? Dressed in a summer weight suit, handsome and colorful and urbane as I could never hope to be.

Elliot turned back to the room, a smile on his face. "I missed you, Griffin."

Griffin appeared in the doorway. No suit coat, no vest, no tie, and the top buttons of his shirt undone. "I'm not certain what to say," he confessed. "I..."

Then he saw me and fell abruptly silent. Alerted by his shift in attention, Elliot turned to me as well.

"Oh!" he said, looking more shocked than an innocent man ought. "I thought you were dining with Mr. Orme tonight."

My nails bit into my palms. There wasn't enough air in the hallway, in the hotel, in the hollow, in the world. Of course Elliot had thought I would be gone for the evening. Why else come here, remind Griffin of everything they'd had, and—and—

And of course I hadn't measured up. No doubt whatever sexual athletics they'd just performed were indeed nothing like what he had with me.

"Whyborne?" Griffin's voice came from very far away. I didn't—couldn't —look at him.

"I'm sorry," Elliot said. "I assumed he knew."

"Knew what?" There. I could speak. Normal words, not the ones trembling on the back of my tongue, begging to be unleashed.

"About us."

"This isn't a conversation to have in an open hall, where anyone might walk past," Griffin said in a low voice. "Come inside my room, at least."

My head spun. I didn't want to go in there and see rumpled bedclothes, or smell Elliot's cologne on the sheets.

Elliot regarded me quizzically. "It's quite all right, Whyborne. I'm not jealous. Griffin and I have always had an understanding. If I were prone to envy, I wouldn't have introduced him to Glenn, would I?"

Something savage rose up inside me, a thing of fire and wind, of fell curses and darkness. The words burned on my tongue, yearning to be spoken.

Elliot wouldn't be half so handsome if flocks of crows hounded him night and day while whippoorwills screeched in his dreams. Then he would believe in otherworldly forces, wouldn't he?

"Elliot!" Griffin's cracked like a whip. "Leave. Now."

Elliot still looked troubled, as if my reaction was honestly unexpected. But he gave us each a quick nod, before hastening away.

"Whyborne. Come inside. Please."

I did as he asked. At least the bed was made. Although he might as easily have had Elliot bent over the chair, or the little desk.

"You slept with your partner. Glenn." I could manage no more.

Griffin sighed. "It wasn't like that."

"I asked you! I asked you if you had, and you said he had a wife and children. You committed adultery!"

"Keep your voice down," he snapped. Green fire flashed in his eyes. "Would you please listen? Glenn and I weren't lovers, or at least, not regularly. We were friends who occasionally tossed one another off in the long nights out in the wilderness, when we chased down some criminal or other."

My mind conjured up all sort of visions of them entwined together beneath the western moon. "Now you are splitting hairs," I grated out.

"Am I?" Griffin folded his arms defensively across his chest. "Believe me when I say I did a great deal more with other men, some of whom, yes, were married. It's not unusual, you know. Many men like us have a normal family as well."

A faint wave of nausea rolled my stomach. "No wonder you laughed when I objected to Christine's talk of marriage. You must think me a fool."

Griffin sighed. "I think you're naïve. I never mentioned any of this to you because I knew you'd never understand."

For a moment, I could only stare at him, outrage stealing my words. "Not understand?" I demanded at last. "How can you say that to me? Of course I understand!"

"No, Whyborne, you don't." He bit off the words: hard and angry. "Your father has the wealth to protect you from ruin. Even if you were caught committing indecent acts in public, he'd just pay off the police and send you on a tour of Europe, until everyone had forgotten and moved on to some new scandal."

"How *dare* you bring my father into this? And you must be mad if you think he'd ever lift a finger for my sake. If he did any of those things, it would be to preserve the family name, not my reputation."

"Even if you're right, the results are the same. And your mother—she greets me and asks me to call her by name. Do you imagine the rest of us, even those who weren't thrown out of our own houses, have such a luxury? You've been protected and coddled, and you don't even see it!"

Coddled? My jaw ached, teeth clenched with rage. "And somehow this excuses having r-relations with Elliot behind my back? Just as you did with all those other men behind their wives' backs?"

Griffin's brows pulled into a tight scowl. "Elliot came by to talk about old times. Nothing more."

My mouth twisted into a sneer. "And talking required you to remove half your clothing?"

"It's blasted hot, in case you haven't noticed! I suppose there were plenty of iced drinks at Orme's residence, but for us common folk, we must make do as we can."

"You call me naïve, but it isn't proper to have been so dressed when he was with you!"

"I'm sorry, but we can't all be born with a silver spoon in our mouth and a stick up our ass!"

The words might as well have been a slap across the face. "If that's how you think of me, this conversation is at an end."

I went to the connecting door and flung it open.

"Damn it, Whyborne!" He followed me, reaching for the doorknob to keep it from swinging shut between us, and I finally found an outlet for the words sizzling on the back of my tongue. With a yelp, Griffin snatched his hand back from the suddenly heated metal.

I slammed the door in his face.

With a splitting headache, I made my way down to breakfast the next morning. I'd slept horribly, replaying the argument with Griffin over and over again. Had I unjustly accused him?

But the way Elliot had spoken, as if he'd meant to just pick up where they'd left off. As if I were the interloper.

Maybe I was. If they hadn't formally ended their relationship, if they'd had an "understanding" as Elliot put it, that they were free to pursue others, then I was just another in a long line of men. Except I was the only one stupid enough to have imagined Griffin's declarations of love meant he'd confine himself to my bed alone.

He'd seemed eager when he returned from Vermont. Had he slept with some stranger while there, while I remained at home, dutiful and trusting as his dead partner's wife?

Assuming she was as unschooled in these matters as I had apparently been. I viciously hoped at least some of Glenn's children hadn't been his after all.

Thankfully, there was no sign of Griffin in the hotel dining room. Instead, Christine sat reading the newspaper and eating hashed potatoes and sausage. "Good morning," she said.

I ordered sausage, eggs, and toast, along with a steaming cup of coffee. "It's one of those things, anyway."

"Griffin was in a foul mood as well," she remarked. "Bolted his food, barely snapped two words at me, and left."

The waiter served my food and coffee. I stared down at the full plate. Would I even be able to stomach a bite? "Do you recall our conversation on the train? I withdraw my earlier objections. Perhaps we should marry."

Christine let out a sigh. "Very well, Whyborne. You know how I feel about moping, so out with it. What have you quarreled about?"

I pushed the eggs around my plate without enthusiasm. At the moment, I couldn't imagine ever being hungry again. "Those I thought to find sympathetic, instead make me feel even more alien. I cannot conform to society's expectations, and yet, it seems, I cannot conform to the expectations of 'men like us,' either. I am called naïve, and coddled, and…and other things."

"Hmm. Well, you're no more coddled than any man, and rather less than some."

I gave her a dark look. "Are you complimenting or insulting me?"

"And as for naïve," she went on, ignoring the question, "I'd rather call you an idealist. Too much classical literature has given you high-minded notions."

"Even Heracles married Deianira."

"Well, you can be sure if we were to wed, I'd never do away with you using a poisoned shirt," she reassured me. "It would be pistols at dawn or nothing."

"Considering I can't hit a target at arm's length, I had best accede to your wishes in all things," I replied. "But don't you see? If I am an idealist, what of you? Society wishes you to mind the home and bear children, even after all you have done. Nor does legend supply many examples on which to model your life. At least you and I have that in common. No one else will ever understand us more than we do each other. Why should we not make our peace with the world and wed?"

I felt her regard for a long moment, but I kept my eyes fixed on my plate. It would not be so bad, if she accepted. Perhaps I would even learn to enjoy travel to distant countries.

She patted my upper arm gruffly. "You're a good friend, perhaps the only one I can claim. But I would never let you make such a sacrifice."

"It was your idea in the first place!" I exclaimed, vexed into looking at her.

"Upon which I didn't act," she reminded me. "Buck up, old fellow. If we cannot find models in our past, we must try to build a future where they can exist, and devil take anyone who tries to tell us we can't. If we grow old and gray together as companions, well, by the time we're eighty, we won't give a fig for society's rules or anyone else's. Then we shall take house together and rail at children who dare to trespass on our lawn."

It dragged a reluctant smile out of me. "We shall be the terror of the neighborhood."

"Indeed. But in the meantime, don't give up on your own happiness quite so easily. Whatever Griffin has done, give him a chance to apologize before you break things off completely."

"You seem rather sure the fault is Griffin's."

"Griffin is a fine chap, but you've been my friend far longer. Therefore, it is my part to take your side in any quarrel."

I couldn't help it; I laughed at her logic.

My mirth was cut off abruptly when the sound of a woman's scream shattered the morning quiet.

Christine and I both reacted instinctively. My longer legs carried me out of the dining room slightly faster, but I was caught in a scrum as other guests and staff rushed to the site as well. At least my height allowed me to glimpse what transpired.

Two figures stood in the center of the lobby. One was Bertie Hicks, dressed for her day's work at the hotel. The other was her husband, Rider.

What the devil?

"Mr. Hicks!" I called, pushing my way through the press. "Excuse me; let me through, please."

"Out of the way!" Christine bellowed, startling guests and staff alike into giving way.

As soon as I was out of the press, I grew painfully conscious of the eyes of the crowd on me. Blast it, perhaps I should have waited...

But one person didn't look in my direction. Mrs. Hicks's screams had fallen silent, but now she clutched her face, staring at her husband while tears streamed down her cheeks. Clearly, something was very, very wrong here.

"Mr. Hicks," I repeated, approaching him warily. "I thought you didn't intend to return."

"Mr. Hicks came to his senses," said a cold, serpent voice, which sent a chill over my skin. Mr. Orme stood in the shadows near the door, but stepped forward as he spoke. "He visited me after you left last night, asking for amnesty."

"I was wrong," Hicks said. And oh God, his voice, placid and cool, nothing at all like the frightened, worried man I'd spoken to in the woods.

He sounded like Orme now. Like the Kincaid brothers. No wonder his wife screamed.

"I grew frightened over childish superstitions," he went on, a fixed smile on his caramel face. "I realized how foolish my fears were, and how much trouble I'd caused. I asked Mr. Orme to forgive me, which he kindly did. Now I'm free to return and put an end to the rumors I stirred up."

Every hair on my head tried to stand up. "And the night in the woods?" I asked. "I was there! I saw Webb. What have you to say?"

"It was dark. We were mistaken." Hicks turned his gaze away from me. "Now, if you'll excuse me, I would like to take my wife home."

Mrs. Hicks's paralysis broke. "No!" she shrieked. "Stay back! It ain't him, Dr. Whyborne! It ain't Rider!"

"Here now!" I exclaimed, when Hicks grabbed her by the wrist.

"Dr. Whyborne." Orme appeared between us, even though I'd not noticed him move. "You have no right to interfere in the business of a man and his wife."

"Curse it, can't you see she's terrified!" Christine shouted. "He has no right —"

"As her husband, he has every right," Orme broke in smoothly. "Dr. Putnam, you are hysterical. As for you, Dr. Whyborne, must I call the Pinkertons and have them confine you to your hotel room? Will that cure you of this habit of poking your nose where it doesn't belong?"

Clearly, he referred to last night. Did he know I'd stolen his little book? He must, by now. I hadn't even had a chance to mention it to Griffin or that damned Elliot, before it had been driven out of my mind.

I stood, frozen and helpless, while her husband dragged Mrs. Hicks out the door. My hands clenched into fists—I had to do something! Summon the wind, or the fire, anything.

But what would it change? Mrs. Hicks couldn't flee, not with an infant dependent on her. And as Orme pointed out, I would be on the wrong side of the law if I did anything to protect her.

Not to mention his threat, which lay in my stomach as if I'd swallowed a lead weight. Orme knew I'd found something last night. Like Rider, before the yayhos had worked their evil on him, a sentence of jail might equate a sentence of death. It wouldn't be as easy to lock me away as it would've been a half-breed Indian, but it was far from impossible.

"You're damned cowards, the lot of you," Christine said contemptuously, raking her gaze over the audience. "Come along, Whyborne. Let's take our leave."

"Watch your step," Orme called after us.

CHAPTER 17

"What now?" I asked, once we were away from the crowd. Christine made determinedly for her room, and I followed, stopping in the hall when she opened the door.

"You are going to Mr. Manning and try to convince him to protect Mrs. Hicks," Christine said as she went inside. A few moments later, she returned, tucking a small revolver into her purse.

"What do you intend?" I asked in alarm. "If you shoot Rider—"

"I don't mean to gun the man down, but if the situation becomes serious, I wish to have something with which to defend myself. But as it is, if he strikes me, Mr. Manning will have no choice but to put him in jail."

I was less certain, but, truthfully, I saw no other plan. "I'll try to convince Elliot to join me at their house as quickly as I can. And if I can't, I'll come alone. Just, please, be careful!"

We hurried out of the hotel; the crowd had dispersed, thankfully. No doubt they thought us both insane, to meddle in what was clearly a personal affair.

I hastened to the Pinkerton offices as quickly as I could. I found the large front room deserted, and the door to Elliot's office closed, but the murmur of voices filtered through the wood.

I had no time to be polite. I gave a single, swift knock and flung open the door.

Elliot stood in front of the window, rather than seated behind his desk. And there, only a few feet from him, was Griffin.

"My God, man!" Away for only the time it had taken to eat breakfast, and already he had run to Elliot.

Griffin's eyes widened. "Whyborne, we were just talking," he said, holding his hands up.

"I don't give a damn what you were doing, Mr. Flaherty." It was a lie, but devil take me if I'd let him know just how deeply his betrayal hurt. No doubt he would only call me naïve again. "Mr. Hicks has returned, but he is changed, just like Orme and the Kincaids. His wife knows it and made a scene. She may be in terrible danger. Christine has gone to save her, and you may either assist us or remain here and rot, the both of you!"

I started to turn on my heel, then remembered Orme's book in my pocket. "And here," I added, flinging it in the general direction of Elliot's head. It missed, of course, and hit the floor several feet away. "Proof Orme isn't himself, either."

I bolted out of the building. Christine depended on me, and I'd wasted enough time looking for help from those who couldn't be trusted.

Griffin called out behind me, but I ignored him. The length of my legs came in handy for once, and I outdistanced him and Elliot easily.

At first, anyway. By the time I'd reached the section of town which included the Hicks residence, I was gasping and panting for breath, and they'd both caught up with me.

I caught sight of Christine—thank heavens, she didn't seem to have gotten into any serious trouble. Instead, she stood outside the house, beside a young black woman I didn't recognize, who clutched a crying baby.

Christine turned at our approach, her face grim. "Bad news, gentlemen," she said. "This is Mrs. Hicks's cousin, who watches her baby while she works. She's been here all morning, and Mrs. Hicks never returned. Neither did Rider."

"You're certain they were coming here?" Elliot asked.

"He had to drag her out of the hotel by the wrists," Christine snapped, drawing herself up and leveling a glare at Elliot. "Not that anyone tried to help her besides Whyborne and me. Where else do you imagine he would take her? Do you *see* any screaming women in the streets, Mr. Manning?"

"Perhaps he took her into the woods, where he's been hiding?" Elliot suggested.

"Mr. Orme had given him amnesty, in exchange for no longer telling tales of yayhos."

"Yes, but according to Dr. Whyborne, he shot Mr. Webb. He didn't have amnesty for murder."

"What?" I spun on Elliot incredulously. "He defended me, perhaps saved my life, and you would have put him in jail?"

"It's standard procedure," Elliot replied. "Besides, do you think I could let an Indian get away with shooting a white man with no inquiry at all?"

I felt sickened, suddenly, and tired. The wailing baby in the cousin's arms had probably lost both parents today. What would it be told once it was older? That its father had dragged its mother away, never to be seen again? Or some merciful lie?

"Even I am not so naïve," I said, and saw Griffin flinch out of the corner of my eye. At the moment, I could barely bring myself to care. "I'm returning to the hotel, where I will review the train schedules."

"Whyborne?" Griffin asked.

I turned away without looking at him. "I'm going back to Widdershins." I aimed the words over my shoulder. "Threshold can burn, for all I care. I'm finished here."

Although an evening train took away the day's allotment of coal, I purchased three tickets for the next morning instead. Two of them I handed over to the clerk at the hotel desk, to be placed in the mail slots for Christine and Griffin. With Griffin's, I included a brief note. If he joined me on the train, I would forgive him. If he didn't, I would know whom he had chosen.

Word of the Hicks' disappearance rapidly spread, and, as I used a borrowed pen and paper to scribble two more notes, I became aware of the whispers. I looked up to find the clerk staring at me, but something about my expression must have put him off, because he hastily turned his attention elsewhere.

Good. I had no patience for impertinent questions at the moment.

I addressed one note to Mrs. Mercer, and the other to Mrs. Hicks's cousin, whose name I received from one of the hotel maids when she passed by. Both notes urged the women to leave town before nightfall tomorrow, and asked them to do their best to convince anyone else who might believe them to take the morning train, if not the earlier one this evening. I left the notes with the clerk at his desk and went up to my room, where I locked the door behind me.

Threshold Mountain loomed outside my window, casting its long shadow over the hollow. I shuddered to think what lay beneath its seemingly calm surface. How long had the yayhos been here? Centuries, if the Indian legends were to be believed. How did they transport the coal they mined back to wherever they had come from? How much of it did they use? Or were they here for other reasons, quite apart from mining?

It didn't matter. Tomorrow night, if Rider had been correct, they'd attack.

I'd done my best. I'd given what little evidence I had to Elliot. No doubt Griffin had tried to persuade him as well, perhaps still was, although I didn't care to speculate on what methods he might be using. Elliot would either come around and use the Pinkertons to organize an evacuation, or he wouldn't. In which case, anyone who tried to rally the town would find themselves trapped in a jail cell, at the mercy of yayhos or Orme.

I'd done all I could. I'd leave on the train tomorrow, and hopefully others would be with me.

What if Griffin didn't come?

Then he'd made his choice. He knew the risks. If he didn't care to leave Elliot, they could...what?

Perish here together?

I pressed my fingers against my eyelids, as if to block out the very thought. I wanted Griffin to be mine again, but even more, I wanted him to be safe.

Could I really leave without him?

I wished with all my heart we'd never come to Threshold.

Someone knocked on my door near lunchtime, but I made no response, and eventually they left. I half-expected Christine's familiar rap, but she was either out, or had given up in disgust as well.

Would we pick up a paper next week, or next month, and find some horror had befallen Threshold? Or would the yayhos simply convert the entire town into their emotionless puppets? Could they do such a thing?

It didn't matter. It was out of my hands. I'd made my best effort. No need to stay here and die with people who hadn't lifted a hand to save Mrs. Hicks. Or to have other horrors visited on me, like poor Webb.

I lay on my bed, and, at some point, I must have drifted off, because when I next opened my eyes, the sun had nearly dropped below the ridge, and someone knocked on the door.

"Dr. Whyborne?" The voice belonged to one of the porters. "I've an urgent message for you, sir."

What could it possibly be? I opened the door and exchanged a small tip for a folded note. "Will there be a reply?" he asked.

I opened the note. To my shock, it was from Elliot.

"Dr. Whyborne,
I've taken a look at the daybook you left with me this morning. I think you're onto something. Please come to my house at half past 7 o'clock, where we can speak in private.
Yrs Truly,
Elliot Manning"

My first impulse was to crumple up the note and throw it away. Surely Griffin and Elliot could combine their investigative powers well enough; my presence shouldn't be required.

But such an action would be childish. There were greater things at stake here than my wounded pride. And Elliot's phrasing, *"book you left with me,"* as opposed to *"book you flung at my head,"* was rather more generous than I perhaps deserved.

"Yes," I told the porter. "One moment, if you will."

I laid the note on the desk and hurriedly penned a response on the hotel stationary, keeping the wording as bland as possible. Once the porter scurried off, I turned my attention to my wardrobe. Less than an hour remained before my appointment, and I wished to make myself as presentable as possible. I might not be able to compete with the handsome Elliot, but I would do my best not to be utterly humiliated at the comparison.

God. I really was a fool.

The looming mountains had already thrown the hollow into an unnatural twilight by the time I made my way up the slope to Elliot's house, a small, single-story affair not too far from Orme's home. It looked to be built with the same eye to quality.

I sneaked out of the hotel like a thief, taking the servants' stairs and exit. If Christine had caught sight of me, she would have surely wanted to come along as well, and this meeting was likely to be excruciating enough without her there to witness it. I'd try to keep strictly to business, but seeing Griffin and Elliot there, together…

Just thinking about it made me faintly ill. I didn't know how I'd make it through with my dignity intact.

Elliot answered my knock promptly and bade me enter. The layout of the house was simple: a single long hall running from the front door to the back, with a parlor and kitchen on the left, and dining room and bedroom on the right. I hung up my hat on the stand in the hall, and followed him into the parlor. There was no sign of Griffin.

"Isn't Griffin coming?" I asked, surprised.

"In a bit. He was looking into something, I believe." Orme's daybook lay on a table, along with a bottle of wine, and two glasses. Several chair surrounded the table, no doubt drawn up for our conference. "Would you like some wine? I've already opened the bottle to let it breathe."

I hadn't eaten anything since breakfast, and barely a bite then. The wine would go straight to my head.

Which might not be such a bad thing. "Yes. Er, thank you."

He poured us each a glass and we sat down across from one another. "You must tell me what you think of the vintage," he said, as if he truly wished my opinion.

I obediently took a sip and found it far sweeter than I'd expected. "It's quite, er, passable," I said, not wishing to seem boorish. Then again, did it matter what he thought of me? I cast about for some topic of small talk which might make our wait less excruciating. "My elder sister is married to an English baronet. She says the French vineyards have quite recovered from the blight."

He settled back in his chair, watching me thoughtfully, his wineglass held loosely in one hand. "I imagine Griffin rather enjoyed the challenge of seducing a rich man like you."

The words shocked me with their bluntness. "I—wh-what?" I managed to say.

"I think you heard me quite clearly," Elliot said with the same charming smile he usually wore. "I know Griffin far better than you. To go from a homeless orphan to a farm boy to buggering the son of one of the richest men in America…he would have found it quite the coup. I remember the first time he successfully passed himself off as an educated man of class. He was so delighted he sucked my cock on the carriage ride back."

My throat felt dry, my mouth full of cotton. I took a large gulp of wine. "I'd appreciate it if you'd stick to business, sir," I gasped, when I could speak again. "I thought you wished to discuss how to save this town."

He ignored me. "I left out a few things in my account on the way to the cave, you know. Like how I met Griffin in a bathhouse, newly arrived from Kansas and taking any prick pointed his direction. The first time I set eyes on him, he sucked one stranger off while another fucked him."

My stomach clenched, acid clawing at the back of my throat. What would Griffin think if he knew Elliot was speaking of him this way? True or not, to just say it in such a cruel fashion…

Or was I being naïve again?

I lurched to my feet. The room spun alarmingly, and I grabbed the back of my chair to steady myself. "Where is Griffin?"

"At the hotel bar, I believe, pining for you. Although why I can't imagine."

I had to get out of here. I took another step, then stumbled and went to my knees. The carpet beneath me had an odd pattern, and I found myself strangely distracted by it. Were those supposed to be flowers? Or faces? A confused lot of faces, crying out a warning I couldn't quite hear…

What was wrong with me?

Elliot placed his glass of wine on the table, and I realized he'd merely held it and swirled it about, not actually drunk any. The bottle had already been opened…and Elliot had set out only two glasses, not three, as there should have been if Griffin had actually meant to join us.

He'd poisoned me.

"Not Deianira but Medea," I said, or tried to say. Only an incoherent mumble made it past my lips. I lifted my hand, hoping to call down the flames, but blackness covered my vision, taking me with it.

Voices.

Light. But blurred, and too distant, and I couldn't keep my eyes open anyway.

"Well done, Mr. Manning." Orme.

I opened my eyes again, saw the knee of his trousers as he knelt beside me, but it all seemed very, very far away.

"What will happen to him?" Elliot asked. He sounded underwater, on the other side of the earth. How odd to think I could still hear him.

Maybe I was dead.

"You know the answer already. He will be given a choice. Whatever his decision, the outcome is the same as far as you and I are concerned."

The creak of a floorboard. "About what Rider told him…"

No, wait, it wasn't Elliot who was underwater. It was me. Cold water in my ears, in my mouth. It was why everything looked strange, sounded strange. I had drowned in a glass of wine.

Darkness. Then movement. The smell of mule. Branches scraping against my face.

I was dead, and they were taking me for burial. Would Griffin come to the funeral? Christine?

I didn't like being dead. There was far more moving about than I'd expected.

The scent of cold stone and dampness in my nose. The family mausoleum?
Would they put me beside my dead twin sister? I hoped she didn't mind I'd
managed to cling to life for twenty-seven years longer than she had. If we were
to spend eternity together, I didn't want her to start out angry with me.

But I'd managed to disappoint everyone among the living, so I might as
well start adding the dead to the list. At least it would be familiar.

If only I'd had the chance to say goodbye to Griffin.

CHAPTER 18

I awoke—truly awoke this time—to find one side of my face pressed against damp, cold stone.

My mouth tasted like the bottom of an old shoe, and my head pounded mercilessly. Bile stripped my throat, and I lay utterly still, breathing in and out slowly, until the nausea passed.

God, I was cold, my fingers and toes like ice. I curled up, shivering, and wished I had a blanket. Where on earth was I? And how the devil had I gotten here?

Elliot had invited me to his house to discuss Orme…we'd had wine…he'd spoken of Griffin…

No, I'd had wine. He hadn't, because he'd drugged the bottle. My head hurt abominably, but at least the rest of my anatomy betrayed no untoward aches to suggest he'd taken liberties with my person.

Where was I? Had I actually heard part of a conversation between Elliot and Orme? Or had it just been a hallucination brought on by whatever he had used to drug me?

Very cautiously, I cracked open eyes which felt as if they'd been gummed shut. I lay on my side, on the floor of a cave, my surroundings dimly illuminated by a pale, green-white light. The stink of ammonia burned my nose. I gave up the struggle and threw up on the floor.

I felt somewhat better afterward, enough to haul myself into a sitting position and look around. The smooth cave walls, with lines of pictographs carved into them, looked horribly familiar. The sickly light emanated from some sort of nitrous fungi, whose threads wove across the damp stone like a blasphemous tapestry, and revealed an assortment of metal tables and cabinets.

Oh God. Elliot had drugged me and—it seemed—handed me over to the yayhos. I was somewhere inside Threshold Mountain.

Had Griffin been wrong all along, and Elliot been altered, like Orme or Rider? Or did Elliot work with the yayhos voluntarily? And why?

It didn't matter. I had to warn Griffin, before Elliot could do the same to him.

Or worse.

The thought of Griffin's danger drove me to my feet, even though I had to lean against the wall for balance. After a long moment, the room stopped spinning, and I looked about for an exit. The floor sloped slightly, which I took to be an indicator as to which direction the surface lay. As I cautiously started toward the smaller tunnel leading from the room, I passed by the tables and cabinets.

On the tables lay strange instruments, whose purpose I could barely guess, accompanied by what seemed to be some sort of surgical equipment. Various effects formed a pile on another table: a bowler hat, numerous shirts which looked to have been sliced off instead of unbuttoned, a white scarf, several pocket watches, a diary, and even a box of magnesium flash powder.

The bowler hat looked sickeningly familiar. Hadn't I last seen it on Webb's head, the night in the hotel? And the flash powder must have belonged to him as well. Everything here had surely been stripped from the yayhos' victims, tossed carelessly aside like meaningless trash.

The white scarf seemed familiar, too. Had I not seen it worn by the maids at the Brumfield House hotel?

I had to get out of here. Tearing my gaze away from the clothing and scattered effects, I hastened to the tunnel, which I hoped would lead me out—

A strange, shuffling sound came from its depths.

I froze, my heart in my throat. The sound was of slow, dragging feet, but with something horribly off about the timing. *Step. Step-step. Step. Step. Step-step. Step.*

I took an involuntary step back myself. My throat closed around the quick, shallow breaths which were all I could seem to get into my lungs. I didn't want to see whatever was in the tunnel. This was a nightmare, brought on by drinking too much wine. I'd wake up in the hotel, or even on Elliot's couch, any moment now.

Why couldn't I wake up?

The nacreous light revealed the figure as it shambled into the room, and I found out exactly what had happened to Mrs. Webb and Mrs. Hicks.

I wish to God I hadn't.

They were mostly naked, but rank horror overcame any thought of modesty, save that the lack of clothes made it far too easy to see what the yayhos had done to them. Between them, they had four legs but only two arms, their bodies sewn together from hip to the top of their heads. Along with their arms and ribs, much of their skulls and brains must have been removed, to graft them together. Their mouths worked in ghastly synchronization, faces slick with mucus and tears. A groan sounded from their mouths, a dumb, animal sound. No recognition showed in their cloudy eyes. Still, they reached for me, one arm ivory and the other dark, and took another shuffling step closer.

I lurched back, a cry of horror and pity locked in my throat. My shoulders collided with one of the cabinets, knocking open the doors and revealing the contents.

Some of the shelves held odd, cylindrical jars, reminding me of the canopic urns the Egyptian pharaohs had used to house their various organs for eternity. Other containers, these of glass and filled with some viscous liquid, held floating disembodied hands, legs, organs, and even a head. The face belonged to one of the missing outlaws.

The head opened its eyes and looked at me.

I let out a shriek and leapt away, nearly colliding with the abomination behind me. I had to get out of here. My chest hurt; I couldn't breathe—

The scrape of chitinous claws sounded in the tunnel leading deeper into the mountain.

The abomination moaned again and shambled painfully away, as if it still bore in its mutilated brains an instinctive fear of what made its way toward us. I couldn't run. Terror had turned my legs to blocks of ice.

A hulking shape came into the room from the lower entrance. As it drew nearer, the dim light of the cave fungus showed me the full aspect of the yayhos at last. In terms of terrestrial life, it most resembled a giant, red species of crustacean, many legged like a prawn. Yet in many ways it was not like that at all, from the bat-like wings to the cone-shaped head, terminating in a nest of squirming tentacles where a mouth should have been. Amidst the ridges of its head, I glimpsed a dozen tiny eyes watching me.

"Dr. Whyborne," it said.

I stared at it in shock. It knew my name. A hysterical laugh tried to force its way out of my throat, as I wondered how one might be properly introduced to an unthinkable horror. Did I shake its claw? Its slimy feelers? Inquire after its mother?

It moved closer, its acidic odor burning my nose like fresh ammonia. "You are a man of science," it said. Its voice was an awful, buzzing sound, mimicking the words well enough I understood them, and yet managing to be utterly inhuman in every substantial fashion.

"Y-Yes," I answered. My voice broke, and I wondered how fast the thing could run, and if there was any hope at all in trying to flee. "Th-that is, I study ancient languages."

The tentacles writhed, and its head shifted color from red to pale orange. "You have no need to fear. There is much you could learn from us."

"Learn?" I repeated stupidly.

"We have many ancient records. We know much of your species you have forgotten." As it spoke, I realized nothing approximating a larynx produced its odd, buzzing speech. Rather, it rubbed together its smallish forelimbs to generate the sound, much like a cricket or grasshopper might. "But we have more to offer a man such as you. What is the knowledge of a single species on a single world? Long have we sought out minds such as yours. We desire to know how humanity thinks, and to lift up certain members of your species. All the secrets of your kind's past will be laid bare to your eyes, if such is your wish, but the wonders of the universe await you as well."

The treacherous laugh tried to break out again. How often had I lamented the loss of the library at Alexandria, the burning of the Codices in the Yucatan, let alone the simple depredations of time and carelessness? What gaps could these beings potentially fill? If this interview had taken place anywhere other than this chamber of horrors, how enticing it all would have sounded.

"You would not be able to travel as we do in your current body, but we have perfected the arts of surgery," it went on.

"S-So I see," I stammered, with an involuntary glance at the abomination in the corner.

"You see only what becomes of those who threaten us. We must protect ourselves, just as you would." The yayho unfurled one wing. After a moment of confusion, I realized it meant to gesture toward the odd metal containers. "You can be an ally. Your brain can be removed and perfectly preserved. Various instruments to allow sight, hearing, and speech can be connected. Perfectly comfortable. You may speak to one or more of those who have undergone the procedure, if you wish to be reassured."

Dear heavens, there were brains in the containers? Living brains, still somehow capable of thought and perception?

"There is no pain," it added, as if it knew my thought. "In this bodiless form, you could travel to the outer planets, to Yuggoth, to worlds beyond this solar system. You could see and speak to beings you cannot currently imagine. Learn new languages, cultures, ways of thinking. Physics and mathematics, should those intrigue you."

Oddly enough, at that moment, I barely even saw the cavern around me, let alone the yayho. I was, instead, a child at my mother's knee, sounding out my first word of Greek, feeling a thrill rush through me as what had recently been incomprehensible ordered itself before my understanding. Or a youth, avidly reading of the archaeological discoveries in the Orient, dreaming back to the time of the ancients. Or maybe a young man, in my first class at Miskatonic University, my mind expanding to soak up knowledge like a sponge, desperate always for more.

Or a man, making fire from his will and a few spoken words.

The thrill of discovery…of revealing things hidden by time or ignorance… burned in me. Surely, Christine felt the same when she opened her tombs and temples, shining light where there had been only darkness for thousands of years. It was not about material gain, about gold or jewels or even mummies to draw the crowds. It was about *discovery*, about *knowing*. About feeling one's own mind expand as new horizons unfolded like the opening of some exotic flower, both strange and familiar at the same time.

Now I had the opportunity to learn things undreamt of by human scientists. To know at least some of the secrets of the universe, things which would otherwise remain undiscovered in my lifetime.

And if I had to do it bodiless, after recent events, such a state seemed less a drawback than it would have only a few days ago.

The yayhos wanted my cooperation...but why? They had me at their mercy. Why not do whatever they wished with me, as they had the Webbs or the Kincaids? Their offer was entirely one-sided: I would gain knowledge, but what would the benefit be to them?

Unless they weren't really making the offer because of my interest in science.

"And while my brain is off in a jar, having adventures, what will the rest of me be doing?" I asked.

"Your body will be well tended and cared for, do not fear."

Yes, I rather imagined it would. Because if they could remove one's brain with such ease, no doubt they could put another in its place. No wonder Orme's handwriting had changed. Had they even replaced him with a human, or one of their own, or some other alien creature which owed them allegiance?

"What do you really want from me?" I asked, amazed my voice didn't shake.

Its feelers squirmed, its head flashing through a series of colors. "We wish to remain hidden," it buzzed. "Your planet has materials we need; your species is not among them. We do not seek open conflict."

"Then why not simply move elsewhere? Coal can be found in many places, some of them still wild."

Its buzz took on a higher pitch. An indication of annoyance at my questions, or something else? "Our mode of travel from world to world is nothing with which your kind is familiar. We must find doorways, places in your world which act as thresholds to step across."

Had I wondered from whence the mountain got its name? Now I rather wished I'd never found out.

"You replaced Orme...to what? Keep any rumors of your existence suppressed?" If they'd had a large enough stock of spare brains, would they simply have replaced the entire town?

"Yes."

"And me?"

"Your family has much power. Influence enough to keep the humans and their machines from our diggings."

That bastard Elliot must have told them about me. With my brain conveniently out of the way, they'd send one of their agents abroad wearing my skin.

Would Father and Stanford suffer unfortunate "accidents," leaving me the heir to one of the largest railroads in America?

Of course the yayhos wanted my cooperation. If I voluntarily told them all about my life, their agent would more easily pass for me. Orme's replacement had been hasty and flawed, but it had been good enough. Mine would have to do much better, at least in the short term, to avoid arousing suspicion.

I needed to escape—but how?

"You've been here for a long time, haven't you?" I asked, stalling frantically for time in the hope some plan would occur to me. "That is, the coal is a finite resource within the seam. Surely it must—"

"Enough questions." I had definitely annoyed it. "All will be answered later. Will you agree to our terms?"

It moved closer, segmented legs flexing toward me. Its ammoniac stink made my eyes water, and I backed away, until my legs fetched up against one of the tables. I reached out to steady myself, and felt Webb's bowler hat give beneath my hand.

"Give me a moment to think," I stammered, my mind reeling for some means of escape.

"There is nothing to consider. Cooperate and learn the wonders of the universe. Do not cooperate, and your brain will be removed regardless."

Its feelers thrashed and squirmed as it loomed over me. I would die here, in this wretched place, and Griffin would never know what happened to me, never know how sorry I was we'd quarreled, or how much I loved him. I groped at the table behind me, even though I'd seen no weapons, in the wild hope there might be a gun or a knife hidden beneath the clothing. Instead, my fingers closed on the box of flash powder.

I flung it onto the floor in front of the creature and closed my eyes, even as I spoke the secret name of fire.

The searing flash of the magnesium powder showed red through my eyelids, even as I turned for the exit. Behind me, the yayho let out a tortured shriek —not the buzzing drone, but something more primal and horrid, piercing as a needle to the ear. The abomination screamed as well, and it was somehow even more awful.

I ran, not daring to look back. How I would escape the cave, I didn't know. My only desire, beating along with my hammering heart, was to get as far away as possible from the monster behind me.

I ran for what seemed forever. Terror gave me the strength of the hunted animal, which flees past the point of ordinary collapse. I didn't slow until I saw, impossibly, what seemed to be daylight ahead. There was rubble, and timbers…

Back at the cave where the geologists had died.

The boulder which had seemed suspicious to Christine and I had been rolled to one side, fitting into a niche, hidden before. Why the yayhos would leave their cave open, I didn't wish to think. I'd worry about it later, once I was safely back in Threshold.

Safely back in Threshold, with Elliot, who had willingly allied with the yay-hos, and whoever—whatever—they had put in Mr. Orme's skull. Not safe at all, really, but I had to warn Griffin and Christine, and anyone else.

I emerged from the cave and into the fresh air. The sun had almost set. I'd lain unconscious for almost a whole day beneath the mountain.

Which meant tonight was the new moon, when the yayhos would attack. I had only a few hours left in which to act.

I didn't know how much light the yayhos could tolerate, but the twilit sky was not much brighter than the phosphorescent mildew within the cavern, so I couldn't count on it holding the creature at bay while I fled. Assuming only one might give pursuit, and not a dozen, or a hundred. How many of the beings in-habited and mined the caverns beneath Threshold Mountain, crawling through the stone like maggots in a bit of rotting meat?

Even one might be enough to end me. I plunged recklessly down the steep slope, branches striking my face and roots seeming to reach up to trip me. I had to warn the town as soon as possible. Even now the yayhos surely gathered their forces—would they come boiling down from the cavern at my back? And what of the abominations? How many of them might be loose in the woods?

My heart pounded frantically in my throat, and I couldn't hear anything over the rough sound of my own breathing, save for the crunch and crack of leaves and twigs under my feet. The sun slipped even lower, and now I had dif-ficulty making out shapes beneath the thick canopy of the trees. Even if I es-caped the yayhos, I'd soon be lost, stumbling in the dark. Curse this wilderness! Why did I ever agree to leave the civilization of Widdershins? Why—

The yayho plunged through the canopy a few yards ahead of me.

CHAPTER 19

A cry of startled terror escaped me. I tried to stop, but momentum worked against me, and I barely avoided careening right into the creature. But its clumsy wings had tangled in the thick branches, hampering its movement. As it sought to free itself, I slipped and scrambled madly along the slope, seeking to get away from it, or at least find somewhere to hide.

There: a pair of boulders, where a single rock had been cleft in two by the long work of centuries. The yayho was considerably larger than I; perhaps I could squeeze inside where it would be unable to reach me.

With no better plan, I scrambled into the cleft. The rough boulders scraped and tore the shoulders of my suit coat, and the odor of rotting leaves and slime rose up around me. I had to turn to the side to fit further back, jamming myself in as deep as I could.

Once there, I froze, struggling to control my breathing. My ears strained for any sound of claws against the forest floor, or of its terrible buzzing, but I heard nothing. I felt like a mouse in its hole, waiting for the cat to either discover it or depart. Where was the thing? Had it not seen where I'd fled? Had it given up?

It reared above me, blotting out the last of the sunlight. Belatedly, I realized it couldn't come at me from the level ground, but I'd neglected to consider whether it could reach me from atop the boulders. Its jointed forelimbs stabbed down, and I tried to pull back, but there was no room to bend my knees. My hat was long gone; a chitinous claw tangled in my hair, drawing a sharp pain from my scalp, and it was all I could do not to scream.

The yayho jerked back, its terrible shriek sounding for the second time in an hour. Green ichor splattered free, staining the rock and burning my eyes and nose with its fumes. For a moment, I didn't understand what had happened. Then I beheld the thin metal blade skewering it through the throat.

The blade wrenched loose. Gurgling horribly, the yayho sought to turn on its attacker, but the slim sword swung again and again, hacking deep into the tough flesh of its neck. When its head dangled half off, it collapsed on the edge of the crack, limbs twitching.

Silence. Then, a light appeared, as if a lantern had been uncovered. Someone slithered off the rock, and a moment later a familiar figure appeared at the head of the cleft.

Relief flooded through me, intense enough to make me light-headed. "Griffin!" I gasped, stumbling out to him.

His sword cane swung up between us, the point of the blade stabbing through my shirt to rest against the skin above my heart.

I halted instantly. "G-Griffin?"

He stared at me, his green eyes wild in the lantern light. All the color had leached from his skin, and I felt his hand trembling through the vibrations of the steel touching my chest.

"Don't come any closer," he warned, but his voice had a broken edge to it I'd never heard before. "Not until I'm sure wh-who you are."

Oh. Oh God. I'd gone to the woods, hadn't I? Just like Orme and the Kincaids and Rider Hicks. How Griffin learned what had happened, I couldn't guess, but he'd come to save me.

No. He'd come to kill whatever walked around in my skin.

I swallowed against a sudden dryness in my throat. "Griffin, please, it's me!"

Tears shone in his eyes, but he didn't lower the blade. "Tell me something only Whyborne would know."

"I-I…" My brain locked, unable to come up with anything at all, let alone something which might satisfy him. My life was quiet and boring—what was there to say? I liked eggs for breakfast? The name of our cat? Hardly something only I could know.

"We're lovers," I said, but of course Elliot knew of our relationship, so the yayhos could as well.

He shook his head. "Not enough," he whispered. Despair settled over his features, and the expression tore my heart and sent terror through me.

Something only we two would know…but what? "You call me Ival."

"Others have heard me use the term."

Blast it! What could I…oh.

"We m-made love the other night—during the storm—you licked my, er, that is, my a-anus," I blurted, my face burning. Then a horrible thought occurred. "And if Christine is with you, for God's sake, just skewer me now and be done with it!"

The sword cane fell from his nerveless hand. With a soft cry, he slumped against me, his hands clutching my lapels and his face pressed against my chest. Startled, I wrapped my arms around him, and felt his shoulders heave with sobs.

"It's all right," I whispered, stroking his hair. I tried to imagine what it would have been like had our positions been reversed; the mere thought of confronting someone—something—else in Griffin's body made me feel physically ill. I held him tight, sinking to the ground so he lay half in my lap.

"I'm sorry," he sobbed into my vest. "I never meant to hurt you. I just w-wanted you to love me, even though I'm not good enough, even though—"

"Shh." The heat of tears soaked through to my skin. "You're speaking nonsense."

"I'm just a farmer's son from Kansas, who's spent the last decade pretending he's someone better, and you're so far above me. I knew it even before I saw your house, knew I didn't have anything to offer a man like you, but I love you so much, and I couldn't…and we quarreled, and I thought—I thought I was going to have to…"

My throat tightened and my eyes burned. "You have everything to offer me. Don't you understand? Before you, I went through the motions of life, but I never really lived until the day you walked into the museum. I care about you, not about where you're from. I thought…after we quarreled, I thought you'd lost interest in me."

"Never. I'm sorry about the things I said."

"And I'm sorry I used the fire spell on the door knob."

We clung together for a few minutes more, until he mastered himself. Pulling back, he wiped at eyes swollen with tears. "We shouldn't stay here. It isn't safe."

"You're quite right." I hesitated, not sure how to give him the news. "I'm sorry, Griffin, but Elliot is working with the yayhos."

"I know."

"You do?"

"How do you think I found you?" he asked. "I'd knocked on your door earlier in the day, but when you didn't answer, I decided to give you time to cool off. When you didn't come to dinner and still didn't answer, I picked the lock and found Elliot's note on the desk. Since I'd spent half the day unsuccessfully trying to convince him to arrest Orme as an impostor, it seemed very odd he would invite you to his house to discuss the matter. I tried to tell myself there was a harmless explanation, but I think even then I knew."

"I'm sorry." Elliot had been my rival—or I'd thought him my rival—but I hated the man for hurting Griffin.

"I went to the house, but was unable to get a reply, which didn't reassure me at all. Christine and I decided to keep watch. Elliot finally returned in the small hours of the night, with mud on his shoes and no reasonable explanation as to where you had gone." Griffin took my hand, his fingers twining with mine. "It took some…persuading…to get him to admit he'd given you over to the yayhos. He tried to convince me he did it to save the town or some such rot."

Fury sparked in Griffin's green eyes. "I was beside myself with fear for you. El-liot told me it was already too late. They would have removed your brain and re-placed it with one of their own, or the brain of a loyal agent. He said when I saw you next, it wouldn't be you at all. I think if Christine hadn't been there, I would have killed him."

"Christine held you back? Why? Did she wish to do away with him herself?"

He smiled wanly. "She wished to avoid either of us ending up in jail charged with murder, I think. We agreed one of us should try to rescue you, while the other warned the town. She let me come for you because…well."

"She knew you would do what needed to be done," I suggested softly.

His fingers tightened convulsively on mine. "God, Whyborne. If I'd had to kill you, even though it wouldn't really have even been you, it would have de-stroyed me. I don't see how I could possibly have gone on."

I opened my mouth to say I knew him to be strong, and he would have per-severed. But a deep boom, similar to the crash of nearby thunder, drowned out my words. It echoed off the mountains, seeming to roll on and on, the trees and the hollows reflecting the roar back on itself over and over again.

"What was that?" I asked.

Griffin's face had gone white in the light of the lantern. "An explosion."

"The mine?"

"No—or at least, I don't think it was. It sounded too far away."

"Then what?"

"I don't know." He rose to his feet and hauled me up after him. "We have to get back to town. Now."

I nodded sharply. "Run as fast as you can. I'll keep up."

When we finally burst out of the choking woods and saw Threshold below us, it was like viewing a landscape of hell. Lanterns bobbed through the dark streets as people tried to flee, and screams and gunfire rent the air.

Yayhos swarmed out of the mine. Dear heavens, how many were there? And how had they gotten into the mine? Had their own tunnels brought them within breakthrough distance to the human diggings? I counted at least three dozen of them, some which stuck to the ground, and others which took to the air, circling above the panicking town on clumsy wings.

More screams and gunfire came from higher on the hill. Abominations shambled out of the woods, reaching multiple arms to grab fleeing townspeo-ple, or simply spreading terror by their hideous aspect. Some of the abomina-tions seemed to have the wit left to operate firearms, and shot into the crowd, creating further havoc.

I came to a halt, overwhelmed by the scene in front of us. What could we possibly do against such a force? Christine was down there, somewhere in the midst of the chaos. How could we find her, let alone defend the town?

"No!" shouted a voice, even above the cries and howls. "You can't!"

Elliot.

Griffin ran toward the sound of Elliot's voice, a snarl on his lips, and I followed.

Elliot and a force of Pinkertons stood in the street near the coal tipple. Elliot now sported a black eye, his lower lip split and swollen. Evidence of Griffin's "persuasion?"

The other detectives looked horrified, pale and trembling, clutching their guns in their hands…and not firing on anything, not lifting a hand to save the town, and, for a moment, I hated them all.

Orme stood in front of them, face-to-face with Elliot. "You will do as you're ordered, Mr. Manning," he said in his calm, reptile voice. "The miners are abandoning the mine. Call it an illegal strike, if it salves your conscience, but your men will shoot anyone who tries to leave Threshold."

Fear and revulsion twisted Elliot's face. "Curse you, that wasn't the deal! They said they only wished to be left alone. They said if we did what they asked, they wouldn't attack the town! I won't do this!"

"You are relieved of duty. Mr. Fredericks—"

Fredericks gripped his rifle. "Devil take you, I'm not shooting women and children trying to flee from monsters!"

Orme's face twisted into a snarl. "Do as you're told, or die with them!"

"He isn't human!" I shouted as we ran up. "It isn't really Mr. Orme at all!"

The thing wearing Orme's skin shot me a look of mingled surprise and venomous hatred. Then, so fast I could barely credit it, he vanished into the darkness.

Elliot's look of shock was almost comical. "Wh-Whyborne?"

Griffin strode up to him and, without the slightest hesitation, swung his fist into Elliot's face.

Elliot went down, clutching at his eye and nose. Griffin stood over him, his overlong curls blowing in the wind, his eyes narrowed with contempt and fury, both hands clenched into fists. "You collaborated with those things! You tried to hand Whyborne over to them! Tell me why I shouldn't just kill you this instant."

"Boss…is it true?" Fredericks approached hesitantly, his eyes wide and uncertain. "Did you really deal with those monsters?"

Elliot slumped back into the dirt. "They said they would attack the town, if I didn't do as they ordered," he said hopelessly. "I saw what they were capable of, and I knew we'd never have a chance against them. I-I tried to save everyone I could."

He seemed a far cry from the exquisite man I'd met my first day here, or even the competent detective I'd unwillingly gotten to know. His hair was disarranged, blood trickled from one nostril, and dirt and muck covered his suit.

I'd thought him perfect. As someone I couldn't hope to match in Griffin's fancy. Now I felt only pity for him.

"Take up arms against them," I said. "You can at least do that."

He nodded miserably. "I will. But we can't possibly succeed."

"You're wrong. Griffin has already killed one, with only his sword cane," I said firmly. Looking up, I discovered the other men watching me. My face grew hot, but I soldiered on. "Th-that is, they aren't immortal or indestructible. It won't be easy, but we can't simply lie down and die. We must save as many people as we can."

Fredericks nodded sharply. "Yes, sir!"

I blinked, taken aback by his willingness to listen. "Er, they hate light," I added. "It's our best weapon against them."

Griffin snapped his fingers. "Lamps! Fredericks, the company keeps spare equipment in the office, doesn't it?"

"Yes."

"Grab as many as you can and get them going. Hand them out to anyone you encounter. It might not be enough to stop the yayhos, but it will at least slow them down."

"You heard the man," Fredericks said.

"One moment," I added. "Does anyone know where Christine—Dr. Putnam—is?"

Fredericks paled behind his big mustache, and my heart filled with dread. "Sh-she's in the jail cell. She was causing trouble—preaching in the square how yayhos were going to come and kill us all—and Mr. Manning had us lock her up."

Griffin aimed a vicious kick at Elliot, who'd gotten to his knees. "There's no time," I said. "Come on!"

"You're right." Griffin drew his pistol in one hand, and held his sword cane in the other. "We have to save her."

We started off, but I paused and glanced back at Elliot. "If she's dead, I'll kill you myself," I said.

Then I plunged after Griffin, into the chaos and blood of the streets.

CHAPTER 20

We ran into a town turned hellish.

The sounds of shattering glass, bullets, screams, and the wet flap of the yayhos' wings filled the air. Some of the residents cowered inside their homes; others fled or tried to fight. A miner swung his pickaxe at one of the yayhos, catching a wing and dragging it to the ground. It broke free and lunged at him. A moment later, it stood with his head clutched in its forelegs, while his body toppled to the side. Griffin fired at it, but it took off again, and I couldn't tell if he'd hit it or not.

Fortunately, it wasn't far to the Pinkerton barracks. The door stood open, so we charged inside—and came to an abrupt halt.

Two abominations stood inside the large front room. One seemed relatively normal, save it now sported four arms. The other, however, was far more terrible, a thing dismembered and put back together all wrong. My gorge rose at the sight, even though my empty stomach had nothing left to eject.

In front of them stood what had once been Rider Hicks, facing the single small cell. Christine stood locked within, her head held high and her expression one of mingled fury and defiance.

"You have caused far too much inconvenience," said the creature in Rider's skin, even as the four-armed abomination behind him leveled its several guns at Christine.

"Christine, duck!" Griffin shouted, and fired a shot at Rider.

He went down, blood and brains painting the floor and the bars of the cell. The abomination turned toward us, its guns swinging around. Narrowing my concentration to a single gun, I set fire to the powder within.

It exploded, fragments of hot metal flying everywhere. The thing let out a shriek, staggering wildly, as Griffin charged the remaining one with his sword cane. Within moments, they were both dispatched.

"Christine! Are you all right?" I exclaimed, rushing to the cell door.

She was pale, but otherwise seemed unhurt. "I'm fine, but good gad, man, what of you? We were certain your brain had been swapped!"

"I'm quite all right," I assured her, as Griffin fetched the key from the wall.

"He satisfied me as to his identity," Griffin said, unlocking the cell. I felt my face heat, and hoped Christine didn't inquire further.

She didn't. "Thank you, gentlemen," she said briskly, as she stepped out of the cell. "I fear things would have gone quite unpleasantly if you hadn't come along when you did. It's good to have you back in one piece, Whyborne," she added, giving my hand a firm shake.

"Your rifle will most likely be in Elliot's office," Griffin said. "But I fear bullets aren't our best defense against the yayhos."

"What do you suggest?" I asked, as Christine vanished into Elliot's office.

He hefted a chair and smashed it against the table, breaking off the legs. "Torches," he said. "Run upstairs and grab some bed linens. We'll soak them in oil and secure them with rope."

I did as he asked, and a few minutes later, the three of us exited the Pinkerton barracks, armed with makeshift torches. "What now?" I asked.

"The community center is large and defensible, with good lines of fire on all four sides," Griffin said. "Perhaps we can rally the survivors there?"

"We have to find some first."

"Come along," Christine said, and led the way toward the nearest houses. "Let's just hope the yayhos don't have any snipers working for them."

We came to the edge of one row of houses. Christine peered cautiously around the corner. "Damn it. There are yayhos trying to break into one of the homes. We can't fire on them from this angle, but if we can make it across the road unseen, we can set up a nice crossfire to catch them in."

"As you say," Griffin agreed grimly. Turning to me, he asked, "How are you holding up?"

"Well enough." In truth, my feet were blistered and my legs sore from the running we'd already done, but I tried to put the thought out of my mind.

"Let's go," Christine said, and dashed across the exposed road.

She made it to the other side without incident. Griffin ran on her heels, and I last. For a moment, I thought we'd make it without alerting the yayhos.

I'd forgotten I needed to worry about the sky above me as well.

The sound of heavy wings gave me just enough warning. I spun, blindly swinging at the yayho with my torch. One of its jointed, insectile forelimbs lashed out, knocking the torch from my hand—and through the broken window of the nearest house.

The thin curtains caught instantly, tongues of flame rushing up toward the ceiling. I let out a startled shout—then another one as the yayho grabbed my coat with its claws, as if it meant to drag me off with it.

Griffin called my name, running out with his torch to fend off the creature. Christine risked a shot, even though it grasped me, and I felt it jerk as she made contact. It released me, and I fell to the dirt of the street as it vanished into the dark sky.

Griffin dropped his torch to the ground; it guttered and went out. His hands closed around my shoulders, helping me to stand. The house was blazing now, and with a sinking heart I realized the fire would surely spread through the tightly packed row.

As the flames licked skyward, the yayhos who had been trying to break into the house abandoned their task, taking to the air instead. Screams sounded from inside some of the structures as the fire spread, and those who had been hiding within now fled in favor of the streets.

"The community center!" I shouted. "Go there now! Run!"

A women in a nightdress bolted from her porch, and I recognized Miss Dyhart, one of the prostitutes I'd met my first night in this accursed town.

One second she ran; the next, she was in the air, screaming as a yayho dragged her skyward. Christine swung her rifle up. "Damn it! I can't see well enough, even with the fire! I might hit her!"

The yayho rose above us, Miss Dyhart's pale nightdress ruddy from the light of the conflagration. Then she was gone, carried off to who-knew-what horrible end.

"No!" I shouted, like a fool. But I could do nothing to save her.

Griffin's hand closed on my shoulder. "We have to get to the community center."

"I'm not going." An odd calm swept over me as I spoke. "I have something to do. You go without me."

Alarm flashed across his face. "Whyborne? What are you up to?"

"We can't win like this, not with them swooping down on people," I replied. "So I mean to turn their wings against them."

"Whatever you intend to do, you must know we aren't about to let you go haring off alone," Christine said briskly. "Especially considering we thought you lost once already. Really, Whyborne, do use your brain, since it's still safely in your skull."

I glared at her, but in truth, her words warmed me. "Very well. I mean to make for the coal tipple."

"The coal tipple?" they both said in surprised unison. Under any other circumstances, I would have laughed.

"Yes. But first…" I darted toward the torch Griffin had dropped. It had gone out, of course, but the end was nicely charred. Picking it up, I headed for the tipple.

The coal tipple was among the highest structures in town, and not far from where we stood. Which unfortunately meant it wasn't far from the rapidly spreading fire, either, but there was no help for it.

It also meant a sniper crouched at the top, in the little tower of the sheave house, had the perfect opportunity to fire on us.

Griffin spotted the glint of firelight off his gun barrel. "Down!" he shouted, hauling me into the relative cover of a wagon, where Christine took refuge with us.

The shot cracked off the sideboard. Christine reloaded her rifle. "Griffin, can you distract him?" she asked coolly.

"What? No!" I exclaimed.

They both ignored me. Griffin darted out from behind the wagon, weaving wildly as he crossed the long open space to the next house. As he ran, Christine swung up over the side of the wagon, sighted—and fired.

There came a faint cry, almost lost beneath the roar of the flames. "Got him," she said, sounding satisfied. As I supposed she had every right to be— even I knew it had been an amazing shot, given the conditions.

"If Egyptology doesn't work out for you, I suppose you can join forces with Annie Oakley," I suggested.

"Danger does nothing to improve your sense of humor, Whyborne."

We joined Griffin near the base of the tipple. "What do you have in mind?" he asked.

I peered up at the towering structure. "I'm going up there," I said, pointing at the sheave house. "And doing what I can against the yayhos in the air."

"Whyborne—" Griffin objected.

"There's no time! Yes, Griffin, I'm going to cast a spell. If you don't like it, you can yell at me later, but for now, please, just go."

"No." Griffin scowled. "We're going to make sure no one comes up behind you."

"I don't have time to argue." I set my foot on the lowest of the rickety steps. "Just promise me you'll flee if the fire comes this way."

I started up the stairs before he could either agree or disagree. Disagree, most likely, but as I'd said, there was no time to waste squabbling. Not when the yayhos circled like monstrous hawks, snatching helpless townsfolk for use in whatever hellish experiments they dreamed up.

I'd never had a good head for heights, so I kept my gaze locked determinedly on the splintery boards in front of me. Unfortunately, the gaps between the steps were large enough I couldn't help but notice how high above the ground I had climbed. My heart pounded, and my poor, abused legs protested this new torment, until I felt sure I'd never be able to make it back down without assistance.

The stairs passed open doors, perhaps meant to allow access to the coal bins. I ignored them, pushing my aching legs higher, until I, at last, gained the uppermost height of the sheave house. The huge pulleys used to haul up the coal jutted out of the center of the floor. The sniper had collapsed against them in death; he had an extra eye implanted in his forehead, and a third arm as well. The rough roof seemed enough to protect from the rain, with a low wooden railing, but not much in the way of solid walls.

Perfect.

Simply drawing the sigil on my palm, as I had done at the museum, wouldn't be enough this time. I needed not only to summon the wind, but to control its course. If it blew from the head of the hollow, it would surely drive the fire to consume most of Threshold. But if I called it from the other direction, back onto homes already burning, the fire might go out altogether, or at least do less damage.

Unfortunately, it would also place the tipple squarely in the path of the flames.

I broke bits of charcoal from the burned end of Griffin's makeshift torch. Falling to my knees, I began to trace the sigil on the rough boards, whispering the words as I did so.

Was that a breeze stirring my hair?

I repeated the procedure a second time, concentrating all of my will on the sigil, on harnessing the very forces of nature to my beck and call. Smoke blew past now, the wind strengthening.

Almost in a trance, I rose to my feet. The wind tore at my hair and whipped the flames, but it wasn't enough. Abandoning my tracing, I stepped into the center of the sigil, flinging out my arms and shouting the words aloud. Making myself the conduit between earth and the sky.

And the sky answered.

A distant sound reached me, like a locomotive at full steam, roaring along the track. It grew louder and louder, slowly resolving into the howl of a gale, tearing through the trees until it poured down into the hollow.

The fire went mad, twisting into huge pillars of flame, all of them bent toward the head of the hollow and away from the wretches crouched in the community center. Black shapes tumbled shrieking from the sky, smashing to the ground or falling into the firestorm to be consumed. Those who escaped crawled along the ground, scrambling on jointed legs in the direction of the mine.

From my vantage point, I could just make out the bulk of the yayhos vanishing into the mouth of the mine. In the town proper, a few scuttled flaming from the ruins, or else were overwhelmed by infuriated miners and Pinkertons, shot and stabbed until they moved no more.

God. Had I done it? Had I driven them back?

Exhausted, I turned toward the stairs—and beheld a frightful figure blocking my path.

Orme.

The flames reflected in the depths of his black eyes. I had thought him emotionless before, but now rage transformed his borrowed face. "You could have had the wonders of the universe opened to you," he growled, and now his voice barely sounded human, as if some cold-blooded thing worked his mouth like a puppet. "Instead, you chose death. So death you will have."

Before I could protest, or even think what to do, he rushed at me. I tried to dodge, but he was too fast. He shoved me violently, and my back collided with the wooden edge of the rail.

Then he was on me, his hands wrapped tight around my neck. Spots exploded in my vision, and I clawed at his fingers. My heart pounded, and blackness began to edge my consciousness.

Orme let out a startled grunt and staggered free. Gasping and gagging, I collapsed against the rail.

Griffin stood there, amidst the smoke and flying sparks, clutching a coal shovel in both hands. Blood streaked Orme's face; Griffin must have struck him with it. But the thing in Orme's skin wasn't down yet, and with a low growl of fury, he charged Griffin.

I sprawled across the floor on my belly, grabbing one of his ankles with both hands. Orme tripped, his shoe pulling free in my grasp. Griffin took the opportunity to strike him again, sending him reeling toward the rail.

The cheap wood cracked beneath Orme's weight. With a last, hoarse cry, he tumbled through and into the fire below.

"Whyborne!" Griffin helped me to my feet. "Are you all right, my dear?"

I coughed, both from my wounded throat and the smoke now billowing around us. "I believe I am."

"Come along." He pulled me from the small room and onto the stairs. The flames were close enough their heat beat against my face, and sparks and ash swirled about us. Griffin half-carried, half-dragged me to the bottom.

"Just a little farther," he encouraged, when I tripped and nearly went down. "We must escape the fire."

It seemed to take forever, but eventually we came upwind of the smoke, and my coughing eased. Turning to look at the town below us, I saw my plan had worked, and the fire slowly died from lack of fuel. The gunshots had fallen silent, although there seemed to be a great deal of shouting. A bucket brigade had hastily formed, passing water from the noxious creek to the buildings which still burned.

Griffin and I exchanged a look. We were both utterly filthy and exhausted, and I felt as though I should like to sleep for a week. But work remained to be done, so squaring our shoulders, we joined the brigade.

CHAPTER 21

I snatched an hour or two of sleep just before dawn, curled up on the porch of the community center, surrounded by men taking their break from the bucket brigade. By the time I awoke, just as the sun rose, the fire was completely out and the other sleepers stirring. My throat ached where Orme had tried to strangle me, and my shoulder and hip protested my hard bed. I pulled on my suit coat, now hopelessly wrinkled and stained, and went down the stairs to stand in the road.

The tipple still smoked, the coal stored inside yet on fire. Only a heavy rain-storm would have a chance of putting it out; otherwise, it and the slate piles would burn until they ran out of fuel. A third of the town lay in ashes, homes gone along with the machine shop. At least the building where the blasting powder was stored had been spared.

All about me sat or stood exhausted, despondent men and women. The dead and wounded had been taken inside the community center. I heard muf-fled moans and the sound of weeping coming from inside. Griffin and Christine sat on the steps of the nearest house, appearing filthy and tired. As I joined them, Griffin gave me a grim look.

"I have bad news," he said. "Do you remember the explosion we heard last night? It was the train trestle leading out of town."

"And the telegraph poles have been felled," Christine added. "It seems we're utterly cut off from the outside world."

Damn it. The yayhos had planned this far too well. No doubt they'd only been biding their time all along, waiting for the dark of the moon to destroy us, just as Rider had warned.

Poor Rider. Had they caught him the night he'd helped me? Or come across his lean-to later? The best I could hope was his brain didn't occupy one of the jars.

As for the fate of his wife, or what remained of her, it made me nauseous to imagine her still down there, a plaything of the yayhos.

Fredericks leaned against the railing of the community center porch. "Do you think them yayhos will come back?" he asked, his voice husky from smoke. "Or did we drive them off for good?"

I stared up at the looming black bulk of Threshold Mountain. "They've been dealt a setback," I said. "As have we. Last night was the new moon, but tonight will still be black enough for them to move freely above ground. I can't imagine they'll simply let us leave to spread word of their existence, not while they still have a chance to wipe us out."

The miner, Bill Swiney, spat to one side. "Then what do we do?" he asked.

A man in a pastor's collar came out onto the community center porch. "We trust in God," he said. "Just as we did last night. He sent the wind, which struck the monsters from the sky, and preserved His faithful."

The tips of my ears grew hot, although, of course, no one knew of my involvement, or would credit it, save Griffin and Christine. "I, er, don't think we should rely on such a thing happening a second time," I said, as diplomatically as I could manage. "The yayhos will have learned from the experience, and, as they say, God helps those who help themselves."

Fredericks seemed equally skeptical. Turning to me, he said, "Dr. Whyborne, your daddy owns a large interest in Stotz Mining. With Mr. Orme gone, I guess you're the boss."

Me? No, there had to be some mistake. How on earth could I know what to do?

Flight wasn't an option—the train trestle lay in ruins, and the only other way out of Threshold was a hard hike over extremely rough terrain, which would take at least a day if not more, even if we weren't attacked in the woods. Under the best circumstances, many of the wounded would never be able to make such a trip. They would have to be left behind, at the mercy of the yayhos, a fate not worth contemplating.

Too many people had already died. Even more had lost everything they owned to the fire. The yayhos would be back again tonight, and likely they wouldn't give me the opportunity to use my wind spell against them a second time. Had they seen me on top of the tipple? Did they know what I'd done?

I looked around at the tired faces, hopeless enough to ask advice from a bookish recluse such as myself. There was a good chance we would all die here in this wretched valley.

What would happen when the outside world found Threshold gone? If the yayhos meant to keep their presence secret, they must have a cover story of some sort. A fire, perhaps, or a mine explosion.

The mine.

"We fight," I said, and hoped my voice didn't shake half as badly as my hands. "But in order to succeed, we must pull together, as we did with the bucket brigade last night. Pinkerton and miner, hotelkeeper and dishwasher. The yayhos are strong and terrifying, but together we can destroy them. Indeed, right now, we have them at a disadvantage."

Swiney stared at me in disbelief. "We do?"

"Their hatred of sunlight keeps them trapped within their underground caves. No doubt they intend to do as they did last night, and emerge from the mine after sundown. But if we move first—if we enter the mine with enough force to overcome their guards and place timed explosives within, perhaps we can at least slow them down long enough for us to escape."

Fredericks nodded slowly. "Makes sense."

Swiney gave me an odd look. "You're not a bad one, Dr. Whyborne." Rising to his feet, he called, "Listen up! I want the best blasting men over here! We've got a plan, and by God it don't include us blowing up with those yayhos. We've one chance to do this right."

"What about the rest of us?" someone asked.

Griffin had risen to his feet and joined me. "How long will preparations take?"

"Not sure," Swiney said. "We'll be wanting as much blasting powder as possible, so we'll have to move it from the storehouse and pack it in carts, to take it in with us."

"We need some kind of weapons for everyone who goes into the mine," Fredericks added. "Bats or picks or whatever we can find."

"And the blasting men have to figure out which pillar is the best for bringing down the roof," Swiney went on. "It's going to take a few hours, minimum."

Although I hated the wait—I wanted the damnable things gone immediately—as Swiney said, we had but a single chance. A mistake with the pillar or the blasting fuses could spell disaster for us all.

Griffin didn't seem happy about the delay either, but he nodded. "Then I suggest those not involved in preparations find some rest. We've difficult work ahead of us."

"Or come to the church and pray," the pastor added, looking a bit put out we'd stolen his spotlight.

There was a great deal of nodding, and the crowd began to break up. "Good job, Whyborne," Christine said.

I winced. "This could still go horribly wrong."

"True. But at least they now have hope." She clapped me roughly on the shoulder, then started up the street toward the hotel. "I'm going to take Griffin's suggestion and try to rest. You fellows should do the same."

An hour later, I stood in my room at the hotel, staring out the window at the peaks outside. Threshold Mountain mocked me with its verdant slopes and gray balds. So beautiful and peaceful on the outside, while untold horrors squirmed beneath the surface. How many yayhos had survived, and even now crawled and climbed through their burrows on chitinous feet?

The hotel had taken some damage, mainly in the form of broken windows, but for the most part it remained whole. The kitchen was busy making meals to take down to the men helping in our defense. At Brumfield's order, the staff had filled a washtub in an empty room on the ground floor, in which I might bathe. The water had been black by the time I'd scrubbed my skin, and I'd left Griffin waiting patiently for it to be emptied and refilled.

As I stared out the window, I heard footsteps come down the hall. Griffin's door opened, then closed, accompanied by the soft sound of the bolt. A moment later, he knocked lightly on the connecting door.

I drew back the bolt and let him in. His hair was damp from washing, and his skin smelled of soap. "Can we talk?"

Disappointed he'd come for conversation instead of other things, I sat down on the edge of the bed and clasped my hands between my knees. "Of course."

He sat beside me. I ached to lean against him, to feel the warmth of his skin, to press my nose into his hair, but I restrained myself.

"I'm sorry I called you naïve," he said. "Not to mention other things."

"You were right to do so."

"No, I wasn't. Or if there was any truth to the words, I should have phrased things better. But I was hurt and afraid, and I lashed out at you."

I straightened in surprise. "Afraid? I don't understand."

Griffin let out a long sigh. "Seeing Elliot again reminded me of a great many things. Of where I came from. Of things I've done. Things I'd hoped to keep from you, because I didn't want you to think badly of me. When I saw how angry you were, I knew I was losing you, and the prospect terrified me. So I fought back, out of some wrong-headed idea I was defending myself, and just made it all worse."

My heart beat faster at his words. "I was equally at fault. I should have trusted you. But Elliot is much handsomer than I, and more worldly, and he wouldn't hold you back from...anything."

Griffin lifted his head and gave me an incredulous look. "Sometimes I have no idea what goes on in your head," he said. "Elliot isn't handsomer, not to my eyes, at least. There's nothing about you I would change."

"My hair? The awful way it sticks up?"

"Is quite endearing."

"My height?"

"Only means other portions of you are in wonderful proportion," he said with a wink. "I also love to see you blush."

"A good thing, since you're adept at making me do so," I muttered.

"And even if Elliot were a god among men, and you were, I don't know, Quasimodo ringing the bells, I would choose you because...because of who you are." He swallowed and lowered his gaze again. "I told you Elliot knew about my confinement. The truth is…he's the one who had me committed to the asylum. It was his signature on the papers."

All the air had squeezed out of my lungs. "Griffin…I'm sorry. I don't know what to say." How must he have felt, to know the man who had mentored him, who had been his lover for years, had betrayed him in such a manner? "Why didn't you tell me earlier?"

"Because it shames me, still," he said, his voice low enough I had to strain to hear him. "I hate talking about it. I hate reminding you that I'm…damaged."

"It's a part of you. Not something I wish had happened, but it did, and there is no shame in it. You did nothing wrong." No, that faithless wretch Elliot had been the one to do wrong. I should have set him on fire when I had the chance.

"Elliot did what he thought best at the time," Griffin said. "And I won't pretend you would have believed me, not without better proof than I had. But neither would you have locked me away and just left me there. He never came to see how I fared; he never even sent a letter. He just walked away, like a child leaving behind a broken toy. You would never do such a thing, not to anyone."

"I should hope not!"

He smiled, soft and achingly beautiful. "Precisely. Tell me what I can do to earn your forgiveness, my dear. I'll do anything, if you'll just be mine again."

His words recalled the silly Valentine's card he had bought for me, now tucked safely in a locked drawer back in our home. How happy I had been when he gave it to me.

"I never stopped being yours," I admitted. "Besides, we were both at fault when we quarreled. Although I was rather put out when I found you in his office the next morning."

"You interrupted another row," he said wryly. "I wished to make it clear to Elliot I was not at all happy about how he had tried to portray our relationship to you the night before. In retrospect, I should have said to hell with Elliot and spoken directly with you instead."

"Quite." But one last thing troubled me, and it seemed the time to get things out in the open between us. "Elliot said you would have found seducing a-a rich man's son an exciting challenge."

Griffin chuckled. "No. I found seducing *you* an exciting challenge." His fingers wrapped around my tie, tugging me closer. "I love watching you in public, so restrained and proper, so seemingly untouchable. All the while knowing I'll have you in my bed later, writhing beneath me and begging for more."

My throat was tight, although not as tight as my trousers against my swollen member. "O-oh?"

"Indeed. And this morning, when you stepped up and took charge of the town?"

I'd felt like a fool at the time, but perhaps I hadn't looked like one. "What about it?"

"I was so hard I worried I wouldn't be able to walk back to the hotel." He glanced seductively up at me through his lashes. "You know, I wouldn't object if you were to take charge of me, as well."

"Oh?" I licked my lips, not sure I could do this without sounding like an utter idiot, but willing to try. "Then t-take off your clothes and get down on your knees."

He obeyed with alacrity. I watched him disrobe, drinking in the sight of his pale skin, of the little freckles on his shoulders. When he dropped to his knees on the wooden floor, I stood up.

"You, er, know what to do," I said.

His fingers brushed over the tented cloth of my trousers and gave me a sly look. "Hmm, no, I don't think I do."

He loved making me say things which would make a sailor blush. "Suck on my cock."

Unfastening my trousers, he drew out my member. Wrapping his fingers firmly around the sensitive flesh, he leaned in and lapped the liquid from the slit, tongue probing for more. A soft groan escaped me, before I remembered we must be cautious, even with the doors locked and no one in the adjacent rooms.

It wasn't easy, though, especially when he ran his tongue up and down the shaft, before finally taking me into his mouth. I wanted to thrust into the hot wetness, but instead I ran my fingers through his hair, gripping it just hard enough to get his attention.

"I won't share you, you know," I told him breathlessly. "For as long as we're together, you're mine alone. You won't touch anyone else, not like this."

He tried to pull his head back to give me a verbal answer, but my fist in his hair stopped him. He nodded as best he could, his eyes wide and pleading for me to believe him.

I did. Nor did I think he'd been with anyone else since we'd met, no matter what that traitor Elliot claimed. "Good," I said, and closed my eyes as he slid his mouth down to my root, one hand cupping my sack. For a moment, I thought about letting him finish me—but no, I wanted more.

I let go of his hair and pulled away. "Help me undress," I said shakily.

He came to his feet, fingers flying over buttons and shoving my bracers aside, until our skin met. He was hard against me, leaking with need, the feeling almost as arousing as what he'd been doing just a few moments before. We fell into bed together, and I kissed him deep, tasting myself on his lips.

The bed was too narrow to be entirely comfortable facing each other, so I rolled on top of him. His hands shaped my shoulders, ran down my back, and gripped my backside. I bent my head to his nipple, even as I rubbed my length against his thigh.

"Yes," he whispered, voice stripped raw with need. "Show me your passion, my dear, please. Show me you still want me."

"Always," I vowed, lips tracing his skin. I slid down, mapping a line with my mouth, stopping to take little bites across his thighs. His cock jumped and jerked in reaction, and he gasped softly.

His thick erection made my mouth water, but I avoided it in favor of his sack. I heard a stifled moan as I sucked first one ball, then the other. The musky flavor of his sex fired my nerves and stiffened me further.

"Take me," Griffin whispered, his fingers twining in my hair as I sucked and licked. "Please; I want to feel you in me."

I had to break off and take a few breaths to calm myself. "Y-Yes."

I almost fell off the bed searching for the little jar of petroleum jelly among my things. When I found it, I gave it to Griffin with shaking hands. He gave me a puzzled look, so I said, "Prepare yourself for me."

His pupils dilated with desire, the emerald only a thin corona. Hastily, he coated his fingers in the stuff, before pressing them to his passage. A little moan of pleasure escaped him, and I watched as he writhed around his exploring fingers, my cock practically pointing at the ceiling I was so hard.

"I'm ready," he panted. "God!"

"Now prepare me."

His eyes widened slightly, and he scooped out more from the jar and spread its slickness over my erection. I had to bite back a moan. "Yes," I whispered. And, knowing how he enjoyed hearing me say unseemly things: "Slick me up thoroughly, so I can fuck you."

He looked utterly wild. The feel of his fingers, firm around my cock, tempted me to simply pump into his hand. But good as it was, it wasn't half as exquisite as what awaited me. "Get on your hands and knees."

Griffin kissed me as if he meant to devour me, his lips and teeth almost bruising against mine. Then he pulled away and did as I'd ordered, dropping onto his elbows with his backside up in wanton invitation. I bit one tight buttock, eliciting a startled gasp, before tracing my tongue across his crease and biting the other for good measure.

"My dear, please," he begged.

Positioning myself behind him, I guided the tip of my cock to the puckered flesh, and pressed. He opened for me, the tight ring seeming to tug me deeper as I breached him. "Yes," he panted. "Love this. God, you're so big."

"Do you need me to stop?"

In answer, he pushed back against me, hungry and demanding. His body felt hot and tight, and the sight of my aching prick sliding in and out of him as I thrust almost undid me. I changed position, leaning forward and wrapping one arm about his waist, my back pressed against his. With my free hand, I caught one of his nipples between my fingers, pinching and twisting until he moaned in pleasure.

He bucked against me, and God, it felt good, from the touch of his skin to the sound of his passion, to the way his body gripped me, as if desperate to keep me inside him. Pleasure built, my balls drawing up tight, and I switched my hand from his nipple to his length. The sensation of his iron-hard cock in my grip, slick with need, sent my desire even higher. I bit his shoulder, hard enough to leave a mark. He cried out in response, shoving back against me, body clenching even as his member pulsed.

It pushed me over the edge, white-hot pleasure shattering my control, hips snapping against his buttocks as I spent myself deep inside him.

I collapsed against his back, stroking to milk a final stream from him. We clung together for several long seconds, our breathing still rough, bodies joined but slipping apart. My every muscle felt limp and loose as I pulled gently free and fell back on the bed. Griffin stretched against me with a happy sigh.

After a few long minutes, my heartbeat returned to normal, and I regained some control over my limbs. All the aches banished by pleasure returned with a vengeance when I dragged myself from the bed long enough to clean up at the washbasin. Once finished, I brought the cloth to the bed and ran it tenderly over Griffin's skin.

"Thank you," he said quietly, when I returned to curl against his side again. He rolled onto his back, and I tucked my head on his shoulder.

I kissed the nearest available patch of skin, atop the arch of his collarbone. "You've done the same for me, many times."

He chuckled. "That isn't what I meant."

"I know." I tightened my hold around his waist. "I love you, Griffin."

"I love you too, Ival," he whispered.

CHAPTER 22

An hour or so later, we walked down to the Pinkerton barracks. Clouds massed to the south and west, and the damp, humid air pressed down on us like a heavy hand. Thunder rumbled, still distant, but promising the storm would be on us soon.

As we passed through the dingy streets of what remained of the town, I stole frequent glances at the man at my side. Griffin looked perfectly calm and composed, but I knew him well enough to note the small lines of worry around his eyes and the slight tightness of the lips I had recently kissed.

We had not spoken much after making love, just readied ourselves in silence. Everything had already been said, I supposed. But I made certain to kiss him thoroughly before we left the room.

Just in case.

"Have you quite made up?" Christine asked cheerfully.

Heat scalded my face. "Christine!"

"What? It was a simple question. I hope the answer is yes. It's very tiring when one's friends are quarreling."

The tension eased slightly from Griffin's mouth as a smile quirked his lips. "I'm sure it was very trying for you."

"Quite. Do try not to be so thoughtless in the future."

"Dr. Whyborne!"

I turned in surprise at the shout. The newspaper editor—what the devil was the man's name? Or had I never learned it?—ran up the road toward us, out of breath and wild-eyed. My heart lurched, and I imagined all sorts of disasters.

Griffin pushed past me, as if he meant to fend off the editor. "What is it, man?"

"The yayhos—the bodies of the ones killed—well—come see for yourself!"

He turned and ran down the road, without waiting for our reply. Puzzled, we exchanged glances and followed him in haste. What was wrong? Surely the awful things hadn't returned to life somehow, had they?

He led the way to a shed; what its original purpose might have been, I couldn't guess. Pausing at the door, he turned to me, his eyes wide with fear. "I came down here to photograph the bodies of the yayhos," he said. "I thought, if we survive this, photos would be worth a great deal to the bigger newspapers. But I came down here, and well, look!"

He opened the shed door, then stepped aside. I approached cautiously, ducking to enter. The foul reek of the yayhos overwhelmed the small area, and my nose and eyes burned. But of the yayhos themselves, only a small puddle of green ichor remained.

"It's like they evaporated," the editor said, when I stepped back outside. "But how? How can this be?"

Christine and Griffin both peered into the shed, as if they thought the bodies might be somehow hidden, even though nothing lay within but shadows and spiders. "The Indian legends said they came from the stars," Griffin said.

"Yes, but surely they'd still be made of the sort of matter as we are." I said, bewildered. "Although the one I spoke to did say they could only enter our world in certain places. I'm no physicist, but perhaps they did come from the stars—just the stars of a different dimension than ours."

The editor looked skeptical, as well he might. Christine poked me in the back. "Just admit you have no idea, Whyborne."

"I didn't hear you offering an explanation," I said, annoyed. "At any rate, at least they don't…don't burst into flame or explode."

"They also don't leave behind much in the way of proof we didn't hallucinate their existence," Griffin pointed out.

I wanted badly to take his hand and offer him some word of comfort. He'd already been labeled a raving lunatic once before, and this must be a blow to him. But the unfortunate truth was we might not survive to be labeled anything except tragically dead.

"There is nothing to be done about it," I said to the editor. "But thank you for letting us know."

Elliot sat in the small cell on the first floor of the Pinkerton barracks, his head bowed and his hands clasped before him. He'd been allowed to clean up a bit, but not change his clothing, and he still wore a suit stained with smoke and blood. His hair was in disarray, and he hadn't been permitted to shave. No doubt, no one trusted him with a sharp blade in his hand.

He looked up as we approached, trepidation giving way to visible despair on his handsome features. I stopped just outside the bars, fixing him with an expression I hoped conveyed the depth of my anger.

"You worked with them the entire time," I said. "Yet you pretended not to believe they existed at all. You lied to all of us and tried to kill me. What happened to the geologists who vanished in the cave? Did you murder them?"

"No!" Elliot came to his feet, his skin pale as chalk. "I wouldn't! It was the yayhos!"

"You wouldn't?" Christine arched a brow skeptically. "Considering you were quite happy to murder Whyborne, I find your protests less than convincing."

"I swear, everything I did was to save the town."

Fredericks leaned against the wall, watching our exchange. "Don't see how keeping mum about them monsters helped anybody."

"My thought exactly, Mr. Fredericks." I glanced over my shoulder at him. "Would you terribly mind stepping outside for a bit? I'm sure they have need for you at the community center."

What he thought of my request, I didn't know. Probably that we meant to dispatch Elliot without any witnesses. If so, he clearly felt no qualms about leaving us to it.

Griffin wrapped his hands around the bars, still staring at Elliot with a cold, condemning gaze. I was devoutly glad it wasn't turned on me. "Those men didn't die in an accidental cave-in—they were murdered. You were with them, and yet you survived, and ended up in collusion with their killers. You don't look very innocent to me."

Elliot buried his face in his hands. "God, Griffin, you don't know what it was like! In the dark, in the cave, seeing your friends tormented at the hands of those—those monsters!"

Griffin's laugh held not even a trace of humor. "Oh, no, Elliot, how could I know what it would be like?"

There was a long moment of silence. Then Elliot raised his head, the expression on his face ghastly with horror.

He hadn't realized until now. Even after his own encounter, he'd never questioned he'd done the right thing by abandoning Griffin to the asylum. My fingers curled into a fist at my side, and I was briefly glad the bars kept me from him.

"Stop protesting your innocence," Christine broke in crisply. "Tell us what you know, or we'll drop you into the mine and leave you with your monstrous friends."

Elliot sank back onto his chair. "I don't know much. But I'll tell you what I can. And perhaps you won't judge me with such harshness."

I doubted it, but I kept the sentiment to myself, not wishing to dissuade him from whatever confession he wished to make.

"We went to the cave," he began. "You know as much. We found the black stone and sent it back to Threshold. But I went inside the cave with everyone else, in case a bear had made its home within. The geologists were puzzled—hell, everyone who knew anything about natural caves was confused by it being so wide and straight. Somebody said maybe the Indians had done some mining here, before white men came, but it didn't seem possible. The walls were too smooth to have been shaped by crude stone chisels." He shook his head and let out a bitter laugh. "When we saw the carvings…God! We thought we'd made a fantastic discovery. Everyone was laughing and clapping each other on the back. We were certain we'd be famous."

Elliot paused, moistening his lips, and when he spoke again his voice had gone hoarse with remembered terror. "We didn't get very far. Just far enough to lose all glimmer of daylight. Then the yayhos came. It was…awful. I shot at them, but there were too many. They overwhelmed us in minutes."

"What are their numbers?" Griffin asked.

Elliot shrugged. "Not many, I don't think. Forty or fifty at the most. At least, such was my impression."

"If so, they all came to fight last night," Christine said. "They weren't holding an overwhelming force behind."

"They don't need more force," Elliot snarled, and a look of mingled rage and disgust distorted his features. "Don't you understand? I've seen what they can do! I saw what they did to the chief geologist. Th-they opened up his skull and took his brain out. They put it in some kind of metal canister, hooked it up to other machines, and h-he spoke to me! Oh God, how he screamed!"

Horror obliterated much of my anger. Bad enough I'd been in the caves alone. To be surrounded by creatures beyond nightmare, his companions vivisected and tortured in front of him…

"And so you handed Whyborne over to them, to have the same done to him!" Christine exclaimed hotly. "And Mr. Orme as well, am I correct?"

Elliot pressed his fingers into his eyes. "I didn't know what they meant to do to Mr. Orme, I swear. At least they discarded his brain. He's mercifully dead. But they seem to have an interest in collecting the brains of learned men. Dr. Putnam may be in danger as well, assuming they have interest in the brains of women."

"They damned well ought to!"

"Lovely," I said. "Perhaps you and I shall have adjoining jars."

"No one is going in a jar," Griffin said, putting a bracing hand to my shoulder. "Is that why you led us to the cave?"

Elliot shook his head vehemently. "No! The entrance had been sealed. I never imagined you'd find a second way in. I thought you'd poke about for a while, get bored, and return to Threshold."

"I still don't understand how you could cooperate with such things," Griffin said.

Elliot seemed to shrink back into himself. "Once they had done…what they did…to the others, they spoke to me. I was sure they would kill me—no, worse than kill me. Instead, they told me they didn't want to battle humanity. They wished only to remain hidden. We had suffered because we trespassed on their domain, but they offered a bargain. I could squelch all rumors of them, help conceal their presence, and they would leave us alone. Otherwise, they would issue forth and destroy us.

"I had no choice! I'd seen what they were capable of! They're motivated by no human mercy; they have no semblance of a conscience. We might as well be not even dumb animals, which might, at least, incite pity in a researcher, but plants to be taken apart and studied. How could we hope to win against them? Even though I hated myself for it, even though my very soul rebelled, I agreed because it would save the lives of everyone in this valley."

He slumped, as if all the strength had left him. "Then we got word Dr. Whyborne was coming here, with a private detective. When I saw you, Griffin...I knew I had to do something. Dr. Whyborne they wouldn't let escape —they couldn't pass up such an opportunity—but I might be able to save you. To protect you."

"Protect me?" Griffin's voice shook in fury. "You consigned me to an insane asylum and abandoned me there! Do you have any idea what they did to me? If you meant to protect me from horrors, you failed long before I ever set foot in this damned town!"

Christine gasped softly. She hadn't known about Griffin's confinement, of course. I cast her a worried glance; her gaze fixed on Griffin, a mixture of pity and uncertainty on her face.

He hadn't yet seen it, as his attention was still on Elliot. I nudged her sharply with my elbow. She started, and I gave a little shake of my head, trying to convey Griffin had not altered from man she'd known only minutes before.

Either I did better than I had any reason to expect, or she knew me well enough to intuit it. Probably the latter. At any rate, she nodded firmly and turned back to glare daggers at Elliot.

"I'm sorry," Elliot whispered. "I didn't know, Griffin."

"Of course you didn't. It would have required effort on your part." The anger had drained out of Griffin's voice, leaving behind only weariness. "Our whole relationship was one of convenience and advantage. I didn't see it at the time, but, believe me, it has become very clear since."

"Griffin, please. I-I care about you."

"Is that why you said such cruel things earlier?" I asked.

Elliot closed his eyes. "When I told you of his confinement, thinking you ignorant? Or about his humble beginnings, in case he had presented himself as a man of class to you? In the hall of the hotel? Driving a wedge between you would make the deception easier to carry off in the end, once the yayhos had replaced you with one of their own. I'd hoped Griffin would put down any alteration in your manner to your estrangement. And as for the night at my house, I suppose I wished to punish you for Griffin's stubborn loyalty to you."

Elliot was even more manipulative than I'd ever guessed. What on earth had Griffin ever seen in him? "I see. And now all that's left is to decide what to do with you."

"Let me help you," he pleaded. "I only did what I thought to be right. Let me make amends by fighting against them now."

I exchanged a glance with Griffin. Elliot had truly made a devil's bargain. He assisted in—or covered up—the deaths of Orme, the Kincaid brothers, the outlaws, the Webbs, the Hicks, and possibly others I didn't know about. Not to mention, he'd tried to add me to those numbers.

At the same time, I believed him when he said he'd thought it the only way to save everyone else in the settlement. Including—or perhaps most of all—Griffin. Now that he knew it had been a false hope, clutched at in the face of despair, I didn't believe he would turn on us again.

"What do you think, Whyborne?" Griffin asked. "Shall we leave him to rot as he deserves? Perhaps if his masters succeed in overrunning the town, they'll find him here. I wonder what will happen to him then?"

Griffin hadn't seen the yayhos' lair. I could describe the horrors of it to him, but it wouldn't be the same. He'd never understand.

Just as I would never truly understand what had happened to him in the asylum, should he ever bring himself to confide any details. I could only acknowledge he'd been marked deeply by the experience, and give him whatever love and aid I could.

I didn't like Elliot…but my brief time in the caves beneath Threshold Mountain had been horrifying enough. What would it have been like to be trapped there for days on end? Surely it would have broken even the strongest of men and convinced him there was no means of escape, save to do the bidding of the creatures.

"Let him out," I said.

Surprise filled Elliot's blue eyes—clearly he hadn't expected me to show any leniency.

"Are you insane, Whyborne?" Christine demanded. "The man is a treacherous rat. He tried to kill you!"

"I haven't forgotten," I said. "Where is the key?"

Christine retrieved it from its peg on the wall and handed it to me with a dubious look. I stepped up to the cell and slid it into the lock. "You will do as instructed, do you understand, Mr. Manning? And if you show any sign whatsoever of treachery, I'm certain any number of men, miner and Pinkerton alike, will be quite happy to stop you cold."

"I understand." Elliot stood up and brushed off his suit, as the door swung open. "Thank you for giving me another chance."

"If we live through this, you'll resign from the Pinkertons, as soon as we reach somewhere with a telegraph." It wasn't a request.

Elliot bowed his head. He looked utterly defeated, and had he not been complicit in such horrors, I would have pitied him. "Yes."

We started away, but he hastened after us and touched Griffin's arm. "Griffin, please, I'm sorry. You have to understand, they would have thought me mad if I'd tried to warn anyone. I did everything I could to save you. Please, say you understand. Say you forgive me."

Griffin wrenched free, his eyes like chips of green ice. "You almost got

Whyborne worse than killed," he said. "For that alone, I would see you hang. Be glad the decision wasn't mine, because I wouldn't have shown you the mercy he has."

He turned and strode away. Christine and I hurried after him, leaving Elliot standing alone and silent behind us.

CHAPTER 23

By the time we descended into the mine a few hours later, the storm was almost on us. Black clouds covered the valley, smothering the sunlight. The wind swirled restlessly, rattling the trees on the heights and flinging handfuls of intermittent rain. Lightning flashed, briefly outlining the peak of Threshold Mountain.

Our plan was simple enough. The miners had identified the pillar whose collapse would cause the most damage, even aside from the explosion. A great deal of blasting powder was already stored inside the mine, everyday convenience apparently trumping theoretical danger. The rest we loaded into mine carts, which would be dragged into the mine by hand, the yayhos having killed all the mules the night before. At least it was downhill all the way.

Once as much blasting powder as possible had been brought in and scattered about, a team of men would bore a hole into the selected pillar and pack it in such a way as to encourage a "blow-out," which I took was something normally avoided. The resulting spark would ignite the blasting powder, any coal dust in the air, as well of any pockets of gas which might have collected.

In order to avoid blowing ourselves up, there would be a long fuse laid to the borehole. The hole would hopefully be somewhere relatively inconspicuous, to keep the yayhos from noticing what we were up to until it was too late.

Which was why we hoped to distract them with a show of force, both to protect the miners scattering the powder and making the borehole, and to conceal our true intentions from the yayhos. With any luck, they wouldn't believe we'd easily sacrifice the riches of the mine, and think our intrusion meant to destroy them during the daylight hours. To that end, the Pinkertons and the main force of the miners went first. Christine and I accompanied them.

What use I would be, I hadn't the slightest idea. But circumstances had put me in charge of things, as absurd a notion as it was, and therefore, I had to share in the consequences of my decisions. Gunfire might set off the coal dust or gas in a premature explosion, so we all carried picks, knives, bats, or boards studded with nails as our weapons.

Knowing Griffin's phobia of underground places, I gave him the task of guarding our backs. The yayhos could not venture out into the sunlight, but their abominations could. If they came around from behind and trapped us in the mine, we'd die in the explosion along with the yayhos.

Griffin hadn't liked my decision, but he'd accepted it. I'd left Elliot as part of his force, because I disliked the idea of having the man in an enclosed space at my back. And because, if I had misjudged his apparent remorse, Griffin wouldn't hesitate to shoot him down like a mad dog.

We gathered at the mouth of the mine. The sloping shaft looked like a gate to Hades, and I was glad the sunlight at least kept the yayhos back from the opening, giving us a chance to get inside. Or at least, I hoped it would, given the heavy cloud cover.

I clutched a makeshift club, feeling like a fool. Christine stood by my side; she'd selected a pick as her weapon, no doubt because its iron head would give momentum to her swing, to make up for any lack of strength in her arms.

Well, any lack compared to someone like the burly miners, not me.

"Everything's ready, boss," Fredericks said.

Swiney, who had emerged as the unofficial leader of the miners, nodded agreement. "Any time you're ready, Dr. Whyborne."

I was fairly certain I'd never be ready. But anything was better than cowering in the community center, hoping we'd survive another night.

"Yes. Er, well. Let's go then," I said weakly.

Christine cleared her throat. "Not the most inspiring call to battle," she murmured.

Oh. My mind went blank, so I settled for thrusting my club into the air. "For, er, Threshold!"

A ragged cheer erupted around me, and a score of throats echoed my cry. "For Threshold!"

The crowd surged forward, and I went with it, caught in the press of bodies.

We raced into the mine, and I barely kept my feet from tangling with the small-gauge rail of the mine cart tracks and sending me sprawling. We all wore carbide headlamps, and the dozens of bobbing beams lent a surreal sense to the scene. I soon found myself running bent over. Christine was just short enough to stand straight, without knocking her hat off her head. "You didn't say it was so damnably cramped!" she exclaimed.

I didn't have the breath to waste on an apology. We emerged from the tunnel, and into the pillar-and-room maze of the mine. If only we knew where the yayhos had broken through.

Shouts sounded before me, mingled with cries of terror and fury. The ammonia stink of the yayhos washed over us, and I desperately hoped their entire force hadn't taken up residence in the human part of the diggings. There came chittering, and shrieking, and the moans of abominations.

I caught a glimpse of a yayho going down beneath a flurry of picks and bats, as the men thinned out in front of me, spreading throughout the maze of the mine. "Push forward!" Christine bellowed, in a voice honed to giving orders to masses of workers on her dig sites. The cry was taken up, even as we plunged deeper into the mine.

It was a nightmare. The tracks for the carts tripped my feet, and the ceiling bent my neck. The yayhos were similarly bent, and couldn't use their wings—but their crustacean legs allowed them to scuttle sideways along walls and pillars, like enormous cockroaches. I didn't see many of them, perhaps two or three, the rest retreating before the dazzle of light our scores of headlamps brought with us. But the front rank was vicious and determined, and the abominations did not fear light.

The man to my left screamed as a yayho jerked him off his feet, its many legs gaining purchase to tear his head free of his body. I swung my club clumsily and landed a blow on its head, at the base of the feelers. It jerked back with a horrible cry, as if I'd struck it in some sensitive place.

Then five of the miners laid into it with pick and board and bat. Green blood coated the floor in moments, and my eyes burned from the fumes.

I turned away, meaning to press forward…and stopped.

Miss Dyhart stood before me.

Coal dust stained her nightdress and her skin, and her hair hung tangled about her shoulders. But her face was oddly placid, and she gave me a tight smile.

"Dr. Whyborne," she said, in a horrible, flat voice, which matched the coldness in her black eyes.

No. My mouth opened, but no sound came out as she shuffled toward me. I remembered her in the bar, bright-eyed and boisterous. How she had kissed my cheek, more like a carefree girl than a hardened prostitute.

I had failed to save her, and now she was gone. This thing wore her skin, and I couldn't move. Not even when she drew close enough for me to see she carried something like a syringe in her hand, filled with poison or sedative, I couldn't guess.

Christine's pick buried itself in her skull, pinning her to the pillar beside me.

I jerked back, club falling from my hands, my heart pounding.

"Damn it, Whyborne!" Christine shouted. She jerked hard on the pick, trying to wrench it free.

A crustacean claw swung out of the dark and dashed against her head.

Christine collapsed into a limp heap. The yayho emerged from its hiding place, legs plucking at her body, and no, God, no, I'd failed Miss Dyhart—I couldn't fail Christine as well.

With an animal cry, I snatched up the fallen pick and swung it with all my strength. The end buried itself in the yayho's segmented head, and I yanked on it as hard as I could, ripping through as much of the organ as possible. The yay-ho flailed, green blood bursting forth, before it collapsed twitching to the floor.

I dropped the pick and hauled up Christine, who let out a muffled moan. "Fall back!" someone cried. "Retreat to the mine entrance!"

It was the prearranged signal, meaning the blasting men had set their charge. I draped one of Christine's arms around my shoulders, holding firmly to her wrist with one hand while I wrapped the other around her waist. I hoped she'd forgive me the liberty, given the circumstances.

"Blast it, Christine," I muttered, all but dragging her with me. "Use your legs! I need your help here!"

She stumbled along beside me, but I couldn't tell how much was deliberate and how much reflex. Swiney saw us and caught her other arm over his shoulder, and together the two of us carried her between us. Behind us, some of the miners fell into a protective formation, guarding the wounded as we retreated.

My arms and shoulders ached by the time we reached the free air. Rain pounded our faces, and the sky had gone dark enough to mistake for twilight. Lightning crashed, dangerously near. Gasping, I staggered forward, and found Griffin in front of me.

"Christine! Is she badly hurt?" he cried.

"I don't know."

"We have to get back," Swiney warned.

We hurried, as best we were able, almost the last ones out of the mine. We scrambled sharply to one side, over and around piles of discarded rock and broken equipment, until we were well out of the projected path of the blast which would issue from the mine's entrance.

Swiney and I carefully laid Christine down, attempting to shelter her from the rain and the blast alike, then crouched beside her behind the screen of rocks. He counted down under his breath, and I followed his example of stuffing my fingers in my ears. My pounding pulse seemed to tick off the seconds along with him.

A troubled look spread over his bearded face. The count grew higher and higher, and it seemed an inordinate amount of time had passed. At last, someone began to shout, and we both dropped our fingers from our ears.

Rising to my feet, I walked back toward the mine, where a group of men milled nervously. "It didn't go off!" one of them cried upon seeing me. "Dr. Whyborne, I swear, we set the charge just perfect! The fuse must have gone out."

"Can we relight it?" I asked, fearing the answer.

The man bit his lip. "It…it depends. The whole fuse wasn't defective, or else it wouldn't have lit off in the first place. If it burned just an inch or two, we might make it. If it burned almost to the bore hole…it's a death sentence for whoever goes inside."

A heavy weight seemed to press upon my chest. "I see."

Silence fell over us all, broken only by the cries of the wounded. I walked slowly to the entrance of the mine and stared down into the blackness. Rain dripped off my hat and ran in rivulets down my neck and under my shirt, sapping heat from my body. We'd risked everything on this single gamble. We either acted this very moment and destroyed the mine and the yayhos gathered in it before they could remove the blasting powder, or we resigned ourselves to the slim hope of surviving the night in the community center, while they attacked from all sides.

And if we made it through tonight, what of tomorrow? There wouldn't be enough moonlight yet to protect us. We'd have to abandon the wounded, run cross-country to save our own skins, and pray we made civilization before the yayhos found us.

Unacceptable. The fuse had to be relit. But what if the yayhos had found it and pulled it out altogether? What was truly needed was someone who could set the entire mine on fire if he had a mind to.

Well. At least the choice was clear.

"Someone has to relight the fuse," I said. The words felt oddly distant, as if another spoke them. "And if I'm in charge, I suppose it had best be me."

I didn't wait for any dissenting voices before plunging back into the mine. I'd never been terribly good in an argument, anyway.

My greatest fear was an army of yayhos waiting for me, in which case nothing would save the town above but a poorly timed fire spell and blind hope. But as I scurried down the slope into darkness, nothing appeared to stop my progress.

As soon as I reached the coal seam itself, I flattened my back against a mining cart. I didn't know if it would hide the glow of my carbide lamp, but I could hardly turn the thing off. Muffled sounds came to me, echoing among the pillars of coal which held up the weight of the mountain. The scraping of claws, the shuffle of a foot, an inhuman moan of pain...

But they were all distant. Had the yayhos retreated? If so, my plan might actually work. And if the fuse was long enough, I might even make it out of the mine alive.

God. I couldn't think about it now. I couldn't worry about Christine, or Griffin, or any of it. I just had to act.

I slid out from behind the abandoned cart and headed for the pillar with the charge. But things which had looked clear on a map were disorienting underground, everything confused by the darkness and my feeble light. Was this the tenth pillar from the wall, or the twelfth? What room was I in?

How had I ever imagined I could accomplish this? Fredericks and Swiney had been fools to put their hopes in me. My father might be a leader of men, but I was my mother's son.

There—something which looked like a thick rope, hanging from the mid-section of one of the pillars. The fuse?

Barely daring to breathe, I crept forward. The ammonia stench of the yay-hos burned my eyes, and I blinked rapidly to clear my vision. Yes, thank heavens, it was the fuse! I hadn't been nearly as lost as I thought. Holding my breath against the urge to gag, I ran to the fuse and picked up the end.

It hadn't burned out on it's own. Instead, it had been neatly cut, as if by a scalpel.

Something sharp closed around my ankle and yanked me off my feet.

My chin clipped the ground, hard enough for me to see stars and taste blood. I found myself dragged rapidly back, over the rough bed of the seam, by some enormous force. I scrabbled madly at the rails, kicking frantically at the same time, but only managed to twist onto my side.

A yayho hauled me deeper into the mine, its feelers working, a score of tiny eyes blinking painfully in the watery light of my headlamp. One of its largest pincers sank deep into the leather of my boot, and smaller pairs of legs gripped my calf.

"No!" I cried, and kicked at it with my free foot. But I couldn't get any force behind the kicks. It whisked me over the rough floor, my coat rucked up around my armpits, my trousers ripping.

Then I saw the perfectly round hole in the wall behind it, and heard the chitinous chitter of a dozen, a score, of its kind. It meant to drag me into the diggings they had made, to open up my skull and scoop out my brain, so I might go mad inside some featureless cylinder—

I clawed at the floor, the skin tearing from my fingers, but I didn't care. It couldn't end like this!

The beam of another carbide lamp cut through the darkness. Griffin stood there, revolver in hand.

Griffin? My breath caught. He had come for me, into the horrible depths, he had—

Had shot his partner Glenn as monsters from beyond were killing him.

"The yayho!" I shouted. "Shoot it! It!"

The revolver spoke, and only then did I remember the danger of discharging a firearm in the mine. The yayho let out a howl, and its grip loosened. Emboldened, I kicked it again and, this time, managed to land a blow on what passed for its face.

There came a second beam of light, and another gun spoke, along with the first. Green blood burst forth, accompanied by a nauseating stench, and the yay-ho let go.

I scrambled to my feet. Already I could hear the restless movement behind, the yayhos and their abominations massing. Griffin ran to me, eyes wide with terror—but he'd come, God, he'd come to save me.

And behind him was the owner of the second lamp. Elliot.

Griffin grabbed my hand, even as he kept his gaze and gun trained on the opening behind me. "We have to run!"

"No." I swallowed against the terror closing my throat. "The fuse—they deliberately cut it once already. It has to be guarded until it...until it reaches the powder."

Someone had to hold off the yayhos. I staggered past Griffin, half dragging him with me, my eyes already fixed on the fuse. "Get out of here," I said. "I'll light it, but there isn't much left. You'll have to run to be clear."

His grip tightened on my arm. "Don't be a fool, man. Light it and flee. You can't fire a gun, which means I have to stay."

No. God, no. I would lose him; I couldn't. "I'm not leaving you," I snarled, grabbing his lapels.

"You have to! Elliot, take him and run!"

"No." Elliot's voice was oddly calm, despite our situation. He raised his revolver and fired at one of the abominations, which had ventured out. They came in force now, boiling up from the worm-eaten heart of the mountain, and our time was almost at an end.

"Damn you!" Griffin shouted.

Elliot shook his head. "You mistake me. Take Whyborne and run. I'll stay behind."

I felt as if all the air had left my lungs. Griffin seemed to feel the same; he staggered slightly. "Elliot—"

"This is my fault." Elliot's beautiful mouth was a tight line now, his blue eyes hard as chips of sapphire. "Let me make amends, Griffin. To the town and to you. Run, and I'll hold them off as long as I'm able."

Conflicting emotions flashed across Griffin's face, anger and grief and other things I couldn't guess. Then his expression firmed, and he nodded. "Do it. And Elliot...I forgive you."

Griffin hauled me after him. We passed the fuse, and I lit it with a few words. What Elliot thought of the spell, I had no idea, nor any time to discover. Griffin and I sprinted back through the maze of pillars and rooms, gunfire ringing behind us as Elliot emptied his revolver into the creatures.

I glanced behind, just as we gained the sloping passage. No light came from above, utterly blotted out by the storm, and the yayhos erupted from their underground lair, like a nest of cockroaches. Twenty, thirty, forty, of them raced through the maze behind us, their wings and crustacean legs buzzing horribly.

They disappeared as we hit the upward slope, running and tripping over the rails. Griffin shouted we were coming, and to be ready, because hell was on our heels, but the boom of thunder blotted out his words.

We burst out into the pouring rain. Griffin wrapped his arms about me, and hurled us both forward, sending us tumbling away from the open maw of the mine.

The very earth convulsed beneath us, an instant before a titanic roar ripped the air. Fire gushed out of the mine entrance, and the blast hurled mine carts and heavy machinery to crash heavily to the earth on the other side of the gorge.

It went on and on, and, for a horrible moment, I thought we might have gone too far and the explosion would kill us along with the yayhos. But the deafening roar receded, becoming nothing more than an echo in the ravine. Black smoke poured from the mine, as if it were the very mouth of hell itself, but nothing living emerged.

Silence fell, almost as deafening as the stupendous explosion which had preceded it, broken only by the sound of rain. Then someone called out, a tentative whoop, and a moment later the air filled with wild cries of joy.

I rolled onto my side. Griffin stared at the smoking entrance, a streak of soot on his forehead starting to run in the rain. I put my hand tentatively to his arm.

He started and looked at me...and a slow smile of disbelief bloomed on his face.

"We're alive," he said, and pulled me into a rough embrace, until the approaching sound of footsteps forced us apart.

CHAPTER 24

A week later, Griffin, Christine, and I disembarked at the Widdershins depot.

The hike out of Threshold had been difficult, but we'd made it, along with a small force of Pinkertons, while the rest of the town remained behind to see to the wounded until help arrived. The denizens of the nearest town had been bewildered when we'd limped in dressed in sooty clothes, for the most part, and all of us sporting at least minor cuts and bruises.

No rational story could cover every aspect of what had happened, from the destroyed train trestle, to the downed telegraph wires, to the mine explosion. And of course we had no concrete proof the yayhos even existed. So we'd spun a web of wild tales, blaming everything from the outlaw gang, to weather, to mishaps, until the authorities merely flung up their hands and declared the whole thing an unfortunate disaster.

"I must say, I didn't get nearly as much accomplished on my manuscript as I'd hoped," Christine groused. "The director will be most dissatisfied."

"I'm sure Dr. Hart will understand, given the circumstances," Griffin said.

"Your knowledge of Dr. Hart is sorely lacking, detective," Christine informed him. The fading remains of an ugly bruise showed on her forehead, just below her hat, but she had recovered from her injury without incident.

As we emerged from the depot and headed to the line of hansoms waiting to be hired, a familiar figure in a dark suit approached us. "Mr. Fenton?" I exclaimed. What on earth was Father's butler doing here?

Fenton ignored Christine and Griffin as if they were no more than luggage I'd brought with me from the train. "Master Whyborne. Your father sent me to collect you."

"Collect me?"

"Indeed. I believe he has some questions as to why you saw fit to blow up a very lucrative mine."

Apparently, the reason I'd given in my letter to Father earlier—that monsters from outer space, which wished to kill everyone in town, had infested the mine—wasn't good enough. It probably wasn't to him. More workers could always be hired, and I was the expendable son.

"The motor car is this way," Fenton said, turning away. Because, of course, I would follow, just as I always had.

"How very nice for it," I said. "Do enjoy your drive back to Whyborne House."

Fenton froze. The scowl on his face had terrified the staff—and me—for as long as I could remember. "Your father has summoned you, Master Whyborne. I wouldn't suggest you keep him waiting."

"And I don't give a fig for your suggestion," I replied with a false smile. "I've already informed Father of the circumstances, and if he doesn't like the results, I *suggest* he not hire Griffin to do his dirty work the next time."

Fenton gaped at me, rather like a large-mouthed frog. I led the way past him to an empty cab, Griffin giving Fenton a sardonic tip of the hat as he passed by.

"What an odious little man," Christine remarked, when we settled into the cab. "He reminds me of those awful lap dogs whose owners think it adorable when they bite the servants."

"You are more correct than you know," I told her.

Before very long, the cab pulled up at our gate. "Goodbye, gentlemen," she said. "Whyborne, I'll see you at the museum. Do try to keep Griffin from accepting any more cases involving creatures from other worlds, if you please."

The cab left us, and we walked through our gate. Saul ran to greet us, meowing loudly. We'd arranged for the cleaning lady to feed and water him each day, but he clearly had missed our companionship. Griffin picked him up and carried him to the door with us.

"Home at last," Griffin said, when we were safely inside. He put down Saul and turned to me, slipping his arms around my waist and tilting his head back for a kiss. I gave it gladly, having had nothing but a few snatched moments over the last week. It was unspeakably good to simply hold him again, without constant fear of discovery. To spend the night in his arms, in as much safety as we might find anywhere, felt like a blessing.

We went up to the study and opened the windows to let in the breeze. Griffin took off his suit coat and sat on the couch with a weary sigh. "I feel as if I could sleep for days."

I settled in beside him, hesitated, then took off my suit coat as well. He arched a brow at me. "First you defy the butler, now you sit about in your shirtsleeves? Whatever will people think?"

"Very funny," I said. I did, however, rise to hang it in my wardrobe, to guard against creases. When I returned, I draped my legs over his lap and slid my arms around his chest, tucking my face into his neck. The scent of Widdershins's fishy breeze drifted through the windows, and the familiar sounds of our home were like a soothing balm spread on my soul.

"I'm sorry," I said quietly. "About Elliot. He did the right thing in the end."

Griffin's breath was a soft, sad sigh in my ear. "Yes. He did."

"And he loved you."

"Maybe."

"And you loved him."

"No." Griffin shifted to press his lips against my forehead. "He was my friend, and I cared about him. I was grateful to him for everything he did for me, and devastated when he abandoned me to the asylum. But I didn't really understand what love was."

"You didn't?"

"No. Not until I came to Widdershins and met you. At the time, I hoped we might be intimate friends. Instead, I found someone who has made me happier than I ever dreamed I might be."

The fingers of his free hand caught my chin, gently turning my face to his. His green eyes shone, and the smile on his mouth was soft and sweet. "You are my joy, Ival, and I love you more than I thought possible."

Emotion tightened my throat. "As you are mine."

"Even if I'm just the son of a farmer from Kansas, who happened to have a talent for mimicking his betters?"

I traced the line of his jaw, until my fingers came to rest just beside the curve of his lips. "You're not just the son of a farmer from Kansas, or even the orphaned son of an Irishman, or anything else."

"I'm not? Then who am I?"

"A good man. A man who wants to do what is best, by his friends and the world. But more importantly, the man I love."

His smile was like the breaking of sunshine through clouds. "I think I can live with that," he said, and kissed me again.

The adventures of Whyborne, Griffin, and Christine continue in Stormhaven, *Whyborne & Griffin No. 3.*

ABOUT THE AUTHOR

Jordan L. Hawk Jordan L. Hawk is a trans author from North Carolina. Childhood tales of mountain ghosts and mysterious creatures gave him a life-long love of things that go bump in the night. When he isn't writing, he brews his own beer and tries to keep the cats from destroying the house. His best-selling Whyborne & Griffin series (beginning with *Widdershins*) can be found in print, ebook, and audiobook.

If you're interested in receiving Jordan's newsletter and being the first to know when new books are released, please sign up at his website: http://www.jordanlhawk.com. Or join his Facebook reader group, Widdershins Knows Its Own.

Made in the USA
Monee, IL
19 January 2023

25690342R00100